The Jungle Planet

A Science Fiction Thriller Novel

Jeff Walker

JEFF WALKER
BOOKS

ISBN 978-1-9994167-3-7

http://www.jeffwalkerbooks.weebly.com

Contents

For Joanna, Jacob and Julia, and the rest of the family—
thanks for all the support over the years.

Jungles

Jungles are one of the most mysterious and dangerous places to find one's self in. Jungles are crowded with various types of plant life; some being poisonous and deadly, to those that are beautifully elegant and full of healing properties. The lush forest feeds on whatever sunlight and rain it can manage, but it is a constant struggle for survival as it perpetuates the expanding growth of its dense canopy.

It also has its share of predators, both animal and plant-based, hiding in the shadows, camouflaged, as if a thousand eyes are watching your every move. Yes, it can be scary. Visiting some remaining ones on Earth could be challenging, maybe even a bit of a daunting task. But, imagine discovering an entire planet comprising out of one. Dreganon V is one of those rare worlds. Nestled in the Parsi System, four jump points beyond Earth, and far from the usual space traffic routes, a habitable world was found with just such an environment. Who would ever have thought an overly vegetative planet like this could exist?

I remember Doctor Lim Rojas, a former botany

professor (from a course I had once taken), telling the class of a proverb he himself had once been told. It came from a village elder, in some remote area of Peru; one that was closest to the mouth of the Amazon Rainforest. He stated: "If you step into the jungle, showing little respect for it, there's a good chance you won't ever come back."

I never gave it much credence, figuring it was just a minor superstition, or some sort of slogan off of a t-shirt he was paraphrasing; But after my encounter on Dreganon V, I understood the meaning behind it, and conceded to such a warning. To be perfectly honest, I never really wanted to go there... not at first. But, the more I had heard about it, researching the survey data from the probes, the more I found myself determined to go see it with my own eyes.

I've been a qualified interplanetary botanist for several years now. To point a fact, I'm the only woman graduate (off world) with dual PhDs in the fields of Botanical science and interplanetary micro-organism pathology; I had been working for AirSurge Incorporated at the time of my studies, and soon became their leading technical advisor in the Interplanetary bio-science division. Some would say that I'm their only qualified leading botanist, perhaps.

AirSurge Incorporated was a dynamic company that located, harvested and processed oxygen for all Earth Core United governed worlds; from starships, to orbital stations, and other various stationed hospitals; They even serviced outer colony bases that required full planetary atmosphere bio-spheres. AirSurge was the leading (if not only) air processing conglomerate for all the human race.

The company sends out vessels to scout for any opportunity where oxygen can be acquired and harvested; Planets, comets, nebula gases... wherever the elements can be used for their needs. That's where Dreganon V (the jungle planet) comes into the picture. It has the highest continual supply of pure oxygen of any other world. The alien vegetation grows on average one point two million hectares per day, that's twelve billion square miles across the planetary surface. The amount of O_2 levels are so high, that an unprotected human would develop hyperoxia within a matter of minutes. Not a really pleasant way to die, choking and rupturing your lungs with too much oxygen. You'd think dying in space would be more unpleasant. No way, this is just as terrible, if not worse.

And yet, even with that scary bit of information, I headed out to that lush garden world, anyway; Perhaps in the hopes I could study and catalogue it just out of sheer hubris. I wanted to be the one to find new species of plant life; to discover groundbreaking medicinal applications, and maybe—just, maybe mind you, to be recognized as the single foremost expert in interplanetary botany and bioscience. I'd be a pioneer in the field and immortalized for all time. Who wouldn't jump at the chance of becoming that?

Well, while I waited for that singular event to happen, I bided my time by joining the commissioned AirSurge harvesters; Contracted ship and crews that verify and process a clean supply of pure oxygen. Sure, it wasn't exactly the groundbreaking job I was wishing for, especially for someone with my established credentials—but, it's all about the money, right? And, oh my, did I ever make a good living working with this corporation. AirSurge is the only supplier of rich, uncontaminated oxygen that the human race so desperately needs to survive.

The journey to Dreganon V was far and long. We had to cryo-sleep along the way to conserve our supplies; Food, water, air... the usual basic needs for any deep space flight. Our Interplanetary Harvester ship, the Skyward Seven, was sent out first (five months ahead), then, an AirSurge Purification Cargo Cruiser would follow behind soon after. That ship was to authenticate our cargo, filter it yet again, and then head off back to Earth to deliver the goods. Seems like a lot of work just to get some breathable air, I know. But, viable oxygen supplies have become more precious than any rare metal or jewel in the entire cosmos, understandably.

The corporation pays a lot for these types of jobs. The danger involved is certainly high risk (anything in space is), but, we all knew that when signing up. It's the price you pay for such a bold adventure, I suppose. That being said, I kind of wished the adventure I was on hadn't turned out so badly. So many things went wrong, so many needless deaths; If only we had known... perhaps our captain would have just outright refused the job. I could just see him proclaiming, "screw it!" while turning the ship about.

Unfortunately, nothing like that happened, and we landed there just the same. If only I hadn't been so damn curious, trying to get samples and exploring an alien planet. I should have realized my inexperience in exploring a wilderness such as this. If only we had just collected the air and left earlier. Would it have made a difference? God, it's like a bad memory that I keep living over and over. The only thing echoing in my brain alongside that nightmare is the awful proverb from the professor who quoted it to me.

"If you step into the jungle, showing little respect for it, there's a good chance you won't ever come back."

Well, if that's true... why was I the only one that did?

Chapter 1

Dreganon V

Five months later...

The Parsi System...

Interplanetary Harvester Vessel, The Skyward Seven, cruised inward as it decelerated while entering the vicinity of the jungle planet's location; The auto-pilot gracefully guided the ship to its target and immediately took orbit around the vibrantly rich green-looking world. The vessel was bulky, with no real aesthetic to give it a more streamlined appearance, a misshapen hodgepodge that was purposely built for endless missions; It sported four large engines that could pivot for entry and takeoff. It also had four extremely large cargo tank tubes surrounding the ship's body. They skirted around it like wide oil drums with thick struts that fastened to the hull. The main drive section (nestled within) was the only part that looked out of place from the rest of the twisted grey-white conundrum. It was sleek and slightly more advanced than the rest of the vessel. The six drum-like containers imbedded in its design showed that more thought was put into its streamlined figure and weren't as overly predominant as the rest of the bulky ship.

Once Skyward Seven reached full orbit, it instantaneously sprung to life, as windows dotted along the sections switched on, while the outer hull halogens revealed more of its detailed structure. Noisy blips and bloops became abundant as each deck awoke with a surge of power. Oxygen hissed out of the ventilation. The vessel was being re-introduced to the life-sustaining gas the human crew needed to breathe. Stations within the bridge, engineering, and various other consoles, had monitors that flickered and scrolled while the programs rebooted.

The interior sections were off-white, with brown stains decorating the sand coloured walls, and had some tarnished chrome accents where hands had worn down its lustre. This was a well-used vessel. Not only did it have all the items needed for everyday living, but it showed a level of comfort one needed to live onboard this *Harvester*. As the ship continued to spring alive, the crew were still sleeping in their allotted cryo-beds built into the side walls; slowly, each pod activated, the automated systems switched on and it gave each individual a rude awakening.

Like children not wanting to wake up for the morning, the various members tried to ignore the bright lights switching on over their heads. They searched for warmth, grabbing the thin blankets barely covering over them, and refused to acknowledge the computer voice repeatedly instructing them to, 'get up'. Quick bursts of cold air shot into their faces, causing them to flinch and open their eyes. This was a means of a deterrent by the computer, a way to continue the process of their awakening, and not give them time to fall back asleep.

Their jobs demanded they be ready for the start of the shift, they were on company time, and this was (after all) a paid venture by them. Captain Dan Sebastian Fruger rose out of his pod first; the man licked his dry lips, flopped his feet to the cold floor, and stretched his weary body. The cracks and pops from his joints caused him to wince slightly. As a man well into his forties, he wondered if this type of job was wearing his body out a bit too thin these days.

The other six members came out of their wall mounted-pods; all looked worst for wear as they gave a general displeased look. No one seemed willing to leave the comfort of their warm beds.

"What-uh-what..." Engineer Allen Kim struggled to talk. "What did we do to deserve this life?"

"You seriously need me to answer that for you?" Captain Dan replied, as he playfully smacked the man on the head. "You signed the contract while drunk, let that be a lesson to you."

"Oh..." He stated back, as the brain cogs turned in his head. "Yeah, I did forget that, shit..."

"Come on, Allen..." Dan slapped his hands. "Wakey-wakey, Mr. Engineer!"

Allen gave a loud yawn while arching his back, along with an equally loud fart. That's what he greeted his captain with as he passed by. Dan gave a sour face to the stench, and Allen chuckled in delight as he headed to the lockers at the end of the room; He found his pants, boots and shirt waiting for him, all neatly stored inside the standing cabinet. He hesitated, putting them on for a second, groggily giving a slight sniff and a look of confusion.

He wasn't sure if he'd cleaned them before going into cryo-stasis, but he soon gave a dismissive shrug, figuring it was no big deal if they were.

Air Collector Technicians Janice Mulahadi, Dillion Polanski and Deacon Bradley, joined the engineer and opened their respective lockers as well. The co-ed arrangement on this ship was nothing new to them. Undressing in front of each other was not uncommon on a ship of this size. There weren't many places for them to dress, and by now, they'd become accustomed to each other's nakedness. One requirement before joining this paid gig was to get a full background check (both psychological and criminal). AirSurge was very strict about that. They wanted nothing or anyone stirring up legalities, especially when it came to deep space assignments. Colleagues needed to respect each other; physically, mentally, and emotionally.

The last to join the group was Katelan Driscoll, the only Interplanetary Astrobiologist/botanist on board. Much like the rest, she had no qualms about undressing in front of her crewmates. Everyone had pretty much got it out of their system over the years. All the whistles, innuendoes and sexist comments, that faded out fairly quickly. They were adults (well, some more than others, Katelan and Janice would muse), but Katelan was the noticeably leaner and healthier one of the bunch. Certainly she had better looking breasts than Janice, in her own opinion, anyway. Scanning the others, it was hard not to notice some poor eating habits that might have contributed to less than ideal stellar physique. That being said, they were still pretty much in a fairly good condition, nonetheless.

"Anybody started the coffee yet?" Janice quipped while hiking up her tight black cotton underwear. "I could use several cups before we start."

"Amen to that," Allen nodded. "I'll see what kind we've got."

"Make sure it's not that company crap again, I hate their cheap ass shit." Dillon grumbled, fumbling to put his white socks on.

"Don't sweat it, Dill," Allen rebutted, giving the man a light slap to the ass. "I made sure I brought my own good, expensive shit." He grinned while buttoning up his grey shirt. "Nothing but the best, gold brand-fine grind Guatemalan coffee."

"Oh, my god... I love you, so very much." Janice stated to him.

"I know, baby, I know..." He winked.

Laughter broke out after that remark. The crew were very good friends with one another; They shared jokes, talked about previous missions (both good and bad), and sarcastically mocked about what they were going to wear for the day. The standard issue white undershirt, black boots, and light brown overalls was the only form of uniform that they had. Nobody seemed to mind, though. Generally, they figured since it was such a dull colour anyway, the dirt and stains would just blend in. Plus, the fact that it made it easier having not to decide what to wear every time they woke up, was just as acceptable.

"How far off are we Cap?" Deacon inquired, as he started combing his thick dark hair.

"We're coming up to stationary orbit," Dan stated, while scratching at his unshaven face. "I just checked with the computer, we've got a few more hours and then we can start the prep for landing."

"Awesome-sauce boss..."

"Where's Katelan?"

"Right here," She responded, while speaking from

9

behind the locker and snapping the last button up on her overalls. "Give me a second…. Hey, grab me a coffee, will ya, Deac?"

She tussled Deacon's hair as she passed by, giving him a wry smirk as she joined the captain. Deacon immediately cursed at her and started his combing regiment again. Dan snickered at their actions, but got back to the matter of business as Katelan stood in front of him.

"You ready to calibrate your equipment before breakfast? Or do you need a few sips of coffee first?"

"Coffee always comes first." She glared. "Why? What's the rush?"

"Not really a rush, per se, I just want to get that done before we set down. I don't want a repeat of what happened last time."

"Hey, that was not my fault," She quickly pointed at him. "If they hadn't given me that uncalibrated equipment, I wouldn't have had to spend all that time tinkering with the settings."

"Well, Katey, that's why I want to make sure. Ya know?" He glanced at her. "I want this to go smoothly. I don't want to spend too much time down there while you figure things out. Hanging around a nebula is one thing, but setting down on an alien world, a class four jungle one at that, there's not much time for us to wait for the machines to start up."

"Fine, okay… I get it." She exhaled.

"Look the minute we land, the ship is going to be bombarded with spores, pollen and growing plant-life that will clog our collectors…"

"I said I get it, okay?" She stressed to him. "I know what we'll encounter. This maybe my first time being on this planet, but I probably know more about what we'll be up against than you do."

"Jungle girl, yeah uh-huh... I know you're the expert and all, but..." He said, with a slight sigh in mid-sentence. "Look, we're all new to this world, we've been to others like it, but not really exactly like it... if you know what I mean." She nodded in agreement. He scratched at his face again in thought, and then shrugged. "I'm just saying, we need to be prepared. That's all, okay?"

"Like I said before," she glared back at him, "I get it. Now, let me have a sip of some damn coffee before I kill you all."

Captain Dan raised his brows and motioned comedically to her as if to respond, "well, shit... go!"

She stormed away, looking annoyed to the point of being totally pissed off, and gave him the middle finger before stepping out of sight. Dan shook his head and gave a long sigh.

"So much for getting back together, or even, us having sex again, I guess."

* * *

As the ship continued to power up and opened the other areas, the crew slowly made their way to those sections and started their routine inspections. They had to ensure there were no punctures or hull breaches of any kind while they were in cryo-sleep. Even though Skyward Seven was fitted with the latest space worthy metallic plating, able to absorb the impacts of dust, micro-meteorites (and other stellar debris), there was still a chance something could get through and pretty much compromise the skin of the ship.

With tablets in hand, checking off each item mentioned, the crew made sure nothing too small or insignificant of a detail was overlooked. This, after all, was for their survival. There had been many accidents in the depths of space; either due to human error, a navigation malfunction, or even overlooking a small hole in the hull. One couldn't take chances being so far out and well beyond help from Earth. So, making sure your vessel is at peak performance was of the highest priority for any person on board.

Katelan took her checklist and continued towards the back. The section had just come to life as she stepped into the room and immediately inspected the computers hooked up to the large collector vats. The calibration was essential for their success. Having reminded her of the last mission, not being properly checked and failing to secure enough o2, Katelan checked and double checked all the sensors this time round.

"The nerve of him," She said to herself. "Telling me I'm not doing my job. Asshole... It wasn't my fault, they should have been perfect the first time."

Allen heard her speak and joined her in the room.

"Quit your bitchin' lady..." He grinned at her. "Stop making it so personal. He's just being a captain, ya know, company man and all."

"Fuck you, Al." She said, giving him the finger. "He's trying to make me the reason for that blunder last time."

"Well..." He hesitated in thought.

"Well, what?"

"It kind of was your fault, in a way..."

"Seriously?" She screamed at him. "I didn't know that they didn't calibrate those... those... fucking things until..."

"Geez, calm down will ya." Allen gestured cutting her off in mid-rant. He quickly handed her a coffee (as if expecting her need for it), and walked away with a wry smirk. "Man, I was just messing with you. Here... get some caffeine in ya, save us the moody moments, and get back to normal... for all our sakes."

She quickly snatched the coffee and took a sip of the brew. It changed her attitude as the flavour hit like a junkie getting an immediate fix. Now that she was in her 'caffeine induced lucidity', she gave him a quick, "thank you".

Allen gave her a middle finger salute as he exited the room. That caused her to giggle slightly; that 'fuck you' finger gesture was like the entire crew's way of saying, 'you're welcome' to one another.

Captain Dan, having seated himself in the cockpit of the main drive, perused his data uplink manifest on a small handheld pad. The company had been in constant contact with the ship and feeding it endless information packets for the crew to catch up on when they woke up. Scrolling through those five months' worth of text messages was almost like a chore for him. The bored expression while reading spoke volumes about his love for this tedious bureaucracy.

He almost missed one important message during that quick *flick and look*. He tapped on the file to expand the attached video message, the minute it appeared the video instantly played. A black heavy set man, sporting the latest fashion of a grey business suit, sat at a desk with a beaming grin on his face.

"Congratulations, Captain Dan, on you and your crew reaching the edge of the Parsi System. The ship notified us the moment you came into its Oort Cloud and gave us a status of when you'd be woken up for the job. I'm the new co-ordinator for all the interplanetary missions for this company; My name is Jacob Russell Dolby, I'm taking over for Mary Sharpton, who was your previous overseer for this specific task." Taking a sip of water for a second, the man then popped up a holographic image that hovered over his desk. It was an image of the planet, Dreganon V, and it rotated slowly as Jacob continued. "She got promoted to co-chair nearly two months back, lots of changes going on here, you understand. Anyway, that being said, we'd just like to inform you that the processing ship is going to be slightly delayed. A malfunction in one container caused the ship to veer off course and had to make a stop at Triton space station for a patch job."

"Wow, that's some delay," Dan mused to himself. "That's like, a whole two weeks from the regular route to reach that station. Must have been some malfunction."

"Baring any further complications, you can expect The Scallion-IPS 44 to arrive with you in three to four weeks after your five day collection cycle."

"Terrific..." Dan grumbled.

"And there is, of course, one more thing to add." Jacob said, as he leaned in closer to the camera. "We would like your bio-scientist, Katelan Driscoll, to collect a specimen of the plant-life for further analysis. Please inform her that the company needs a complete detailed bio-reading of it for our geneticists to look at back home." He then relaxed back into his chair and grinned again. "That's all for now, thank you so much and I look forward to meeting you in person some-day, perhaps."

The transmission ended with Jacob nodding with a wink. Dan turned off the holo-imager and sat back in his chair in frustration. He wasn't pleased with the delay, more so, he wasn't pleased with the fact he'd have to tell Driscoll she'd have to collect a sample to bring back to their scientists back home. He knew she'd get paranoid or feel as if they were questioning her competency. She'd flipped out before when giving her findings to the company, only to have them go over it with a team of other bioscientists to confirm what she'd given.

"Shit," He cursed to himself. "This is just making my day better and better."

Chapter 2

The Crew Of Skyward Seven

Hours after combing through the sections and marking off their lists, the crew finally re-assembled in the cafeteria that was between ship operations and their lockers. The kitchenette was built into the wall on the side, it had everything needed to prepare a meal or get a quick fix for the day. That included a large coffee maker and tea dispenser. Katelan poured herself another cup of that special coffee of Allen's and sat down with the rest.

The captain tapped his tablet and flung the hologram image to the centre of the round table. It expanded to show the translucent vision of the planet, scrolling with data of weather patterns and a flashing red dot symbolizing their vessel in orbit of it.

"Okay, let's talk about our landing everybody." He said, using his right index finger to spin the image. "It's on the far side on the upper left quadrant... here..." He tapped at it, causing a blue icon to appear. "There's less foliage in this part, and it's fairly close to a body of water. If—that is—indeed water."

"It's not," Katelan chimed in. "Don't even think of using it as a water source. With this much vegetation and pollen, it's more likely turned into a thick goop of sap. The rain pools and it becomes stagnant in the plant life, they just suck out what they need and deposit their..."

"Shit?" Deacon finished for her.

She gave him a disapproving glance. "I was going to say, excretions... but, whatever."

Janice snickered, "Got it, don't drink the poopy water. Anything else we should know, boss?"

The captain rubbed his scruffy face and leaned back in thought.

"Well, we're going to have to activate the landing cutters. We need to cut a path downward until the ship can safely land on... uh... whatever type of ground it has."

"There is no ground." Katelan stressed to him. "The planet is completely made up of jungle. There's no earth of any kind to set upon. Just compacted vegetation on the surface and to its core. If there's even an actual core to be had."

"Right," Dan exhaled. He hated her cutting in while he was talking. It was a nasty habit of hers. Still, he continued on as if it didn't irritate him. "So, when we get to the surface, I want constant rotation teams for scrubbing the collector intakes and cutting the vines from the ship. Having seen the visuals from the probes that landed here years before, they got overwhelmed in a matter of minutes."

"It grows that fast?" Allen glared.

"Yep," Katelan nodded. "This isn't like the jungles of the Amazon or the ones on Cassian Two, the vegetation here is in a constant state of flux. I'm rather keen on studying the development and the hyper re-productivity."

"I bet you are." Janice rolled her eyes.

Before Katelan could comment on that, Dan switched off the holo-image and stood up.

"Okay, kids—let's start the prep-work and get moving. The other ship will be here in a matter of weeks, and we need to make sure there's enough air to process for them. So, let's pitter-patter and get at her."

The crew nodded to his instructions and headed for their assigned tasks. Janice and Katelan shared one last disapproving stare at one another but soon let the matter drop as they too got into their work mode.

Katelan and Dan found a quiet section of the ship where no one was around at the moment. He had asked her to join him for yet another quick 'talk' (of a sort). The second they were alone, Katelan grabbed hold of Dan and started kissing him. He reciprocated back and allowed the passion to grow more intense while caught in the embrace; but suddenly (and without warning to her), he stopped and eased her away.

She looked surprised by that sudden action and glared at him.

"What? You don't want to do it?" She shrugged while pursing her lips. "Seems like we've got time..."

"No-no, look, that's not why I asked you here."

"Oh?" She arched a brow.

"I mean, sure, I want to do this..." He gestured lightly at her. "But, not right now. The company left a message asking that you bring a sample back."

"Yeah, I know." Katelan passively shrugged. "I always bring a sample back with me. I'll give them a full report on the findings..."

"They want to look at it themselves." He quickly stated. His eyes fixed on hers and showed his pain in telling her the news. "They want their geneticists to do the full research on it, not you."

"What?" She glared at him. The disbelief in her face caused Dan to lower his gaze. "Are you fucking serious? Are you telling me they don't trust my judgement? I'm the goddamn specialist in this field, Dan!"

"I know, I know..." He passively acknowledged, holding out his hands to quell her anger. "Look, they didn't exactly come out and say just that... but, I could tell that's what they were stressing upon. Even with all those degrees you have... they still don't trust an off-worlder like yourself."

"Fucking Earthers!" She screamed, slamming her fist to the door frame beside them. "I can't believe this is happening to me again. Assholes... Fucking assholes the lot of them..."

Dan brought her in for a hug and allayed her anger as she began to tear up. Once again, because she wasn't a proper citizen of Earth, even after she was awarded the highest achievements in her field, the strict peers from the, 'Earth Club Only' science division, continually blocked her from getting any further recognition. The jealousy among that group was unprecedented. It practically borderline on them being racist, a growing sentiment that seemed to get stronger in the scientific community. Though she couldn't fathom why that was.

"Hey," Dan said, cradling her face. "Don't let them get to you. Want to stick it to them? Huh? Then do the research yourself. Show those bastards what you can do. Let them do their research, present the results, and then you come in with yours right after." He kissed her lightly and wiped a tear from her cheek. "You science the fuck out of it and ram it up their asses."

That comment caused her to laugh. She calmed down instantly and finished wiping her tears.

"Science the fuck out of it..." She snickered, while repeating his comical statement. "God, you're such an idiot."

"Yep," He nodded. "But, would you want me any other way?"

They shared another laugh then hugged one another. Dan wasn't just the best lover she'd ever had, but he was a friend she could rely on to give her the honest truth. Their love/hate relationship was an odd one, for sure, but she wouldn't trust any other man like she did with him. Dan was her rock, an argumentative pain in the ass rock, but the only one she could count on.

"Come on, let's get going, save the sex for later." Dan winked.

"You had your chance," She snickered with a final kiss to his lips. "Too bad you missed it."

She walked away with a large grin on her face. Dan stood there with his arms raised up in disbelief.

"Why is it always hot and cold with you?"

"You love it, come on..." She winked to him over her shoulder. "Now stop bitching and get back to being a captain, captain."

Dan shook his head and exhaled. "Way to go, Dan. Way to go."

* * *

In the lower engineering section, Dillion was chatting it up with Allen (keeping the conversation as light as possible) as they proceeded with a final inspection. The two were busy shouting out favourite movie titles, with women that had hot roles in them, occasionally interjecting random insults about their choice. For them, this was normal fun. They had a good friendship that went beyond their working lives. They'd always call each other about a new book they read, a sporting event they wanted to attend, and even go on double dates with women they managed to hook up with.

Janice would always refer to the two as *"The Space Bros"*; an inseparable and insufferable duo that would always laugh at in-jokes only they found amusing. Even though she wasn't in the room with them, she could still hear their voices carrying through the bulkheads of the ship. It made her instantly tap on to the internal ship speaker and voice an opinion of her own.

"Will you two idiots shut the hell up! Christ's sake, I can hear you giggling ninnies all the way up here in the fucking cockpit."

"Janice!" Allen gleefully responded, as he reached over to the wall communicator nearby. "Don't be jealous, babe. We're just having a bit of fun."

"Jesus Janice, stop being such a killjoy." Dillion said to her. "We're just keeping it light, okay? Geez, what's up your sour skirt?"

"You are—ya dumb twat," She argued back sharply. "You're annoying the crap out of me up here. It's impossible to think with you two shouting out your stupid movie quotes and sexist shit."

Dillion ridiculed her answer and made a face. Allen shrugged at his reaction and tapped on the ship's comm again to answer her.

"Do you need another cup of my awesome java, babe?

Or maybe... something else to ease that tension away from your..."

"Don't even finish that sentence, Al." She quickly stated. "I'll write you up so fast on charges, you'll be singing that tune from your cell on the prison world of Tersa Minor, giving your new boyfriend a taste of that sweet virgin ass."

Dillion exploded with laughter and pointed at Allen. "Oh, shit dude! She pegged your ass on that one, oh my gosh!"

The engineer was smirking at her answer, "Aw, Janice, babe... you broke my heart."

"If only you were as good as your coffee, sadly, I think I prefer to plant my lips on that, rather than you."

"Oooh! Dang!" Dillion howled again.

Allen found the comeback slightly amusing, but then motioned at Dillion to shut the hell up. Clearly, she wasn't in the mood for his antics. Allen cleared his throat and rephrased his answer in a more pleasant manner.

"As you wish, my sweetest darling angel. I shall, as ever, defer to your infinite guiding wisdom."

There was silence over the comm channel, as Allen wondered if she was still thinking of writing him up on those charges she threatened him with. Finally, the silence broke as she gave her answer.

"Ugh, unbelievable... You're such a dummy. But, I guess... for now, I still love you. Now, cut the nonsense and let's get on this thing."

"That's what she said." Dillion snickered.

"Yeah, I did say that, moron! Duh!"

The comm instantly switched off and the two men were left giggling about the whole conversation. Dillion so loved annoying her. So did Allen, to a point. He at least could get on her good side and smooth things over. But Dillion was the thorn in her side, always.

"Is she ever going to break up with that other boyfriend back on Earth?" He asked Allen.

He gave a slight sigh and rubbed his face in frustration at that question.

"Fuck if I know, man. Something tells me this might end the minute we get back."

"Yeah," Dillion nodded. "I think that's her plan all along."

"You think I'm an idiot for hooking up with her?"

"Nah," He said with a smirk. "It's your life. Who am I to question such things."

"True dat... Heh! Thanks, Dill..."

They clasped each other's hand in a unique bond of friendship. The typical signal that seemed to suggest, *I got you, bro.* Dillion finished the gesture with slap to his right shoulder and pointed back to the engines.

"Let's get this done, before your lady starts screaming at us again."

"I hear that..."

The two men chortled while completing their final check.

* * *

For such a small crew on a ship like this, the relationships were getting complicated and full of emotional baggage. Dillion (and perhaps a few others on board, like Allen) understood that things tended to get a bit weird on long missions like this. People are human after all, sexual tension always seems to lead to affairs in one form or another. At least Dillion wasn't part of this twisted sexual romp, possibly Deacon as well, though, he wasn't really sure where Deac's preference tended to go.

Dillion had thrown a random question at him once, specifically about what kind of *'experimenting'* he did during his teenage years; The response he got was a wry stare and a tightly lipped "screw you" for his troubles. Deacon acted more like a devoted celibate priest on these jobs, rarely did he ever talk about sex or the possibility of any relationship with anyone on board. Maybe that was a better way to be on these types of long missions. Reserve all that energy for that special someone back home and keep all that trouble out of your life.

"Everything is a go down here." Dillion radioed to the cockpit. "Heading up to my station now."

"Rodger that, Dill," Captain Dan responded. "Try not to get lost on the way."

Dill snorted at his comment. "Yeah-yeah... that was a long time ago, okay? I was still a toddler then. Let it go already."

"Ya still are one now..."

"Har-dee-har-har..." Dill mocked. "By the way, Are we there yet?"

"Just yanking on your diapers, sonny. Get to your station and buckle up. Maybe we'll stop for ice cream later."

"Ugh, grown ups." Dill groaned as he signed off.

Chapter 3

Satellite Analysis

The AirSurge Advanced Satellite Surveillance Drone (AASSD-0453) that was sent three years ahead of them, took passive scans of the planet prior to Skyward Seven's arrival in the system. Katelan's small black data pad uploaded all the information being sent from it, and scrolled through the various reports the drone had acquired. According to them, Dreganon V was not the typical jungle world many scientists had speculated it to be. There were many theories and possibilities about its environment, to be sure, but not like what she was reading about now.

Katelan had previously researched AirSurge's limited scientific observations about this planet, there was nothing too specific about the general ecology, or any detailed facts about the world itself. The only thing she did know was that it was overly abundant of plant-life, that the world was nothing but jungle forest surrounding its globe. From that, she could give a basic breakdown of what to expect to the crew, as she did at the meeting earlier. However, there were things she wasn't expecting to find out based on this satellite's find.

The spectrum of the various gases graphed in its report were almost standard to that of most bio-diverse worlds had; that of carbon, oxygen, nitrogen, and methane. But, these were of ones she'd never encountered in her professional career. They produced ten times the amount necessary for such an atmosphere, highly concentrated and over abundant of their releasing of emissions of it. Katelan scrolled back a few times in the report to make sure she wasn't misreading the numbers. Once it was confirmed, she carried on to the next file and pursued them as well.

It astounded her to know that the plants were extremely tolerant to concentrated air pressures, especially an O_2 environment; that meant that this atmospheric dependant organism was only suited to be this type of extreme setting. It intrigued her analytical mind, wondering if the animal life was just as adaptable. She flipped through the other scans, eyeing the sections that might shed some light on this quandary... only to find that there was no other bio-life readings—just the vegetation.

"That's odd..." She stated, glaring away from the tablet. "There should be some other type of life—insect, mammalian, or another form of adaptable species..."

She opened up the other files; her finger quickly swiped them away as she read through the data, hoping to find anomalies or errors that the satellite could have misinterpreted. But no—there was none to be found. The information was flawless and of very high quality. AirSurge's technology was always a cut above the other survey companies, in terms of planetary scans and quantum AI analysis programs, that is. But, something didn't feel right to her, anyway. The fact that there were no minerals, solid land masses, or soil of any kind for rooting (at least, none that the satellite could detect), increased her level of curiosity about this bizarre ecosystem.

"Guess this is why I'm so important to the company." She thought in passing. "I'll have to touchdown and physically inspect the specimens for myself. I'll have to get a lot of samples, though," she nodded, while glancing up in no particular direction, "yeah, maybe four or five... depending on the types and species of plant. I'll bring my portable electron-microscope, attach a few apps to enhance it to a minilab, but... it should do the trick, until we can get my full lab set up."

Katelan poked at her tablet a few more times, placing the files back into the main data queue, and then pulled up the half completed checklist. At that moment, a call came over the ship-wide speakers.

"Five minutes everyone!" Captain Dan stated. "Five minutes... get to your assigned seating and get ready for landing."

A high pitched alert squawked soon after and the warning like flashed from above. Katelan proceeded to her chair next to a console with a built-in monitor. From there, she could view all the telemetry of the atmosphere and record anything the satellite might have (or could have) missed during its pass. She thought about the conversation Dan and she had moments ago. It pissed her off that she was still being treated like an intern bioscientist, an off-world woman that had more brains than the entire lot of her male peers back home.

"Hrmft!" She grumbled, folding her arms tightly. "I'm gonna give these guys a run for their money, that's for damn sure. How dare they fucking hold me back, for what? Just because I overlooked the production levels of oxygen on the last planet, I'm going to be punished for it? I can't believe they awarded the find to that click-group bunch of corporate scientists of theirs, spiking the ball on the discovery and mocking my credentials in process. Those assholes held it over my head and laughed at me for the oversight. Not this time—no fucking way... not this time."

The flashing light above switched colors; the bright blue automatically became a deeper red, signalling to all that the transition time from orbit to that of the landing was about to commence. Katelan found the seat belt harness, slipped it over her body, and clicked the buckle, giving it a tight tug to make sure it was secure. Once that was done, she eased back in the chair and placed the tablet into a station dock on the console. There was some idle chatter over the ship-wide comms; the various crew members were calling out their procedure checks and informing the captain of their readiness.

Katelan closed her eyes for a moment. She wanted to let go of the anger. Every time those memories of the oversight came up, it made her doubt herself; specifically, about her ability as an Astro-biologist, that she wasn't truly up to par, as many suggested from that incident. She did her best to let it go and focused back on her task at the moment. She spun around in the chair and activated her station. Instead of worrying about the past, she would concentrate on the future, and the mission on the surface below.

"This is Katelan," She stated to the captain after tapping the comm-button. "I'm ready here, the AASSD is linked and Skyward Seven's computer is in the green to back up the telemetry."

"Make sure you calibrated it correctly this time..." Dan's voice responded.

"I got it, okay?" She frustratedly barked back. "I'm not making the same mistake twice."

"Ease up, girl!" Allen interjected into their conversation. "Keep your pantyhose on, geez, man just wants to know if you're good."

"Fuck off, Allen..." Katelan responded bitterly. "I don't need your input as well, ya stupid nob."

"Wooo..." He stretched out in response. "So scary, I love it when you talk dirty to me."

"Okay-okay..." Dan's voice cut in. "Let's keep it professional people. I'm activating the Nav-computer now..."

"Make sure it's calibrated as well... captain." She sarcastically inferred to him. "Wouldn't want you to mess this up either."

There was no response. It was possible that he was too busy to answer her, or—just didn't feel like giving a response. Dan was a good captain, a good lover, but defiantly not as in-tune to her emotional state as he should have been. Sometimes, he was just downright stupid in that regard, saying things he didn't or shouldn't have, or joking with the others at her expense. Yes, she knew it wasn't intentional on his part, just his typical idiotic-man brain not functioning properly. She still loved the dummy (as much as any woman could with someone like that), but, she just wished there was more to him than just good company and a good lay. Perhaps she was expecting too much.

"Not a whole lot of choices out here in the cosmos, or on this ship... it seems." She thought, while tapping on the flat-console keyboard with a long sigh. "Ah, well... such is the life of Katelan Driscoll, whoo-hoo..."

Chapter 4

The Landing

S tationed in the craft's cockpit, the three seated in a
row (Captain Dan, Deacon and Janice) belted themselves in and began working the various controls
and computers. Every person on this ship had pilot training,
it was a way to ensure that (should it ever happen) if the
captain or AI was incapable of operation of the craft, one of
the crew could take over immediately. There was no need
for a first officer, or second pilot, since they all had the basic
skills of working the controls.

Dan always felt that to be a copout by the company.
They just didn't want to pay extra for another well-trained
pilot. They could just get regular crew, for regular pay, and
not have to deal with the Space Pilot Union. That union
demands that pilots be given additional hazard pay and
planetary rights to any world they discover. Companies like
AirSurge would rather not share any profits, planetary
rights or deal with cocky pilots who might end up costing
them billions of dollars.

Dan had waived his rights to such things. He didn't care

to have planets named after him, or deal with legal woes when butting heads with major industries. All he wanted was to fly a ship, get paid, and rack up all the vacation time he could get. AirSurge was only more than happy to accommodate him on that criteria.

"Give me a vector, please." He said to Janice.

"Zero-nine-five by two-one-six." She responded. "Velocity angle is at thirty and everything is five by five."

"Thank you..." Dan nodded, entering it into the computer beside him. "Deac, what's the latest weather report?"

"Looking good, clear sky on approach. The O_2 levels are high, but not combustible if we do cause a burn in entry. Must be all that greenery keeping from being dangerous—or blowing up the whole planet, at least. Other than that... we're good to go."

"Thank you, Deac." The captain entered that into the computer as well. There was a moment of waiting, and then the computer gave a slight ping with a green checkmark on the screen. "The Nav-computer has approved the computation. I'm proceeding with the landing. I've got the wheel and preparing for descent."

"Aye" The other two nodded.

This sort of procedure was necessary to relay vocally. Pilots need to communicate their intent so that it's recorded in their black box. All space vessels have black boxes (much like old airplanes did in the past). That way, if there was an accident or some sort of human error, the investigators could understand how or why it happened. Dan took the controls in his hand and began easing down on them slowly.

"All crew, prepare for landing." Janice instructed over the intercom.

In various sections of the ship, each member had a seat

they could use; Katelan was at the back, sitting by the collectors, Dillion was in the Landing Cutter room as he prepared the lasers, and Allen was underneath the main drive in the engineering deck. He checked all his computers and glimpsed at the engine levels, rising and falling.

"We're in the green here." He signaled to the cockpit. "Power levels are good, no feedback, landing is a go."

"Understood," The captain acknowledged. "Okay, people... here we go. In five, four, three, two..."

The ship entered the atmosphere. The belly side took most of the heat as it flared underneath. That being the most well-shielded part of the craft, Allen (stationed in that section) was well protected from it, even though was getting rather warm as the ship continued entering the planet. Dan and the computer worked in synchrony to keep the ship steady. He steered towards the location and the AI maneuvered the thrusters to the best angle needed. The ride got slightly choppy, the ship rumbled and quaked, but the crew seemed unphased by the motion. They've done this so many times, it was almost normal to experience such jolts.

"Katey,' Dan radioed to her. "How's the equipment?"

"It's fine." She grumbled at him. "Just shut up and land will ya."

"Rodger that..." He stated, a slight grin on his face.

"You two ever going to kiss and make up, daddy?" Deacon glanced at him.

"One day, junior..." He snickered at him. "One day..."

Skyward Seven finally broke out of the fiery entry and cruised through the clouds, through the main cockpit window, they could see the immense jungle appearing before them.

"Holy mother..." Janice gawked.

"Wow... oh... wow..." Deacon replied.

"Welcome to the jungle folks." Dan smirked at them.

For miles upon miles, there was nothing but green Amazonian-type foliage. Huge, broad-leaf-like trees practically covered the entire area as if they were sheltering the rest of the plants from the light. Sitting at their seated stations, the rest of the crew could see the visuals on their flat screen monitors nearby. Each one gawked at the awesome spectacle and marvelled at the sheer wonder of it all. Katelan, being the botanist, was already studying the plants with a keen eye.

"I don't see much in the way of variety," She said, not realizing others could hear her over the communicator. "Not much in the way of color or pigmentation on some of those plants..."

"God," Janice uttered with disdain. "We haven't even touched down yet and you're getting all scientist on us."

"Just an observation, Janice..."

"Whatever," The woman snickered back. "I bet you can't wait to get all your little scientist tools and microscope, and skip around the forest looking for new flowers."

"Okay, people," Dan sternly stated. "Let's keep it professional. Save that nonsense for after we land. Dillion, you ready to start trimming?"

Dillion maneuvered his swivel chair to the computer station, with two control sticks in hand, he clicked the top buttons and watched the screen in front of him.

"Ready and willing, boss! What's the shape you'd like? I can do a star, crop circle, Bart Simpson..."

"Just rectangular, please and thank you," Dan said, his eyes rolling at the stupid suggestions. "Big enough for the ship and us walking around it..."

"Got ya, one boring rectangle coming up."

As Skyward Seven got closer to the landing zone, four

laser turrets unfolded from the sides of the ship and shot a fine beam of white light. The lasers sliced through the thick canopy below and created a perfect rectangular shape all the way down. The vessel eased into the cut section and lowered itself deeper and deeper inward.

"Have we reached the bottom yet?" Dan asked Dillion.

"Uh... no," He responded, with his eyes focused on the screen. "Still slicing through, man, this is pretty damn thick, dude."

Katelan linked up to his screen and watched it with interest. She could see nothing but deep dark jungle, and the occasional flash of the white light illuminating parts of the dense forest.

"Dill, you're getting pretty close to a part that looks stable, stop the cutting already."

He acknowledged her and turned off the lasers. The ship touched down on a patch that was full of their chopped vegetation. With a slight bump, the landing struts managed to keep level and was now resting comfortably for the captain to ease off the controls.

"Touchdown!" He proclaimed.

The crew cheered and began getting out of their seats. The three in the cockpit switched off their controls and gave each other a high-five for a perfect landing.

"Good job, everyone," The captain stated over the comm. "Now comes the really shitty part... let's start up the collectors and strap on the suits."

Groans of disappointment and negative replies followed his words. Dan ignored them (of course), the typical response from a crew that detested working. It made him wonder why they signed up for this job in the first place, if that was the case. He took a few moments to stare out at the deep-dark jungle before him. The dark greenery beyond seemed ominous, forbidding and down right spooky to him. But, he'd been in places like this before. Other worlds had similar dense forests like this. Yet this one seemed to give him more of that, "creeped out" feeling. The more he focused on it, the more it felt like it was looking back at him.

"You okay there, Dan-o?" Deacon said, patting his shoulder, jerking the man out of his trance-like gaze.

"Huh? Oh, uh... yeah," Dan glanced up at him. "Just had a brain fart or something..."

"Jesus," Deacon chuckled. "Brain fart? I haven't heard an expression like that since I was a toddler."

"Yeah, I expect the word fart was pretty much the staple of your upbringing."

"Dang, Dan!" He glanced with a double take. "Ya'll getting nasty on me, or what?"

"You asked..."

"Yeah," Deacon shrugged as the captain got up and walked out of the cockpit. "I guess, I did, yeah..."

* * *

While everyone was getting into their environmental suits (more suited for oxygen environments rather than the vacuousness of space), Katelan started up the air extractor and primed the collectors for its storage. The high-pitched whine of the machinery caused some to flinch momentarily; it had been sometime since any of them had to endure that kind of ear piercing noise. Once she was done setting it up she started putting on her suit as well.

"Hey, who's doing the scrubbing this shift?" Katelan asked the group.

"You volunteering?" Allen glared at her, while locking his helmet into place.

"No," She sneered. "I'm not volunteering, I'm just asking."

"I'm doing it first, Katey." Deacon said with his hand raised. He was fully suited and his air was on. The pulsating sound of his breathing could be heard as he spoke. "Then, after break, it's Dillon's turn..."

"Shut up!" He reacted with a smack to Deacon's helmet. "I'm not doing it this time. Fuck, I'm always after you on that duty. Give it to Janice... or even her..." He pointed at Katelan.

"It's going to be you, dimwit." Deacon said, pushing him. "You and I are the only ones strong enough to scrub that shit off."

"Oh, fuck, you did not just call me weak." Janice said as she came into the room. Her suit was nearly finished, she held the helmet in her hand and scowled at the men. "You want a break, Dill, fine, ya pussy. I'll do your shift then. But if you ever call me weak again..."

"I didn't call you anything..."

"Everyone shut up!" Dan barked at them all. He was fully suited and his helmet light was on. It blinded everyone as he turned to talk to them. "Dill, you're on the scrub duty after Deacon. Janice, you're on cutting duty with me. Allen, keep an eye on the pumps, filter and the O_2 levels, and Katey..." He walked over to her and motioned with his hand. "Get out there and start doing what you're supposed to be doing."

"Which is what? Exactly?" Janice ridiculed.

"Being a fucking scientist!" He said sharply back to her.

Janice winced from his loud voice (transmitting through her comm-channel) and let the matter drop. Dan continued to keep his eyes on Katelan, as she soon gave him a passive salute and strapped on her helmet. The air switched on and the head lamp flickered to life.

39

"Let's get this job going already." Dan said, as he turned away and motioned for them to follow.

The entire crew walked into the adjacent airlock. The inner door closed and sucked out all the remaining air pressure inside. Once that depressurized, the outer door opened and the rush of the rich oxygen of the planet blew inside of it. They slowly made their way out of the ship as the ramp lowered for them and came to a rest on the ground.

Now that they had a full view of what this planet actually looked like, they stood stunned by the depth of the greenery and oversized leaves of the plants. Katelan couldn't help but lower to her feet to touch the freshly cut pieces the ship landed upon.

"Amazing," She said. "It's so massive, the texture looks rough... yet my hand glides over it as if it's smooth."

"The pollen is thick." Deacon motioned. "Look at it, floating in the air all around us. It's so light and minuscule, I bet the breeze brings in a continual cycle of this stuff."

"My vents are already clogging." Janice said. "We should have asked for additional suits."

She rubbed the side areas of the helmet where the protruding vents were. The pollen collected on it like sticky candy, she opened a spot so that her helmet could eject the carbon dioxide she was producing. Deacon shrugged his shoulders at her and tried to help rub off the building filth.

"Yeah, but you think the company would just say, 'oh, absolutely, we'll spend more money on you guys, sure.' Not fucking likely..."

"Cheap assholes, right?" Janice snickered in agreement.

The group continued to spread out and explore the area. Captain Dan turned to look at the ship and inspected the large collectors towering high above. From that view, he could see the pollen and spore mix anchoring to the hull.

He shook his head in disapproval and resigned himself to get back on the mission.

"Enough sight seeing," He said, turning to the crew. "Let's get going. The longer we stay here, the more we're all going to be covered in this shit. Deac and Dill, get up there and start scrubbing the collector vents. Janice, you and I will walk about the ship and start our trimming duties. Katey…"

She stood up and tried to rub some of the spore off of her hand. Dan helped her brush it off and tapped on her helmet.

"Get your sample, start scanning the plants, and maybe, just maybe mind you… We'll take the Bush-cat out for a walk."

"Sounds like a plan." She grinned.

The Bush-cat was a robotic suit designed to traverse deep forests and marsh-like environments. The promise of taking a stroll in it made Katelan even more geared to get started in her side project. Cataloguing the indigenous life (plant or animal) was a prime concern for AirSurge, they didn't want anything affecting their profits. If it was a danger to the ecosystem, taking all the O2 for themselves and basically leaving this world with nothing, well, it wouldn't look good for them.

The Bio-Moon Pact came about ten years ago, after an incident was exposed by environmentalist investigators. Planets, moons, and any life bearing planetoids were subject to intense scrutiny when corporations harvested them for resources or used them for disposal. Basically, they were not to endanger life on any scale, microscopic or otherwise. They had to prove it was safe, without a shred of doubt, and keep those ecosystems intact for the next generation lifeforms to use.

Environmentalism became top priority on Earth after

losing many battles of their own over the centuries. Rich polluting industry leaders that continued to harm the planet (regardless of the strict laws) were often charged and executed by a committee of those victimized by their negligence. AirSurge wanted to maintain their good standing with all in Earth Core United, by being the leading environmentally conscious corporation that set the standards for all others.

Katelan had no misconceptions about their true nature. They do it to look good for political reasons, for profit margins and to generally keep the ECU off their backs. But, at least it kept them honest... of a sort, she thought. They were cheap when it came to benefits, pensions, and basic worker wages. Like Katelan, one had to prove your status in education in order to get top pay. It wasn't fair, but, with so many looking for work beyond Earth, it was acceptable enough.

"Just stay within the border of those trees," Dan said to Katelan, whom even now was busy scanning the foliage with her small handheld device. "I don't need anyone getting lost or falling out of sight somewhere."

"Those aren't trees," She pointed at them. "That's just a really tall thick stem, maybe even a cluster of vine, but it's not a tree."

"Uh huh..." He nodded with little interest. "Just don't go past them. Got it?"

"Aye-aye, sir..." She saluted mockingly.

Dan rolled his eyes while he and Janice started up the cutters. They began trimming down the vines that were reaching out for the ship's struts. The plant life was fairly aggressive, but, it was no match for the super-advanced trimmers.

"God, I love this part." Janice announced as she easily chopped through the vegetation.

Dan shook his head at her. Janice's overly enthusiastic face while laughing at the slaughter was a tad disconcerting for him.

"Jesus, what a psycho..."

Chapter 5

Technical Difficulties

A llen strolled over to the furthest part of the vessel and pressed a button on a small remote in hand. It opened a compartment on the aft side section, and what came out of that sizeable space was a folded up vehicle. A grappling arm brought it out and placed it gently in front of the engineer. Once the grappler retreated into the compartmental space, Allen tapped the remote control button again and the vehicle unfolded to its full height. Taking off his helmet and placing it next to his feet, he took a checklist pad from the adjacent wall. There were several within reach, but this one was labelled Bush-cat Operations.

The Bush-cat (or land walker) was aptly named for its unique look and design; it had four legs, a small winch-cable on the back (that looked like a tail), and a dual seat head that was shaped like a feline head. Whether that was intentional, the crew didn't seem to care too much, but Allen couldn't help but wonder (when eyeing it) if that was the original inspiration for this specific vehicle. Giving it a slight pat on the right side leg, and faking a scratch to it as well, he smiled at the Bush-cat pridefully.

"Who's a good girl? Hm? Who's a pretty lil' girl... ya wanna go outside? Yeah? Wanna go for a stroll kitty-kitty-kitty?"

He giggled at his own words and popped the door to the left side seat; a small ladder came down, and he climbed in. He started glancing about the machine with the checklist in hand. The inside wasn't huge. In fact, it was only large enough to house two people. The entire Bush-cat was about the size of an off-road truck, like the ones back on Earth, but it stood almost to the ceiling of the vessel when the legs were at their full length.

To accommodate this factor, the hydraulics would activate and retract the size of them, giving a crouched position. Again, imitating an Earth cat, as if it were ready to pounce. This made it easier for the crew to gain access and inspect the land walker in its entirety. Allen continued to check off certain points and took notes on the fuel status, drive functions, and other tedious details one needs to make sure it's working right.

Katelan (still suited up) casually walked into the same room and watched the man with a smirk. He was whistling a tune and occasionally scratching the ear of the machine's head. It sported two satellite dishes that looked like cat ears; both were triangular and pointed, with minor arrays sticking out of them. It was a good thing this back section was large enough to house such an interesting piece of technology. The floor where it stood had two retractable hatch doors that could drop it outside once checked over.

Katelan couldn't wait for this thing to get out and start a proper survey of the planet. She mimicked the sound of a cat meowing, causing Allen to glare back in surprise. Once he saw it was her, he snickered and meowed back mockingly.

"I thought the captain ordered you to stay back in the pump room?" She motioned with her thumb.

"When have I ever listened to instruction properly? Or you, for that matter?"

The two laughed; Engineers were all the same, and bio-scientists like her, for that matter. It must be something in their mindset when it came to authority-type figures. Or, like he said, perhaps it was just them. Allen quickly dismissed the comment and gave her a proper answer.

"I'm just making sure this thing is working, it's been awhile since we've used it. That was, what? Five years ago on Taurus Two? Now that was a long survey mission. Especially on a planetoid with a heavier gravity than most worlds..."

"She's had quite the stretch on her warranty, I'll say that much." Katelan admitted. "So, what's the verdict? Can we release her into the wild yet?"

"Man, you are so impatient."

"I just want to explore, ya know?" She said, giving the machine a pat to the leg as well. "There's a lot of jungle out there. I really want to cover as much ground as possible, do some surveying, maybe collect a lot of samples..."

"Yeah..." Allen said, stretching out the word. "About that..."

"What? What's the matter?"

"Well, I'm not so sure this Bush-cat would work too well here. I'm concerned about the type of environment it has to contend with."

She cocked a brow at him and took off her helmet. They didn't need to wear them inside the ship, but she wasn't planning to stay too long indoors. She wanted to get back out as soon as possible.

"Oh, come on, Allen. The Bush-cat has been in worst

places than this. It's gone through desert terrain, snow covered landscapes, heck, it even sliced through forests way the hell thicker than this place."

"True..." Allen conceded. "But, have you actually looked at it out there, it's kind of... murky and muggy, if you know what I mean."

"Uh, yah," She belittled. "It's a jungle dude."

"That's not what I mean."

"Yeah-yeah, okay..." Katelan snickered. "So, what are you talking about? Are you worried about the overabundance of pollen-spores? Or the fact there's so much moisture out there that it's turning into a sticky paste? Or..." She cocked an eye at him. "Do you mean, that it could clog the engine vents too?"

Allen seemed mildly surprised she did notice that fact. Of course, that quickly subsided as he forgot whom he was with—science-botany major, with more degrees than anyone on board.

"Right," He nodded. "I'm glad you're paying attention out there. But, it's not only that, though. I noticed the landing struts when we stepped out, they were sunk in to the ground, a bit farther down than usual."

"And?" She said, rolling her hand for him to the get the point.

"We're basically on a giant compost heap." He stated. "I couldn't feel anything really solid when I first stepped out. It felt more like, well, like a damp sponge in a way. Is that normal?"

"For this place?" She shrugged. "Maybe, I dunno, I'll have to inspect outside. But it's not uncommon for jungles to drop a lot to the floor. Even in the amazon-forests, back on Earth, the amount of dead foliage would carpet the ground."

"But," Allen interjected. "You could still feel something solid to walk on there, right? Even with all that crap spread about, you could still know there was some sort of earth underfoot, correct?"

"Sure," She nodded. "There could be solid land underneath out there too, we just don't know how far down. There is a hell of a lot of plant-life out there, overgrowth is bound to make this place super-dense in terms of pollination. The rich oxygen atmosphere probably perpetuates the constant turnaround factor."

Allen, again conceding to her observations, nodded with a look of reservation. He signed off on his checklist after giving the winch a tug and folded his arms while pursing his lips in thought.

"I'm not sure we should take this out there, not yet, anyway." Katelan's glare of confusion caused him to elaborate. "The spores and that other floating shit out there, even though we'd be protected sitting inside of it, the engine vents, like you said, would be compromised. How do we prevent that from clogging up? We could go a few feet and it would overheat the engine. If that happens, and we're so far away, how do we get it back to the ship? We'd have to pick it up after we completed filling the air tanks."

Katelan could see his point. Even from just stepping out for a few minutes, she noted how super coated her suit was. The pollen and spores practically choked the suit's vents and left a faint film on her helmet. She looked at him, then at the Bush-cat, and then back at him again.

"We could give it a test run, see how bad it gets?" She said. "I mean, it's survived dust storms, marsh waters, snow and ice build up..."

Allen could see where she was going with this and quickly cut in, "Yeah, but that's different. Those weren't as much as a problem as this place. Ice and snow melted from the heat pumping out of the vents, and sand... well, yeah, it could gum it up the works, but—not as much as this stuff would. I mean, this is really, really sticky shit, Katey."

Tapping her lip in thought, Katelan circled about and tried to think of some solutions. Brushing off the gunk from the vents and filters was a hard enough task in on itself, the air extractors being the prime concern for this mission, but they could do without the Bush-cat if they wanted to avoid anymore extra work. She realized that someone would have to be perched on top of the vehicle and scrubbing off the land walker as they traveled. That wasn't going to be at all possible.

"Damn..." She murmured in mid-circle. Her eyebrows furled with frustration. "I really want to get out there in this thing, ya know? It's got a mini-lab installed in the back. Plus, I could get a ton of samples stored inside of it."

"Look," Allen said, hearing her disappointment. "We could place it out there, like you said, and see how much of that shit gets in. But, it gets into the engine, we're going to have a heck of a time cleaning it out. We'd have to scrub not only the vents, but the motor, the pistons, check the fuel line... lots and lots of problems." Katelan twisted her lips and gave a drawn out exhale in frustration. Allen shrugged at her response and continued. "You want to be sure, and I want to be sure it won't do that. But, I'm telling you right now, this isn't like sand or ice, or water, this is bio-matter. It's sticky, gummy, nasty stuff that could contaminate all the inner-workings. It probably won't get too far without clog-ging up and breaking down."

"Wouldn't this be the same for our ship engines?" She inquired.

"Nah," Allen smirked. "I closed them off the minute we touched down. So, long as we don't go flying about the planet, we should be golden. Can't give the same guarantee for the Bush-cat."

"No, you're right..." She nodded. She stopped pacing and arched her head back slightly. "It pains me not to have that thing out there, but, if it's going to be yet another problem to deal with..."

"That's the reason I was giving it a full inspection." Allen passively gestured to it. "We'd for sure have some–technical difficulties–when running around in this thing. I was hoping I was wrong. I dunno..." He gave her a coy glance and squinted. "But, hey, if you still wanna try, anyway? It's your call."

Katelan eyeballed him for a second, mulling over the thought, but soon shook her head afterwards. She strapped on her helmet once more and gave a passive, disappointed sigh.

"Maybe later, I guess. Right now, we need to focus on getting the air tanks filled. Got to meet that quota, right? So, my little science jaunt will have to be on foot, for now."

Allen tapped the remote and the Bush-cat folded up again. Even he seemed a tad bummed out by it.

"You'd think the company would give us a heads up of what this might mean on our equipment." He said, while tapping the next button on the remote. The compartment opened up again and the swivel arm came out to pick up the Bush-cat. "Did their probe not give a full scan on this place before we got here, or what?"

Katelan placed her hand on his shoulder and smirked. "You know as well as I that they didn't care about that. All they're concerned about is getting the purest oxygen and making a profit on it. Probe data doesn't mean shit to them, but, if it's got a good O2 count? Then they'll send others to figure out the rest. That means us. We're the lab rats, right?"

"Guess so..." Allen snickered as he patted her hand. "Speaking of which, I think I'd better get back to the pump room, I'm sure our fearless leader will bust a vein if I'm not tending to it."

Katelan nodded in response and headed out of the room. Pausing briefly, she turned to Allen and pointed at the machine returning to its compartment.

"I still think we should still test it out later, okay? Never hurts to give it a try, anyway."

"Damn, girl, make up your mind, will ya?" Allen said, giving a wry look. "Yes-no, no-yes... Is that the ambiguous scientist talking or the typical female brain part of you?"

"Oh, god, Allen," she grumbled, rolling her eyes as she turned to leave. "It's no wonder you're super single, with stupid comments like that."

He laughed at her response. As she headed down to the next section, he shouted back to her.

"You know I love you, Katey! I'm just fuckin' with you!"

There was no reply. He took a moment to enjoy getting the last words in and twirled the remote in his hand like someone wielding a gun, and then placed it in his suit's leg pocket. He picked up his helmet off the floor and headed for the pump room.

"See Allen?" He said to himself. "Nobody gets you, but you. That's why I love me so much."

* * *

The crew was hard at work trying to cut the surrounding jungle and keep the ship clear of any obstacles, especially the air tanks. The minutes flew by as they toiled away on their tasks. Despite being so dysfunctional, with their assorted egos, their team effort was far better than one would think. The group knew their jobs, they had a good working mentality of what was required, but when it came to interpersonal relationships, they weren't as skilled. Dan wasn't sure why they were like this. He had hoped they could get better as the missions continued, bringing them closer as a team and creating more of a family unit.

"Those damn, egos..." he thought to himself. "If we could just let some of those personality traits go and just get along better—bah! Who am I kidding?" He glanced around at them casually and shook his head. "This is like being with a bunch of salty pirates. At least we're trying to get along, mostly, could any other extractor team say otherwise? Probably not, they're probably rotating their crew frequently, allowing no one to stay too long."

"Hey boss!" Janice said waving at him, cutter tool in hand. "Your girlfriend over there is in my way, could you please smack her on the ass for me to nudge her out."

"Why don't you?" He glared at her.

"She'd probably think I'm making a move on her... better your hand than mine."

The woman's smile made him grimace with disapproval. Janice was always ribbing him about them hooking up. Was that jealousy, he wondered? Maybe she wanted to make a move on him and resented the fact that an 'overly educated pre-madonna' did so. That's what Janice would often call her. It seemed overly bitter to constantly make that remark. Did something happen to Janice to make her so resentful towards highly educated women? Maybe a former lover dumped her for one?

Speculation was all well and good, but for now, Dan gave her no response to that stupid comment. He just waved her off and continued doing his task. Janice's smile diminished and shrugged her shoulders. Guess he wasn't in the mood for her type of banter.

Chapter 6

All In A Days Work

Katelan took her time to marvel at the scenery. She walked carefully through the thick brush and touched the wild plant life with a curious eye. The various leaf sizes and flowering blossoms darted about overwhelming her senses. The contrast of colours and plumage was mesmerizing and beautiful to behold. She'd almost forgotten to take samples as she wandered about. Giving her head a quick shake from the splendour, she bent down and used her handheld device to extract a part of the greenery.

The fairly small device had an LED screen imbedded and the capability of acting as a miniaturized microscope. It showed the sample's composition with an enhanced the view of its cellular structure, she tapped the screen and zoomed in further. Now could see the tiny molecules and DNA lattice work in real time. Pulsations within the high-lighted structure made her eyes flare.

"Fantastic..." She uttered to herself.

The more she eyed it the more her smile widened. This was like nothing she'd seen before. The replication of cells was constant. This plant life seemed to be constantly in flux and always evolving. That explained the rapid growth and aggressive nature she figured.

Yet as she zoomed in more, she noted something else in the structure, a type of protein strand she'd never seen in any Earth-type plant. It seemed to create its own internal food. Unlike sunlight or water (a source most plants tend to process), this had a photosynthesis capability that wasn't quite like most botanical life. The strands weren't something she'd ever encountered in her studies, or even discovered on other worlds.

That caused her to pause in thought. Looking away from the device for a moment, she glanced about the dense jungle before her. She slowly nodded while taking in her own internal assessment and gave a low, barely audible sigh. There was no other type of lifeforms on this world, at least, none that she'd seen so far. That puzzled her greatly.

Granted, they've only just arrived, and still hadn't done a complete survey of the entire planet, in full. But, from her experience, having been in many environments (such as this), there should always be something; Foraging animals, various bugs flying about or crawling on the ground; but no... there wasn't anything of the kind.

"A singular plant-based life ecology." She hypothesized in her mind. "With no herbivores, insects, or any type of damaging factors to curb the growth and evolution. It can't be... it's impossible, right?"

Katelan was hoping she was wrong before jumping to such conclusions. But glancing about, with ears poised for any noise, she found the endless jungle to be as quiet as anything. It sent a slight chill up her spine. There was an occasional breeze that caused the leaves to rustle, and the creaking of vines as they stretched out, but nothing else. No creatures calling out or birds chirping over head, not even the hiss or slithering of lizards that would love this type of environment.

"Kind of creepy, ain't it?" A voice said behind her.

She turned about to see Allen standing behind her in his enviro-suit. Katelan didn't hear him come up from behind, but then, she was preoccupied and busy in thought. Allen snickered at her shocked expression and gestured.

"Sorry, didn't mean to make ya jump."

"Did you put pillows on your feet?" She scowled at him. "You almost gave me a heart attack."

"It's the blanketed floor of veg that does that." He said, pointing to the ground. "Like I said, a giant compost heap underneath, maybe there is no solid floor. The plants absorb the sound of our heavy footsteps, see?" He showed, putting his foot down on it. "It's more like a sponge."

"I guess that make sense..." She shrugged. "Still, don't come up on me like that. Or else I'll have to put a bell around your neck."

Allen snickered at her suggestion and nodded. He took a few steps ahead of her and gazed about with his hands resting on his hips.

"Fuck, what a place, huh? Hard to believe there's a ton of air here and yet—nothing else is breathing it. Other than the plants, that is."

"Yeah, it's one for the books, I'll say that much." She eyed him for a moment and then put her tool aside. "I thought you were supposed to be watching the pumps and maintaining the O2 filters..."

"I was," He nodded at her. "Their in the norms for now, I just needed to stretch my legs and get a bit of the view before heading back to my boring job. Deac and Dill are scrubbing the vents, making sure all that shit floating about doesn't gunky up the works. A monkey could do my job, pretty much. But, at least I get paid for it."

"Holy shit,' She batted her eyes at him. "You get paid? Is it in bananas?"

"Yeah," He coyly glanced back with a wink. "Only the best for a guy like me."

The two snickered about it for a second and then headed back to the ship. But, just as Katelan looked back to the jungle for a second, her eye caught something in the distance. A shape in the darkness that quickly vanished. She did a double take and grabbed Allen's arm in alarm.

"What... what the hell was that? Allen! Allen did you see that?"

"What?" He said, looking annoyed as she tugged on his arm. "What are you on about?"

"There," She pointed. "Out there, on the horizon line..."

Allen squinted to where she was directing him and shrugged his shoulders. He couldn't see anything, other than more dense green jungle.

"Probably just another vine moving about," he said. "There are tons of them trying to latch onto the ship."

"No, I saw something, I swear something moved..."

"I didn't see anything," He grumbled. "The only thing moving is me—as in, back to the ship. Come on... we'll do more exploring later."

Katelan looked back and then back to Allen, who headed off to the ship. She briefly closed her eyes and tried to get a grip on reality.

"Right... nothing there." She asserted to herself. "Get it together Katey, you can't lose it out here."

She took a deep breath and relaxed her mind. Allen called to her to follow, and she quickly obliged. They joined up and softly marched in unison back to the vessel.

* * *

"Scrub-scrub here, scrub-scrub there, and a couple of tra-la-la's, that's how we clear the day away, in the merry ol' land of..."

"Oh, will you give it a break!" Deac grumbled to Dillion. He wasn't amused by his comical singing. "Just scrub the damn vents and keep your musical references to yourself."

"Hey, you scrub the way you want, and I'll do it the way I want." He grinned at him. "Sheesh, go be grumpy somewhere else. It's my turn, why don't you go oil those rusty arms of yours."

Deac didn't bother to respond. He just gestured with his hands in frustration and stepped off the top of the ship. The built-in footings along the hull were deep enough to aid him down, as was the railing that was welded to the side. The minute he got to the ground, or whatever they landed on, he turned to see Katelan and Allen return.

He placed his hands on his hips and scowled with disapproval. "Where the hell did you two take off to? Huh? I know she's loving all this, but you're supposed to be keeping the pumps monitored."

"Yeah—yeah..." Allen jeered lightly. "It's fine, trust me. As long as you guys keep up the scrubbing off the gunk, the filters will do the rest."

"So confident..." Deac rolled his eyes.

"All in a day's work, my friend." Allen grinned and bowed. "Any other bitching you wanna express to me?"

Captain Dan showed up just in time before Deacon brought his fist to Allen's helmet. His hand blocked the punch and glared at the two of them with anger.

"Grow up!" He exclaimed to both. "I've had enough of

this kid-like bullshit behaviour! Allen, get your ass in that pump room and stay there till I say otherwise, ya got me?"

Allen was about to argue the point, but the captain asserted his bitter glare and motioned his head for him to go back in. Deacon muttered something to the man as he left, but Allen didn't catch it in time.

"Deac, take your break and then get back up there to relieve Dill once he's done his part of the scrub." Deacon nodded, reluctantly and headed in as well. Dan turned to Katelan and pointed at her small device in hand. "Well? What's the verdict?"

"I'm not done yet..."

"What's taking so long?"

"What do you mean, what's taking so long?" She sarcastically retorted back. "I just got started. We need to do a proper exploration out there to get many more samples. This isn't just a 'tap and go' kind of thing, ya know? I need to compare results, do more testings, get viable samples of water, the air, pollen..."

"Yeah-yeah... I get all that..." Dan motioned his hand. cutting her off. "I'll get one of the guys to join you on an excursion in a few hours. Think you could just give us a hand in the meantime? Might go faster if we at least get one tank filled with air."

"Sure..." She grimaced. "But let me do a scan of the nearby area first. I want to see if there was a body of water close by. I want to know what the plants are drinking on this giant compose heap."

Dan snickered at that comment. That pretty much summed up this place alright. Plants upon plants were being buried underneath each other. If the thick fog of pollen and spores hadn't prevented them from lifting off their helmets to breathe the air, they'd probably instantly notice the ripe smell of decomposition of vegetation. A *'compost heap'* was spot on to what it would be like. Luckily for them, they had to wear their suits with breathing filters. That cuts down the odour considerably.

The running gag of "who cut a fart?" got old real fast, especially when getting a sudden whiff of it from time to time as it permeated onto the ship. Katelan ignored the vulgarity, especially when it leaned towards many-a-joke of one's bodily functions. She'd been used to it by now, but never tried to match the dry wit of the others when it came to that sort of low brow type of talk. Yet, she wasn't a snob about it either though. When it came to pitching in and helping with some duties, especially if the others needed it, she wasn't above getting her hands dirty.

Katelan might have been privileged in education, but she was still one of the crew, despite the off-hand remarks the others would make about her.

"So, where do you need me?" She said, while turning off her device.

"How about scrubbing?" Dan motioned to the ship with his thumb. "Maybe give the two morons a lesson on how it's properly done..." He paused for a second and looked at her. "Unless, that's beneath you, helping us poor stupid men, right? Can't all be geniuses like you."

"Shut up," She responded, tapping at his helmet playfully. "Give me a broom and get out of my way, ya dumb man."

He smiled at her reaction and motioned as if he was handing her an invisible broom. She accepted his mockery, grabbing the non-existent tool, and then motioned as if she was bashing it over his head. The two laughed as they playfully continued the pantomimed violence.

* * *

Two and a half hours later,

The entire crew sat at the rounded table inside the ship and moaned about their sore joints and muscles. The work had been tedious and gruelling. The constant scrubbing of the vents, replacing the large industrial sized filters and chopping the vines had tuckered them all out. A grouping of coffee cups, used plates of food and various meal bar wrappers, littered the table space.

Dillion had fallen asleep as Dan and Janice talked of previous missions. Allen, never one to pass by a moment for practical jokes, started drawing whiskers on Dill's face. He chuckled about it, as the man was oblivious to what he was doing. Katelan tried to make him stop, but was too busy laughing. Deac was stoic as always. Mildly sipping on his cold coffee and looking like he needed to be somewhere else in that moment.

"Deac!" Allen stated, noting the man's obvious dissatisfaction, and threw the marker to him. "Unpucker that sphincter, will ya? Just have a moment to relax."

"We've got a schedule to keep."

"Yeah," Allen shrugged. "So? We'll get back on it. Relax, man... geez."

"Break was over fifteen minutes ago." Deac stated. "We've got to get back on it before AirSurge arrives with the transport."

"We've got plenty of time." Katelan said, trying to persuade him. "Besides, you guys promised to explore the planet with me."

"There's no time for that."

"Says you..." Allen dismissed.

"He's right, though." Dan stated, ending his conversation with Janice, and stood up, adjusting his pants. "We do need to get back on schedule. However, I did promise Katey we'd go exploring to gather more samples for her research."

Dillion suddenly awoke and joined in the conversation. "I vote to go exploring..."

Janice burst out into laughter when she saw his face. The whiskers and kitten-looking design was too cute for her to resist mocking him about it. Dill wasn't sure what she was going on about, until Katelan handed him a mirror and the look of surprise washed over him.

"Okay, so, the kitty here votes to go with Katey." Dan passively gestured. "Anyone else?"

"I'd love to go..." Allen smirked. "But, guess I'm too valuable to wander off. Engineers never get the chance to explore and have any fun."

"Poor you..." Janice said, making a sobbing face at him.

"How about you Janice?" Dan motioned to her.

"Fuck, no..." She answered sternly. "I'd rather watch paint dry, thanks so much."

"Well, then," Dan said, puffing out his chest. "How about I make you go? As your captain, I could make it an order. By law, you'd have to do it."

"Oh please," She balked. "You know me, I don't give in to that threat, besides, you won't do it."

"It's done," He said, slapping his hand to the table. "I hereby order you to go with Katey, to be miserable and bored."

Chapter 7

Exploration

I n all their travels, the crew of Skyward Seven, had never really gone exploring too far by foot on most of the worlds they sat down upon. Not to the extent they were supposed to, anyway. Occasionally, they walked about the area close to the ship, took in the sights, used the *Bush-cat* to travel about in, or shot hi-res images of the landing site. AirSurge had mandated that all crews should explore each planet they set upon. It was part of the environmental policies the government enforced on them. The company, even though they were trying to look compliant, tended not to follow through on it too much. If there was an audit due, sure, they'd make it look good, but really—it was at the discretion of the captain and crew.

This planet, however, was a different story. AirSurge notified Captain Dan that it was *'strongly recommending'* that he and the rest of the crew were to aid Katelan in her specimen collection. That meant they had to explore—on foot, by *Bush-cat*, or both. Dan wasn't sure why the company pushed so hard on this point, but, after noticing the air quality once it was filtered, he understood. Pure oxygen like this was a godsend. The plant life was perfectly regulating the world's atmosphere like a superhuman lung. He wondered if they were considering transplanting some of the vegetation to Earth, and recreating the forests to help with our atmosphere.

Now, Dan is not a scientist. He's not even interested in botany like Katelan is. But he's not a stupid guy, he knows enough of how the corporate mind works. If he had to truly guess what their intentions were, his money would be on creating a sustainable O_2 factory that would pump out pure breathable air they could ship closer to home. Katelan concurred with his thoughts on it, even though she could crunch the numbers and *'bio-science the facts'* better than he could. But he was essentially correct, the company was all about the profits and not about *doing good for the people of Earth.*

Marching out together (Dan, Janice Katelan and Dillion), they set out into the depths of the jungle and examined everything this world had to offer. The pollen was still super thick, sticking to their suits and helmets, causing them to pause every now and then to wipe away the crud building up. Even their vents were clogging up faster the deeper inwards they went. Janice wasn't having any of it.

"Fucking shit! Fuck! Fuck! I hate this shit!"

"Stop blowing a gasket, Jan..." Dillion grumbled. "It's just nature, for Pete's sake."

"Nature my ass!" She exclaimed at him. "I can't see crap through this fog of stuff mucking up my view."

"Guess we should have left you back home then, huh?"

"Up you, jerkwad!" Janice glared. "Why the fuck didn't we take the stupid *Bush-cat*, anyway? I would have preferred being in that thing."

"We've only got the one, and it only fits two, so... there's how many of us here? Huh? Janice?"

"We all didn't have to come, ya know." She scowled. "I did volunteer to stay behind, right? I didn't want to go. Damn it! I can't scrape this off!"

"Allen isn't sure the Bush-cat can work in this environment." Katelan stated. "We'll have to give it a proper test later..." She took out a small item from her right side leg pocket and handed it to Dan. "Give her this, it might help."

"Thanks," he said. "Here Janice, I got ya..." He came up in front of her with a small spray container and used the liquid to clean the gunk. "This is a lubricant that should lessen the stickiness. Katelan whipped up a batch before we set off."

"You're welcome, by the way." She said to them all.

"Bio-scientist at work, huh?" Dillion snickered. "I'd like to know who you tested that on before using it for outside applications."

He gave a wry wink at her, and then quickly glanced over at Dan. That caused Katelan to shake her head with dissatisfaction. The sexual implication was unnecessary and childish. She stomped her way over and slapped the back of his helmet.

"I can't cure stupid, ya know," She said. "So don't even try being smart with me."

"Ouch..." Dillion smirked.

Janice gave a sigh of relief as Dan managed to clear away the green-ish, slime ridden-goo enough for her to see. Janice looked amazed as the pollen simply bounced off and failed to adhere to glass.

"See..." Katelan said to her. "I know what I'm doing."

"For now, sure..." Janice winced. "We've got a way to go yet, don't get too cocky there, lil' missy."

Dan took lead of the group and singled for them to follow behind. Using a laser blade cutter, he chopped, hacked and cut a path for them to walk through. The stumps and vines were severely thick, it took several chops before he could even make a dent. This concerned him, as it showed on his face, and turned to Katelan with a shrug of his shoulders.

"This is going to take forever, Katey." He said, panting hard already after a few swings. "You sure you want to go in further?"

"I know, Dan," She nodded. "But just a bit more that way, I noticed a water pond on the visuals before we landed... or something like it, could be a ways up. I want to get a sample, and then, maybe, we can take a short break, ok?"

"Right," Dillion balked. "Picking flowers along the way... fun, fun, fun."

"We'll be out here for hours..." Janice bemoaned. "Took us three just to make it this far."

Dan turned back with some reluctance, but proceeded to slice away. Dillion offered to take turns with him, as did Janice as well. After a few more hits, and a few more sore arm aches, he gladly took them up on the offer.

* * *

The slow, steady progress was gruelling for them all. But, after yet another hour of cutting through the trail, they finally came upon the pond-like water pool. Once they saw it, everyone collapsed in joy. Katelan thanked Dan for his muscle, even as he attempted to rub them from the strain.

"Yo, we helped too..." Dillion said.

"Yeah, for a bit," Katelan said to him. "Then you let him go on for the rest of the hour."

"I'm a lover, not a cutter..." He grinned, panting heavily inside his suit. "Damn, I think I'll sleep good tonight."

Katelan checked on Dan's suit vitals and helped him to sit up. Wiping off the excess pollen goop, she managed to get his breather vents clear enough for more air to filter in. He nodded in thanks and motioned for her to get the sample immediately. She took some vials out of her side leg compartments, and unscrewed the lids. She came to the water's edge and was just about to dip it in, when Janice called out to her.

"Woah! Wait a minute! Take a sweep with the sensor pad before you go near there. What if there's a big fucking piranha waiting for you?" The woman got up, looking more like a drunken sailor, and wobbled over to join her. "You can't even see what's in that... that stuff... ya know? Could be a creature waiting and drag you down with it."

"Wow, paranoid much?"

"As you should be." She glared at her. "Seriously, think before you leap. That's the problem with all you science geeks... no, clue about the consequences until it happens."

"Wise... words..." Dillion struggled to utter out of breath. "She's got a point."

Dan conceded as well. "Give it a quick scan, just in case, Katey."

The woman rolled her eyes at their caution. But, she obliged their warnings. She had seen no evidence of other lifeforms on this planet, and was resolute that nothing animal or insect had ever evolved on here. She took the scanning pad Janice was handing her and waved it over the area she was in. Nothing *blipped* or *bleeped* to say there was any multi-toothed nasty beastie waiting to bite her. The only thing it did show was more plants growing at the bottom of this very deep water depot.

She showed them all the result with a quick wave of the pad, and handed it back to Janice. The woman took another look at it before putting it back in her right side pocket and motioned her to proceed.

"Ok, we all good now? Is everybody's sphincter relaxed?"

"Get your damn sample, would ya?" Dillion grumbled.

Katelan dipped her hand in with the sample vial, and scooped up enough water to fill it. She closed it up, placed it back in her side leg compartment and stood up proudly with her hands on her hips.

"There, that wasn't so bad now, was it?" She turned to face them and shrugged. "Okay, let's head back."

The entire group moaned at her happy attitude.

* * *

Back on the ship, Allen continued to monitor the tanks as they filled up with fresh O_2. The readings were incredible to him. This was going to be the best haul they had in a long time. He switched on his music selection (now that there wasn't anyone there to complain about it), and danced about while fiddling with the controls to maintain the levels coming in. Deac surprised him suddenly, as he stepped into the room, in his space suit, covered in pollen goo.

"Jebus, man!" Allen squawked, holding his hand over his chest. "What the fuck?"

"Are you coming to help me out there, or what?"

"Dude, I'm here." He gestured to the controls. "I've got to keep them steady, ya know? Can't just be out there leaving all this unattended. It could leak out, blow up... or some kind of shit. Right?"

Deac gave out a long sigh. "I'm scrubbing alone out there. I need a break, it's been nearly six hours. And nobody is back yet."

"Really? Six?" Allen blinked back. "Wow, time sure is flying, huh?"

"No shit... look are you going to help or not?"

Allen motioned his hands up at him to relax. He tapped on each of the valves, watching their needles to see if they spiked from it, and when he was satisfied they were good, he turned back to face Deac.

"Okay, fine." Allen conceded. "I'll do some manual labor as well, sheesh! Take a stress pill or something Deac, man, you're way too tense."

Instead of saying something back or giving him the finger response, Deac stomped out of the room and unhooked his helmet. Allen seemed amused by the whole confrontation, snickering to himself about the situation and singing, "You've got a friend in me". Just before he headed out to get into his suit and start his turn at scrubbing the vents, Allen suddenly realized that Deac had come in to the ship before decontaminating himself.

The floor was littered with the vegetation spores and left a trail behind. He cursed the man under his breath for being so stupid. The protocol was that they were to clean themselves down before entering the ship. There was a decontamination chamber off to the side of the entrance that all crew have to use before coming into the main section. Deac forgot and just stormed in like an idiot. That didn't sit well with Allen, who even now, bent down and started scraping off the spore-goop off the floor with a piece of paper he found.

"Damn it, Deac!" He screamed out the room's door. "You're making a mess of things!"

"What?" Deac harped back. "I can't hear you..."

"I said, you're an asshole! And you're a slob!"

"Yeah-yeah-yeah..." The man's voice trailed off.

"Shit, stupid, mother fuckin..." Allen grumbled, holding the paper with the spore still on it. "I'm gonna make you eat this right now."

As the man walked out to confront his idiotic crew member, the goop on the floor started to wriggle and grow. A small leaf formed out of the tiny spore pod, unfolding, and stretching out. More followed, as each glob on the floor did the same. A vine appeared to connect each one and their stems pulsated with purple veins as it drank in the ship's air.

* * *

"Come in, Skyward Seven... over?" The captain repeatedly tried to hail the ship over his communicator, but there was no reply. "Yo! Who's minding the store over there? Come on, guys! Are you reading me?" Static was all he got back as he trudged through the thick brush with the rest of his fellow explorers. "You better not be fucking with me... I swear... damn it, Allen! This isn't funny!"

"Maybe they're outside, Cap?" Dillion shrugged. "You know it's hard to hear anything when they're slicing up the veg and cleaning off the vents, right?"

"Yeah, maybe..." He nodded back. "Man, would it kill the corp to give us a new transmitter though? Something more powerful than this ancient hardware? When's the last time we had an upgrade on it?"

"I don't think we have enough hands and toes to count

that far, Dan..." Janice snickered. "It's been awhile, a good long while."

Katelan was trailing behind them all as she continually eyed the sample in her hand. Giving the odd shake, she tried to watch the debris in the liquid as it floated about. It was definitely spores, from what she could see, much more of them in a concentrated state. She stopped listing to the group yammer on for all the time they'd been heading back. So when Captain Dan's hand suddenly waved at her in the face, she snapped out of her focus on it.

"What?" She glared at him.

"I asked you a question," He stated, standing in front of her. The rest of the group had stopped to look at her. "Stop looking at that shit and answer me."

"What was the question?"

"Do you think the jungle is interfering with our comms?" Dan motioned about. "Is this crap cutting our signal or what?"

"Uh..." She had to pause in thought for a second, as if flipping through a book in her mind. Her eyes darted slightly as she mentally looked for the answer. "I suppose the density of the plant life is blocking the signal. Much like mountainous terrain, it's probably bouncing the transmission back. Guess we never considered this foliage to be so thick as to block such a thing."

"So what do we do?" Dillion said.

Janice shook her head and motioned her arm at him. "We keep walking, numb nuts. Ain't much we can do in this type of situation. It's not like we do anything else."

Dan looked at Katelan with a raised brow. He wanted to know if Janice was correct in that statement. She gave him a slight nod in agreement and placed the sample vial in her side arm pocket. It was insulated enough to keep it from spoiling and wouldn't get damaged from the padding inside.

"We could expand the range if we launch a drone in the sky," Katelan suggested. "But, with the spores and pollen clogging the instruments, it wouldn't last in the air for too long."

"And that won't help us in the here and now." Dan exhaled in frustration. "We're going to have to limit our outings from here on. Only groups of two at a time, maybe keep closer to the ship for the time being."

"We can always maneuver the ship elsewhere..." Dillion said.

Dan shook his head and walked past him. "No, that would be a waste of fuel, energy, and time. All of which we don't have too much of. Let's just head back and brainstorm more about it later."

"Let's hope the two geniuses haven't blown up the ship or killed each other..." Janice smirked.

Dan motioned for them to continue and the four pressed on into the deep, dark jungle of Dreganon V.

Chapter 8

Something In The Air

The sun was starting to set in the distance of the lush jungle environment. Katelan and the others were tired and trying to make their way back to the ship. Captain Dan hadn't the strength to slice through any more of the greenery. Katelan had volunteered to do the honours, seeing how everyone was complaining she did the least amount of work getting there in the first place (Janice being the most vocal about that fact). So, she took the tool and hacked away as best she could.

The darkness was starting to set in and the foliage was becoming harder and harder to see through. She had to be careful of where they stepped. There was no way of knowing if another pool of mossy-type water, like the one they just came from, lied elsewhere beyond. The route they originally took was now regrown. The plants had aggressively reclaimed that space Dan ploughed through. So now, once again, they had to make yet another tunnel for all to walk in. Dan was right about the thickness of the stems, they were hard and difficult to chop off.

Katelan was growing tired fast as she sliced over and

over. Even in the dark, the quietness of the jungle was damn eerie to her and the others. The only noisy thing was them; The sound of their footsteps crunching the leaves, the slicing swoosh of the saber, and their breather apparatus pushing out their carbon dioxide. Dillion looked about with concern.

"What a place," he grumbled. "I don't think it's worth the effort to get all that oxygen from here, to be honest."

"Well, that's not for you to decide." Dan stated as he followed alongside, rubbing his sore muscles. "You want to get paid? Maybe get some extended vacation? Then, ya gotta do what ya gotta do."

"Geez, somebody put that phrase on a company motivational poster." Janice quipped sotto voce.

The group caught her lighthearted sarcasm and shared a quiet chuckle as they soldiered on. Katelan went on to *slice and dice* through the thick jungle, occasionally stopping to catch her breath, and then attacking the unforgiving brush once more as she regained her wind. This would be the pattern for a few more minutes, surprising even herself at how much endurance she could muster for the task; but something caused her to pause suddenly and raised a hand to halt the others behind her.

Like a rabbit on alert, Katelan froze in her spot and swivelled her head about. Captain Dan and the others looked confused, as they also tried to catch whatever she was worried about. Janice wordlessly shrugged at Dan as he glanced her way. Dillion did the same likewise, he wasn't sure what was up either. Dan turned his attention back to Katelan, who still hadn't moved a muscle.

"What is it, Katey?"

"I heard something..." she said, peering into the darkness ahead. "It's very faint, but, I hear it..."

Dan tried his best to listen. There was only absolute silence, other than their own breathing.

"There's nothing," He shrugged. "It's probably just your imagination."

"No..." She shook her head. "It was like, a voice... in the air, or maybe... like a whisper..."

"Maybe you cut a fart and didn't realize it." Dillion snickered.

"Really man?" Janice said, giving him a back hand to the helmet. "Back to charm school for you, mister."

Katelan ignored the others and sharply looked at Dan in the eyes. "I swear, it was a voice..."

"Okay..." He gestured in response with palms out. "Okay, I believe you. So, what do you want us to do about it? Do you still hear the voice now?"

She paused for a second, even lowering her breath slightly so that she could listen, and then shook her head. Dan nodded in reassurance and calmly took the slicing blade from her hand.

"Ok, so, maybe it wasn't what you thought it was." Dan said to her. "And even if it was, a voice, there's nothing we could do, right? We need to get back to the ship, with the sample, and strike out again another time."

That was a logical assessment from Dan, Katelan couldn't disagree with it. She was tired. Maybe it was just as he said. Dan took point again and motioned for her to take up the rear. She nodded without question and cleared her side helmet vents of the pollen clogging them up. Each of them did the same, forgetting about the build up mounting, and gave one another a thumbs up to signal they were alright.

"Okay, people, let's get a move on." Dan instructed, and

then turned back to slice more of a path. "It's getting darker out here, and I really want to get back for a beer."

"Amen, I'm all for that." Janice snorted.

"Wait, we've got beer on board?" Dillion said with a confused glare. "Why am I the last to know about this?"

"Just a figure of speech, ya dummy..." Katelan said, giving him a slap on the shoulder. "Besides, you think we'd let you near any? It would be gone before we could even keep it cold."

"Hey, I can't help who I am." He waggled his brows at her.

"Being stupid?" Janice rebutted. "Or being the resident drunkard?"

"Both..." He grinned.

Everyone laughed in unison. It was just the bit of light comedy they needed to brighten the journey. The gleeful group shared a tune, one that Dan whistled and caused everyone to follow along in kind. Dan was a fan of the classics, especially the old time-y ones, like Eminem—*Without Me*. Dan always had a few tunes stored in the ship's memory banks and played them during long flights in-between solar system jumps.

He wished he had uploaded some to his environment suit's comm, but he thought this would be a short walk, no need to get the team riled up from him playing his *old man* music, as they would say. For now, whistling would have to be his only outlet. Thankfully, the others understood his archaic melody and joined the chorus. But as he struggled to maintain the beat (slicing the veg along the way), a growing concern came in his mind and looked at the path with some doubt.

"This is taking too long," He grumbled to himself. "We should had been at the ship or seen it in the victim by now."

Giving a slight glare back to Katelan (preoccupied with keeping up with the rhythm of the tune), Dan thought more about the situation. "She's hearing voices, that's not good at all. I remember people going mad on such long exploration missions. God, I hope that's not happening to her."

Katelan caught him looking and gave a smile. He nodded and quickly focused back on cutting through the greenery.

"Damn it, I should have marked the path we came through earlier..." he thought to himself. "Come on Dan, just a bit further, you can do it."

Back on Skyward Seven, Allen and Deac were busy tending to the ship. They managed to clear the large vents and trimmed down more of the growing vines as they drew closer inward. Both men looked exhausted and were sweat laden from the workload. Allen took a moment to sit at the base of the ship's ramp and took in some deep breaths.

"Fuck, I'm tired, dude..."

"Where the hell is everyone, anyway?" Deac said, leaning against the ship's left landing strut. "How much longer till tank two is full?"

"Um..." Allen struggled to think. "Another hour or so..."

"Aw, come on!" Deac roared, with a string of profanity afterwards. "Are you serious? We did practically two hole tanks on our own."

"I know, right?" Allen lay back onto the ramp. "Where are those mother fuckers? What could take an entire solar day to look for?"

"They should have used the *Bush-cat* and cut the time factor down."

"It only sits two, Deac." Allen grumbled. "Two might have been fine in that thing, sure, but the others would have to sprint like the wind to catch up to that behemoth."

"So, why didn't two just go then, huh?"

"I don't know, man!" Allen screamed in frustration, sitting up with a look of angst. "I'm not the captain of this team, I'm just the lowly engineer of this lot... so, don't ask me stupid shit like that, okay? Geez..."

Deac threw down his cutting tool and stormed over to Allen. "I simply asked a question, Allen. I'm tired too, if not more, seeing how I've been out here doing this more than you have. But, hey, what does it matter, right?" Deac threw up his arms and turned away. "You know what, screw this, and screw you, man. I'm not doing any more, you got that? I'm done, finished, over... I'm going inside and having something to eat."

"I ain't yer poppa..." Allen shrugged, giving a mild snort at his comment. "Do what you want, I'm just as done, if not more."

They both gave a passing glare to each other, one that took longer than should have, and then Deac finally headed inside the ship. Allen made sure he was out of the way as the grumbling co-worker stormed past. He wanted to trip the son-of-a-bitch as he came close, he had a hand ready to do so as he sat there, but pulled away before following through on that thought.

"Best not to make it worst." He thought.

For a group that practically lived, worked and had vacations together, one would think they would be a solid team that could tolerate each other's behaviours by now. But, when you're doing stretches of time and long distant missions like this, with nobody else to talk to (other than the same people over and over), the occasional butting of heads and ego clashes tend to go in circles. You can only stand to talk to someone for so long, before you get totally bored with them. At least, that's Allen's theory, one he was only happy to share with the rest of his crewmates.

"God, I could really use a drink right about now." Allen grumbled. "I should have brought a bottle of whiskey with me... or a six pack of beers."

That wouldn't have gone well if he did though. Alcohol and recreational drug use was prohibited by the AirSurge corporation, especially on time sensitive missions like this. They needed the work done with no drunken or stupefied crew, less liability in the long run, but, more so for their corporate image. Unbeknownst to AirSurge though, many Harvester crews were bringing it aboard and using it when they managed a good score for themselves. Though off ship, of course.

But Allen was used to Dan Fruger's captaining, being a stickler to the rules, he instructed them all upfront of his '*no drinks or drugs*' policy before signing them on. If you wanted to work for him, you had to abide by his mandate, and so Allen freely accepted it. He'd be dry as a bone until they returned home, and then get blitzed out of his mind for a week or two. For now, though, he would have to deal with it as best he could till then.

* * *

Beyond Skyward Seven, the sun finally disappeared over the horizon of the jungle planet, the dark creeping in to full blindness and the surrounding plant-life seemed to fade out, as if muted by the lack of sunlight touching them. Suddenly, other colours appeared, neon-like pinks and blues peaked out of the shadowed depths, showing a beautiful array of phosphorescence that highlighted the surrounding area.

It was if someone flicked on a switch and all the night lights came on in unison. A strange a bizarre occurrence that seemed to be overlooked by the crew. As Captain Dan and the others trudged on with their headlamps guiding their path, only Katelan seemed in awe of such a splendid sight. She reached out to touch one of the plants; a strange glow that seemed enticing, giving her an urge to draw closer to it. But, as her headlamp shone upon the tantalizing broadleaf, the glow dimmed away and returned to its typical green colour.

Examining with a keen scientific eye, she wondered if this was an attractor for other plants nearby, a reproductive display that only certain nocturnal species of vegetation could achieve at this phase. Recording it with her holographic camera, nestled in the arm-comm unit of her suit, she stepped back and allowed the plant to glow once more. It did, with a greater brilliance than before.

"Amazing..." She grinned, giving a slight chuckle in amusement. "It's so beautiful."

"Yeah, sure," Janice said, looking about at all the different types surrounding them. "Beautiful now, probably deadly later, right? Isn't that how it always seems to go?"

"You watch too many old Earth movies, Janice." Dillion snickered. "Afraid a plant is going to suck your blood or something? Blah-blah, I vanna swallow you, Blah-ba-blah!"

"I bet you do..." Janice glared at him. "Perv..."

"Let's keep it moving people..." Dan said with authority, as he grew tired of the bickering.

They quickly regrouped themselves and forged ahead.

* * *

It had been about twenty minutes since Allen and Deac had given up on doing any more work. The sound of the air collector switching off caused him to stir slightly. The fact that the other pump didn't kick in made him sigh loudly. He wondered if the other tank's filters were clogged now, something he wasn't really looking forward to changing—yet again. He remained lying on the ramp, thinking about that fateful day when a shot glass would be in his hand once more, when suddenly, Deac yelped out something incoherent from inside the ship.

He dismissed it at first, thinking maybe Deac was still acting up, having his temper-tantrum and wanting attention. The man cried out again, only much louder and calling Allen by name. It startled Allen as he sprang up and glared over his shoulder.

"Aw, what's a matter now, man-baby?" He sarcastically belittled. There was only silence. That made Allen stand up and carefully step closer inside. "Yo, Deac! What's a matter? Ya stub yer toe, or something? I'm not coming in to kiss it better for ya."

Again, there was no reply, yet Allen waited patiently for one. Still nothing, not a sound. A concerned look washed over his face as he slowly stepped deeper into the ship. He wondered if this was a ruse of some sort, a practical joke to get back at him for yelling earlier. As he entered the main living space, where the eating table and lockers were, he noted where Deac's helmet was; it was sitting on the side of his chair, the one spot he always took because it was closest to the lockers, while his boots (no doubt kicked off in anger by him) lay about on the floor.

"This isn't funny, man." Allen warned. "I know karate... Judo... and other shit like that..."

Well, no, he didn't, actually, but he wanted to sound like

he did. He hoped Deac wouldn't try anything stupid and poised his hands up, trying to look like a skilled fighter without actually being one in reality.

"Deac?" He called again. "Come on dude, I'm not in the mood for this now."

Stepping further inward, past the lockers and towards the back of the vessel, Allen kept looking about, eyeing corners and hidden sections where he might try to pop out at him. But there was no sign of the man. He lowered his hands, feeling it was a waste of false pretences anyway, and gave up the search. But as he did, a hand suddenly appeared from behind and gripped onto his shoulder, causing Allen to shriek in shock.

Chapter 9

Lost

"What do you mean, you don't know where we are?" Janice gave a stern glare at Dan and tapped her foot as she eyeballed him. "I thought you told us we were close? What the fuck, dude?"

"I thought it was taking longer than usual..." Dillion griped.

"Hey, I'm doing my best here, alright!" Dan bitterly shouted at them all. "It's not my fault this jungle tends to regrow so fast we can't retrace our original steps."

"We should have marked our way, damn it!" Janice vocalized once again. "We've been out here for hours, man, fucking hours!"

"She's right..." Katelan cut into their conversation. "We should have used some flares as markers. It was dumb of us to come out this far without some sort of..."

"Oh, brilliant fucking idea!" He screamed over to her. "Hey, who's the genius scientist on this mission, huh? Why didn't you start putting out markers? You've been in jungles like this before, right? Don't you usually have that in your bag of tricks, *lil' Miss Know-it-all?*"

Katelan looked at him in surprise. That was the first time he'd ever dared to talk back to her in such a tone. She thought he was on her side, always, but now, he's looking at her as if she was nobody special. Janice, Dillion, heck, even Deacon would belittle her for being a *know-it-all* science woman, but she never expected him to be that way towards her, not ever. Katelan wanted to cry. She held it back, though. "Why give that asshole the satisfaction?" She thought.

Dan caught his words and recoiled slightly with shame. He could see the look of disappointment in her eyes. He was going to apologize, until, Janice started cutting in with her own insult to him.

"You son of a bitch! She's not the leader of this team, you are! Don't be bad-mouthing her for your own incompetence. If you had half a brain, you would have known to bring the right provisions for the journey. But, no... oh, no... why would you ever think that far ahead?"

"Oh, man," Dillion giggled. "Where's the bag of popcorn, I need to enjoy this..."

"Shut up, Dill!" Janice fingered to him. "I've had it with your sass, too."

"Calm down, bitch!"

"What did you fucking call me?" She bitterly glared at him. "What? What did you just fucking call me, asshole?"

"Enough!" Dan screamed.

He held out his hands and silenced the two. He looked over at Katelan, still mad at his words, and gave him a passing glare. Dan let out of breath of frustration and tried to talk sensibly.

"God, all we ever do on these missions is bicker, fight and continually go at each other's throats. Figuratively and literally, guys. I'm tired of it. We're family, a tight knit crew that's been together way-way-way too long, it seems. Yes, we're stuck in the middle of nowhere." He then glanced over at Janice, "Yes, I take full responsibly for the lack of thought on this," he said to Katelan, and then looked over to Dillion. "And yes, I know... it took longer than usual, Dill."

"Okay, then..." Dillion shrugged at him. "So, what now boss? You'za thinkin' we'z-a gonna die?"

Dillion, forever the comedian of the group, always try to include some culture references to stymie any overly tense conversation. That made Dan roll his eyes and chuckled slightly. He knew what that was from. Though, he wasn't much of a Star Wars fan enough to know which movie that actually came from.

"We're going to wait until light." Dan stated, totally dismissing Dill's comedy routine. "It's way too dark to make our bearings, plus, we can follow the angle of the sun to make our way towards the ship."

"How long is the rotation of this world, anyway?" Janice pondered aloud.

"Well," Dillion glared up at the night sky. "I figure it's in the ballpark of eighteen hours, maybe twenty, the sun sets pretty damn quick. That was like two hours ago..."

"It's got a twenty hour rotation." Katelan stated to him. "We've been out for nearly over eight hours, the night started two hours of that, so another six to seven hours before dawn will come up, maybe."

"Seven hours?" Janice winced. "Fuck! That's too long a wait. We should keep walking, maybe we'll get lucky and run into..."

"We're going to keep getting more lost doing that Janice." Dillion exhaled with mild annoyance. "I vote to park our butts down and maybe catch some sleep."

"But what about the others?" She glared over at him.

"They'll wonder where we are. Maybe they'll get into the *Bush-cat* and come looking for us, right?"

"Those two?" Katelan snickered. "Bet they're passed out from all the scrubbing. Probably pissed off we didn't come back in time to help."

While the conversation about correct planetary time continued amongst them, Dan checked his wrist air gauge counter, choosing not to voice an opinion on matter. He noticed it was hitting the red line. The suit O_2 levels were nearly exhausted, it only had under half an hour of air left. Having spent most of it doing a majority of the heavy cutting, he was now realizing time (whatever this planet had) was running out.

"Guys, what's your O_2 levels?" He asked the group, breaking their idle chatter. "I've only got half an hour left."

"Shit..." They all stated while checking their own.

"I'm nearly at that mark..." Janice said.

"Same..." Dillion acknowledged.

"I'm low too..." Katelan grumbled. Suddenly, she peered up at them all and smacked her helmeted head lightly. "Oh, geez, really? We're surrounded by oxygen, guys. We just need to switch the flow filters from output to input."

"But," Dan tilted his head slightly. "Won't we die if we do? Ya know, from the concentration of the amount out here?"

"Not if you set the filters to the lowest setting." She pointed to the LED screen on her arm. "It's adjustable, thankfully enough. See here? Just bring it down so that the suit can regulate the flow." Everyone watched as she did it and then adjusted theirs. She nodded once they did and breathed in as the filters switched. "It might be a bit stinky... sorry guys."

"Oh! Oh, god!" Dillion yelped. "It smells awful! Geez, I thought it was bad before! This is ten times worse!"

The others agreed as they breathed in the foul odour. The looks of horrified and gagging faces made Katelan snicker. She helped each member to adjust their filters further to lessen the stench, but not completely, that was how the air just was, unfortunately.

"Think of it like being on a farm colony, yeah?" Dan said. "Space cows, and such..."

"Whatever," Dillion grumbled. "I'm going to be smelling this for months on end, I bet."

"At least we can breathe normal now," Dan said, squatting down and resting against a tall jungle root sticking out of the ground. "Maybe even get some shut-eye, right?"

The group all took a spot, trying to find a comfortable area, and kept themselves in a circle. Their headlamps all pointed at each other and illuminated their faces. Dillion seemed blinded by them and held up a hand to block it.

"We should have dimmers on. These things do have dimmers on them, right?'

"You want a lullaby too, ya big baby?" Janice huffed. "Just close your purty-lil' eyes. I'm not switching this off until the morning. I wanna be able to see whatever comes out of that dark, man. Ain't no way I'm going to be dragged out by whatever lurks out there."

"You watch too many movies, Janice." Dan grumbled, folding his hands together and closing his eyes. "There's nothing other than plants on this planet. Right, Katey?"

Katelan said nothing, but nodded with a distracted glance. She wondered about that fact. They hadn't been here long enough to know if there was, or wasn't, something else alive on this world. She made it a point to stay awake as long as possible. Dan instantly fell asleep. Soon, Dillion and

Janice followed as well, but not her—not right away, eventually though, she couldn't keep her eyes open and reluctantly drifted off.

* * *

Whispers and voices plagued Katelan's dreams. Images of the jungle world swept through as they continued on in their mumbled tones. It was hard to make out what they were saying, it was if the sound was coming at her from every angle. Even as she could see herself running through the thick maze of wilderness, the voices taunted her every step. It was as if they were summoning her to a specific direction.

As she passed through the endless branches, oversized leaves and flowers blooming in her wake, she saw figures standing around just out of the corner of her eye; Humanoid beings, faceless, shadowy and blending perfectly with the jungle's backdrop. It terrified her and wanted this nightmare to stop. There were screams coming from behind her, as the voices merged and overlapped. They were of Allen and Deacon, Janice and Dillion, and finally, Dan, whose was nearly loudest of all.

She wanted to scream herself, to ask them for help, but found she had no voice to do so. The other voices, the taunting whispers from before, continued on, they followed the sound of her heartbeat; it was strong, rhythmic and gaining strength as she continued to struggle deeper into the jungle. She could feel an invisible hand pushing against her back, getting forceful with each step, and increasing the stride until she reached a rounded opening.

Once there, she found a wide hole waiting. It was deep

and dark, with the sound of those voices emanating from it. She wasn't sure what it wanted from her, what she was suppose to do. She tried to go around it, but, could not do so. The invisible hand once again pushed her—it sent her straight in, and she let out a scream that carried on forever.

* * *

"Wake up! Wake up, Katey!"

She awoke to find Dan standing over her. He was shaking her and trying to stop her screaming. Katelan was confused momentarily, trying to make sense of what just happened. When she finally realized this wasn't part of the dream, she instantly hugged him and wept.

"Jesus, what the hell?" Janice said, walking over to them. "That was loud enough to hear throughout the entire jungle!"

"I-I-I thought I was falling..." Katelan whimpered. "I was falling so far..."

"You're not falling, alright?" Dan said, taking hold of her. "You're okay, Kate, you're okay."

Dillion stretched his arms out with a long yawn and gawked at the others. He noted the daylight bleeding through the dense foliage and glared at them with confusion.

"Morning y'all..." He grinned. "Something happen while I was out?"

"You slept through that?" Janice gawked at him.

"Through what? What did I miss?"

"Seriously?" Janice rolled her eyes and turned her attention back at Dan and Katelan. "Just the sound of someone screaming... which you'd never hear, mister deep-sleep."

Katelan let go of Dan and tried to regain control of herself. She wiped the tears off her face, gave a few calming deep breaths, and thanked them all for their concern. Dan still looked confused as to what just happened. As did they all.

"It was just a stupid dream." Katelan said, rising to her feet. She fiddled with the arm controls and regulated the airflow again. "I'm sorry everyone, really..."

"No-no-no..." Dan gestured at her. "You don't get to shake this off so easily. Spill it, Katey, what was it about?"

"Dan..." Katelan stated, holding out her hand to stop him from pressing the matter.

"Just tell us already, will ya?" He reacted in frustration.

She could see none of them, especially Dan, would allow her to let it go. With reluctance, she nodded and tried her best to give a basic run down of what it was all about.

"Okay, fine. The dream was about me, being lost in the jungle..." Janice snickered and gestured to their predicament now. Katelan conceded to that fact, but continued anyway. "I was alone, but there were voices calling to me. It felt like the jungle itself was pushing me to a spot, as if it wanted me to go there. I could hear you guys in the background..."

"That's good, right?" Dillion shrugged. "We were there for ya..."

"No, Dill," she exhaled. "You guys weren't there. Just your voices. You were all screaming—in pain, or being... killed."

"Shit..." Dan uttered.

"Yeah," Katelan nodded. "Like I said, not the best of dreams. Then I was brought to a deep dark hole, and pushed into it, right to my own death."

"Fuck, I hate those kinds of dreams." Dillion stated.

Janice elbowed him for uttering it. "What? I'm just being honest here."

Katelan looked at Dan, who just seemed to sympathize and gave her an understanding pat to the shoulder. Nothing need to be said between them. He knew her well enough to not drag it out any further. He quickly switched the subject and turned to the others with instructions.

"Okay, well, let's not go on about this anymore. Dill and Janice, let's have you guys on cutter duties. I think it's time we find our way back to the ship. Katey, you go behind them and I'll be behind you."

Everyone nodded and took their positions. Dan gave the cutter tool to Janice and let her take point. Dillion helped to clear the brush as she started slicing away. Before Katelan could start walking, Dan held her back for a moment and spoke privately.

"You sure you're okay to go on?"

"I'm fine..." she grinned at him. "It disturbed me a bit, but, I'm over it, really."

"I'm worried about you..." He stated, stroking her helmeted head lightly.

"Don't be," she responded, removing his hand. "Let's worry more about doing our job and getting the hell off this planet."

Giving a simple nod in return, he agreed with her. She turned away and walked through the area the two in front had just cleared. Dan kept a cautious eye on her. The concern on his face never wavered, and wondered if he should scrub the mission and return home. But that was an impossibility, the company would hold him liable, and the crew wouldn't get paid for anything. For now, he would have to just keep vigilant and make sure she wouldn't lose it out here.

Other captains reported crew going insane on long, gruelling missions like this. Some sort of psychosis that develops when workers are overly isolated or stressed out on deep space explorations. He hoped that wasn't happening here, with her, or with any other member of his crew. But most of all, he hoped it wouldn't happen to himself either.

Chapter 10

An Astrobiologist's Dream Come True

Walking along the freshly cut path Dillion and Janice were making, Katelan sauntered behind them and paused frequently to inspect the foliage and flowering blooms on the trail. "How Professor Lim Ragas would love this kind of environment" She inwardly thought. "So many new species of plant-life from continual cross-pollinations, so varied a flower, with petals displaying unique colors." It truly was a dream come true for any botanist or bio-science professional. This planet was vibrant and diverse, with rarities never seen by any human eye, until hers, that is.

She remembered attending all those virtual university lectures Doctor Lim gave: Hybrid genome structures and self pollination abnormalities, types of floral symmetry and design significance, and of course, her favourite subject— Astrobiology. That one, most of all, is why she took the job with AirSurge. They were heading out to those strange new worlds, where new botanical discovers could be made. Now, at long last, here she was, standing on the new world—an alien jungle of unlimited potential.

Katelan couldn't wait to get back to the ship. She was excitedly eager to start up her lab and delve into the biochemistry makeup of these genetic wonders. She was mostly keen on giving the water sample (the one she took prior) a closer inspection as well. She took it out of her sleeve pocket and studied it as they continued to walk on. The small vial of water looked murky and clouded. She gave it a few good taps and watched the greyish-green flotsam float about; a mixture of spores, pollen and other unknown bits.

There was something about this sample that bothered her though, something she just couldn't seem to put her finger on. The water looked far too grey, milk-like, as it were. No matter how she turned or pivoted the container, the water wasn't clear enough to see through. That was strange. If this was from some swamp or bog on Earth, one could still see some sort of separation or clarity of the water near the top. But no, there was nothing at all. Even when she let it settle, the sludge inside never rested to the bottom. Was this a natural source? Was that pond always there? Or was this from a previous rainfall that was still dissipating?

The more she gazed at it intently, the more she could see floating around inside. Yes, something was most definitely not right with this stuff.

"What's the matter?"

Katelan popped out of her focus as Dan spoke. She didn't realize he was so close beside her and did a double take in reaction.

"Uh, what? Oh..." She fluttered her eyes briefly. "It's nothing, just thinking... you know, bioscientist, right?"

"Uh-huh..." Dan glanced at her. "Spill it, I know you too well for that kind of dismissal."

"No really, I'm not..."

"You get so involved in the work, Katey, I know you well enough to know what's going on in that overly smart brain of yours."

She had to concur with that fact. They had been together for a good number of years. A relationship that was both professional and personal. Neither one wanted to admit they were more than just intimate friends, or *fuck buddies* as Dillion would often point out, but definitely in the realm of exclusive boyfriend and girlfriend.

"I'm concerned about something," She said to him. "This water doesn't look like water..."

"Huh..." He said. "Well, maybe it's not, maybe it's just sap. You know, kinda pooling together in one spot."

"Yeah," She nodded, mildly surprised that he made good observation. "That makes sense, sure. I thought that as well. But, most plant sap tends to be thicker, less watery-looking..."

Dan thought for a moment, occasionally moving freshly chopped branch out of his way as Janice went on hacking away in front. Dillion was just as sloppy chucking them around, but, not in their direction. Dan grunted as he pitched it away.

"Liquid chlorophyll, maybe?" He asked with uncertainty.

"Yeah, that's another good one I thought of too," She nodded, giving a wry smile at the man's attempt to know what he was talking about. "But, no, I think that would be far too much in one spot. Besides, I doubt the surrounding plants would have let that enriched nutrient go to waste."

"Okay," Dan blinked. "So, what do you think it is then?"

"I'm not sure." She stated, while looking ahead. "That's why I need to inspect it in the lab."

"What about that device clipped to your side?" Dan pointed to the small hand scanner.

She looked at it hanging off her belt and shook her head. "It's not enough, I need the ship's computer to help cross-reference with other Earth-based species as a comparison. It might give me some insight on the viscosity and general properties of something resembling it."

"Of course..." Dan shrugged.

She gave a smirk at his answer. Yeah, he wasn't into this kind of science, botany and astrobiology, that wasn't really something they had in common. They had a sexual attraction to one another, but, that was pretty much it in terms of anything else. At least he tried to show some sort of interest. Most of her former boyfriends wouldn't even give that much. But, beyond the sex they seemed to enjoy off and on, there was no reason to maintain a steady partnership. Not that they didn't give it a good try.

Dan kept his eye on her as they walked, and to that of the vial she was still holding. Katelan was preoccupied with studying it, moving the liquid back and forth, as if she was waiting for something to happen if she kept doing the motion.

"What I wouldn't give for a coffee and a sandwich right now..." He uncomfortably stated, trying to change the subject. "Guess I should have packed a picnic for us all."

"I agree," Janice chimed in. "With the coffee part, anyway."

"I'd kill everyone here for a sandwich." Dillion bluntly stated.

"Great," Janice sarcastically mocked at his words. "Remind me not eat anything you prepare in the future."

Dan snickered at their responses, but noticed Katelan

wasn't doing so. He tapped on her helmet slightly and gave a look of concern.

"How bout you? Coffee, sandwich—anything?"

Katelan placed the vial back in her sleeve, and gave a disappointed sigh. "We shouldn't have come out this far, I should have just collected something closer to the ship. I'm sorry."

"It's okay," He smirked at her. "I made the call, not you. As captain of this bunch, I should have foreseen our getting lost into consideration. Guess that makes me a really crappy captain."

"Nah," She grinned back. "Just makes you a typical man... not looking at maps, not asking for directions..."

"Geez, that's sexist..." Dillion interjected in their conversation.

"Shad-up you!" Katelan mocked, picking up a fallen thick leaf and chucking it at his head. "You're sexist all the time."

"That's the damn truth..." Janice agreed. She laughed and gave him the finger. "Choke on that reality, Dill."

Dillion gave one back to her and drew out a long sigh. "I get no respect in this group, none."

Everyone started laughing. They were tired, cranky, and giddy, all at the same time. The hunger and dehydration was definitely setting in. All four members continued on through the super-thick alien environment; swinging cutters, snapping branches, and stomping out roots as they made their way to (what they hoped) would be the direction of the ship.

Chapter 11

Unexpected Events

"Oh, thank you God!" Janice exclaimed in appreciative joy. "We've made it back."

The weary (and starving) explorers had indeed found the ship once again. Dillion ran up as fast as he could and mockingly tried to kiss the side of the vessel's hull. Dan and Katelan both sighed with relief and headed for the ramp, which to their surprise, was still open and now overgrown with vines.

Janice laughed at Dillion's antics and expressed her own affection to the ship by patting the closest landing strut. She also noticed the lack of trimming done as she pulled a few vines strangling the landing gear.

"Lazy assholes..." she sighed. "Bet they're still asleep inside."

Dan motioned at them all to head inside. It was time to get out of the suits, get some much needed grub, and go inhale some cleaner air than what they've been taking in. Katelan was the first to head in, but seemed puzzled that neither Allen nor Deac came to greet them. At the very least, she expected them to run up in anger for abandoning them there all this time. But, there was no one. Dan soon joined behind her and glared about inside.

"Where is everyone?" She said to him.

"Probably out looking for us." Dan said, walking past her and opening the inner airlock door.

He stepped inside and gestured her to follow. Janice and Dillion followed behind and waited as the door shut behind them. The ship usually would start its decontamination protocol; venting out the atmosphere, exchanging the air, and then giving a green light for them to remove their helmets. It concerned them all that none of that took place. Dillion tapped the other door and tried to glare through the small round window.

"Yo! Numb nuts! Are you going to let us in or what?"

"Give it a second, Dill..." Janice grumbled. "Maybe they've had some problems while we were away."

Dan didn't think so, he came to the door and thumped on it hard. "Allen! Deac! Come on, guys, stop messing around and let us in already!"

At first, there was only silence, it made them all briefly look at each other with concern. Then, a voice said something behind the door, but nobody could figure out who was speaking. The hydraulics *whooshed*, and the door slowly started opening upward. Standing on the other side of it, was Deacon.

"Deac? What the hell, man?" Dillion scowled at him.

"Sorry, we've had some issues." He responded.

"Issues?" Janice mocked. "We need to decontaminate, what's going on? You two idiots break the damn ship or something?"

Katelan noticed Deac's suit, it was covered in green-yellow spore-pollen, and she could barely make out his face through the helmet. Dan authoritatively stepped past the slime-ridden crewman and entered the ship without removing his gear. Looking inside, he could see that everything was covered in the same goop as Deacon was. It made him angry.

"Jesus! What the fuck did you guys do?"

Katelan and the others walked behind him and eyeballed the inner ship as well. Nobody could take off their enviro-suits, not while the outdoor elements had practically taken over the interior. Dillion and Janice cursed up a storm as they noticed all their things had gotten contaminated. Katelan turned to Deac, standing beside her, and threw her arms up at him.

"You morons! Look at this place! It's gonna take weeks for us to scrub all this shit off of everything in here. Who left the door open? And where's Allen?"

Deac remained standing beside her, showing little to no reaction to her complaints. She glared at him again and folded her arms, waiting for an explanation.

"Allen isn't here." He stated. "Don't know what happened to him. I guess he's outside looking for you."

Janice sat down on a chair covered in pollen. It stirred up the dusty-like substance and hung about her like a fog.

"Unbelievable, just fucking unbelievable..." She said, shaking her head. "Deac, how did this happen? What were you two doing?"

Deac (still standing quite still) answered her without turning in her direction. "I needed help, Allen couldn't hear me so far into the ship, so I opened the door and marched over to him."

"And you too got into a fight," Janice finished for him.

"Yes..."

"Fantastic," She grumbled. "Hell of a time to pick on one another."

Dan was still seething from the stupidity of it all, but apprehensively glared at Deacon for a moment. The man hadn't moved a muscle since they entered. It seemed strange and rather odd to the man. Deacon could be very hot headed, passionate even, especially when being accused of something. Yet, now, he's passive and speaking *'a matter-of-factly'* to them all.

"Katey, see if you and Dillion can locate Allen out there." Dan said. He did his best to remain calm while asking, and continued to stay focused on Deacon, standing motionless. "Let's, uh, make sure he didn't run too far away from the ship."

"Aye-aye boss..." Katelan mockingly saluted. "Come on, Dill..."

"Damn it," Dillion disappointedly said. "I really wanted to have a sandwich. I'm starving..."

"We all are, honey." Janice bemoaned. "Now shut up and go find our engineer. We're gonna need him if we're going to get this place back to normal."

As both Dillion and Katelan passed by Dan and Deac (not bothering to glance at them), Janice stood up and wiped her ass off from all the pollen-spore stuck on it.

"Fuck, this is some god-awful crap. Deac..." She glared over at him. "Make yourself useful and grab a scrubber, will ya?"

Deac simply nodded and walked away to the back section of the ship. Dan watched the man with scrutiny and twisted his lip in thought. Janice noticed his concerned face and shrugged her shoulders at him.

'What's a matter with you now?"

"I'm not sure," Dan grimaced slightly in a low breath. "Something is off about him."

Janice snickered, "Yeah, what else is new buddy..."

* * *

Katelan stood outside the ship and studied the growth that had asserted itself all over. She was puzzled at the amount in such a short time. They had tried to clear a few spots before heading in, but now... it had regrown as if they hadn't touched it at all. It was very disconcerting to her. She remembered the vial in her suit's arm pocket and took it out to make sure it was still good. The swirling goop of water mixed with pollen reminded her of an ancient lava lamp she once had as a child.

Placing it back inside the pocket, she then crouched down to the growth and slowly brushed at it with her hand. She studied the leaves and roots that stretched out before her. The curious botanist mindset took over, as she carefully inspected the plant with an inquisitive eye.

"It's so damn aggressive," She thought to herself. "Regenerating at such a quick pace, it's so unnatural, compared to Earth and other world forests."

Instinctively, she took the small hand scanner from her utility belt; the one she had used earlier to do a quick look at the surrounding plant-life nearby. She focused it on the root itself and tried to make out the holographic that displayed before her. Eventhough this device could perform magnifications beyond that of any normal microscope, and could even intensify to the molecular level, with images showing the genetic structure. It still wasn't enough to get the full scan she'd hope to get from this unique plant-life.

Buried deep within the ship, in boxes and storage containers was her lab equipment. They were supposed to be set up before stepping out onto the surface. But Katelan was far too excited to begin, and she totally forgot about it the minute they did set foot onto the world. Katelan realized she was acting more like an overexcited explorer and not like the skilled bioscientist she was.

"Well, so much for that then." She thought. "I'll just have to make do with this for now."

She adjusted the images on the holographic screen, marked each one to be filed and recorded it for later, and expanded the generated 3D display of the genetic pattern. Her eyes focused on the one area she'd seen before in the previous scan.

"There's that odd protein strand again." She mumbled to herself. "But, it's bigger this time... clustered, with other things attached to it. What are they?"

Dillion finally stepped out with a scrubber device in hand. Like a lumberjack, puffing out his chest and giving a pleased sigh, he surveyed the area, and began using the powered tool on the slime-ridden ramp to clear a path. The high-pitched whine from the device caused Katelan to jolt a little, she wasn't expecting to hear it so suddenly, especially when lost in thought. Dillion came closer to her and tried to use it around the woman.

"Beep-beep lil' lady..." He snickered.

She ignored his typical antics. But then, suddenly, she glance up for a split second. Something had caught her ear, a faint sound, something being muffled by Dillion's machine. She strained to hear it, and waved her hand for him to stop. When he didn't acknowledge, she quickly placed one hand on him, and motioned her head toward where she was glaring. Dillion, rolling his eyes at her mannerism, did as requested and listened with her.

"Do you... do you hear that?" She said to him. "That noise, just now?"

Dillion squinted for a second, straining his own ear, trying hard to listen. He simply shrugged his shoulders.

"No, actually, I don't hear a thing. It's pretty silent, Kate."

"No, Dill..." She motioned again with her head. "Really, stop and listen for a second. Trust me."

He let out a disappointed grunt and did as he was instructed. The two remained motionless, silent as the jungle itself, but Dillion still couldn't hear a thing. He was about to say something to her, when suddenly... he heard it. It was a voice, a barely audible one at that, calling out from far away and sounding like someone in horrible pain.

"Shit..." Dillion said, his eyes growing wide. "Is that... is that, maybe..."

"Allen!" She stated with a look of realization.

The two immediately bolted in the direction and called out his name repeatedly. Dillion stopped short for a second, "Wait, Katey!" He said to her. "We should tell the others!"

"No time for that," She screamed back at him. "We'll radio it in on the way. Come on, Dill, let's go!"

Dillion looked at her, then back at the ship, then back at her again. He was confused on what to do. He soon relented, cursing under his breath, and tried to follow behind as she ran further beyond.

* * *

Inside Skyward Seven, Dan continued to scan the surroundings of the ship. The place was a mess with the goopy-green slime of pollen/spore, and even started growing some small vines out of clustered roots that sprouted along the consoles and floors. It baffled him on just how fast this stuff spread and grew. It's one thing for it to be outside of the ship, easier to clean off and keep in its own environment, but an absolute nightmare to contend with inside their living space. He tried to rub his forehead in frustration, forgetting he was still locked inside an enviro-suit, giving a sigh while looking at his hand.

"I'm so god-damn hungry..." Janice stated. She used the scrubber device to clear a few sections of panel, constantly banging and butting it everywhere in frustration. "I just want to get out of this suit so I can at least take a pee as well."

"Yeah," Dan passively stated, while still gawking. "Our suits can filter out anything, if necessary..."

"Oh, hell no," She stated, flopping the machine hard to the floor. "I'm not doing my business in this getup. I'd rather hold it than walk around with piss in my boots!"

"Where's Deac?" Dan asked, not giving Janice's comment any heed.

He quickly headed towards the back of the ship, while Janice was still complaining about the idea of relieving herself in an enviro-suit. As Dan scanned each section he entered, he called out Deacon's name and waited for an answer. Nothing came back. He came to the engine room, hoping the man was there, or maybe even Allen... who knows. But as he stepped in, he noticed a large dead plant sitting in the room. How did he know it was dead? Well, it was brown for one. Nothing on this world was even remotely brown, other than the leaves on the ground they stepped on outside.

The plant was also splayed out on the metallic floor, looking like it had been ripped apart or shredded. It was an odd sight to come across in the room. He bent down to examine it closely, occasionally fingering the leaves and broken stem. But as he sat there looking perplexed, he could feel a presence behind him and spun about. There was Deacon, with a large shovel-pick in hand, ready to strike it down on him. Dan was quick to react and managed to stop his blow just in time. The two struggled for control over it, pushing and pulling, neither one giving in.

"What... what are you doing? Deac?" Dan strained to hold him off. "Have you lost your mind? Fuck!"

Deacon said nothing, he continued to force himself down onto the captain and desperately tried to kill the man. Dan managed to swing his leg out and kick the man off of him. Deacon fell to the floor on his back. Dan leapt onto him in that weakened position, snatched the shovel out of his hand, and bashed it on the man's head. The sound of the helmet cracking caused Deacon to flail about, he tried to grip the shovel again, but Dan was too enraged and continued to pound down on him.

Finally, the helmet shattered, Deacon's suit immediately depressurized and was exposed to the alien world's overly abundant air supply. The man frantically gasped and tried to cover his face, as if it would help in some sort of way, but it was a futile effort. With a few last desperate violent gasps, Deacon collapsed instantly. Dan kept the shovel poised over his head, ready to deal another blow, and watched for any movement to give him the excuse. When nothing happened, he dropped the shovel-pick, and a wave of horror washed over his face as it sank in. Dan's eyes grew wide. He couldn't believe what he'd done—he killed him, Deacon was dead.

Chapter 12

Mimic

"Holy shit! Holy shit!" Dan repeatedly rambled on with a horrified expression. "Deac... oh, god... oh, fuck! No... no, man! No!"

The ramification of what he had done finally shattered his mind. Dan was at loss on what to do next. He was still in denial of what had transpired, looking briefly at the body and then the blood-soaked shovel. In desperation, he called out for help.

"Janice! Janice! Oh, fucking christ! Janice!"

Janice, after hearing his repeated calls for her, came running in and saw the carnage. She was in total shock of what was before her; Deacon's lifeless corpse with Dan standing over him, he dropped the murder weapon to the ground, and she saw nothing but blood all over the two of them. She gasped at the sight and was at a loss for words.

"W-w-what the..." She sputtered. "What did you do? What did you fucking do?"

"He was attacking me!" Dan frantically stated to her. "He tried to kill me, Janice!"

"What do you mean?" She barked back. "Kill you? Why would he do that? Have you gone insane?"

"No!" He firmly responded, glaring back at her. "I didn't go insane, that piece of shit did!"

Janice didn't know what to do. She was overcome with disbelief and horror. She turned her back for a minute, sobbing lightly and trying to come to her senses. Once she was finished, she turned back to face him and pointed.

"You'd better start explaining yourself, right now, Dan. Right this fucking minute..." She quickly ran over, picked up the shovel, and held it out defensively. "Don't you dare come near me until you do, you got that? Not one fucking step."

Dan nodded and raised his hands up. He tried to collect himself and took a few deep breaths to calm down. He was still shaking from the ordeal, but tried his best to curb it for her sake.

"I told you, he attacked me, Deac tried to murder me."

"So you say..." She motioned the shovel at him.

"It's the truth."

"Give me more than that, you son of a bitch!"

Dan held up his hands further, trying to calm the woman, and did his best likewise. He took a few deep breaths and looked straight at her.

"I came back here to find Deac, when he didn't respond I investigated further. That's when I noticed that dead plant on the ground over there and decided to look at it. Before I could get up, Deac came up from behind, jumped on me and tried to take me out with that shovel you've got in your hand."

Janice looked at him, then at the shovel, and back on him. She wasn't sure what to believe in this moment. The blood was still covered on the tip of the tool and dripping onto the metal floor slowly. Dan desperately waited for her to answer back (he could see she was struggling to comprehend his explanation). She let go of the shovel, letting to smack to the ground, and straightened her back with a more relaxed glare.

"I'll need to confirm your story with that of the ship's video feed, but..." She eyed him carefully. "I'll take your word... for now."

Dan nodded in agreement. Well, what else could he say or do in that moment? He looked guilty as hell to her. So, rather than trying to convince her over and over, he'd just have to let her see it for herself. Janice glanced down at Deac's body.

"Now, what do we do with him?"

"Let's bring him to medical," Dan passively gestured. "We can examine him there."

"We're not doctors," She stated abruptly. "We've only had minor first aid training..."

"Yeah, but we've got Katey." He stressed to her. "She's got the know-how to deal with this... or something similar to it."

"Dan," Janice tilted her head, giving a wry look. "She's just a biologist, you ninny. Not a real doctor."

"Don't let her hear you say that." Dan snickered. "Come on, at least let's get his body to the Med-scan bed."

"Yeah, right..." She nodded, looking unsure of where or what to grab of the body. "Sorry, buddy, no disrespect."

As she lifted him up, the look of amazement washed over her. He was light, lighter than she would have believed. Even Dan had an astonished gaze as he held on to the body's ankles. Deacon was not in the best of shape. He was nearly six feet tall of pure girth, and so, he should have weighed a ton. They were baffled by the relative ease they could move him about. Janice and Dan brought the corpse to the medical section. It wasn't so much a section, or a room of its own, but a slot in the wall that opened up and unfolded the equipment needed.

A ship of this size required maximization of all its space. The medical bed stuck out as the scanners, computers, and other items needed unfurled out of their confined compartments. Once they placed Deac's body down onto it, the scanner immediately activated and began projecting the holographic interface. The computer queried him as to the emergency. He flicked through the various options and selected the one called: *Autopsy/Examination Procedure*

"How long will this take?" Janice inquired, unsure of the procedure.

"I'm not sure," Dan grimaced. "I've never had to do this before."

The two said nothing further as they watched, both were still in a state of shock, and were mesmerized by the automated station as it continued the task. The machine did all the work; lasers cut the suit, while small robot arms came out to remove the clothing and took samples of the corpse. All Dan and Janice could do now was wait.

* * *

"Allen! Allen!"

Both Katelan and Dillion were screaming in unison as they jogged about the dense jungle. Their voices were being projected by their suit's intercom, augmenting it to a level within a radius of sixty feet. The thickness of the plants tended to contain the sound, essentially bouncing it back towards themselves. Dillion gave up screaming after a while, after realizing this.

"He can't hear us, Katey."

"Allen!" Katelan screamed again, totally ignoring Dillion's defeated state. "Allen! Where are you?"

"Will you stop already!" Dillion said to her. He stopped for a moment and placed his hands on his hips in frustration. "I'm tired, and this is getting us no where."

Katelan turned about and threw up her arms. "Oh, so that's it? You're just going to give up? He's our friend, Dill... our friend and crewmate we've known for many years..."

"No," He asserted with a finger. "I'm not giving up, but there's no way we can find him in this flippin' brush, okay? We need the others help. The two of us aren't just going to stumble upon him, come on! It's literally looking for a needle in a haystack... or... the jungle equivalent of one, whatever..."

Katelan frowned at his comment, but then nodded in agreement. It would take a lot to search for one missing person in a place like this. They, themselves, were nearly lost in this never-ending labyrinth of greenery. She conceded the point and walked over to him.

"Okay, yeah..." She proceeded to nod. "You're right, sorry. We should head back and see if the others have had any luck. Maybe he's back already, right?"

Dillion complied and started the journey back to the ship. Katelan followed behind and looked back with a somber glare. She couldn't understand where or why Allen would take off like that. She wondered if he was just wandering about taking samples for her, or, blowing off some steam after Deac and him had a fight. The latter being more plausible, Allen wasn't one for taking people's crap when they got in his face about something. Deac was overly opinionated, so it stood to reason that the two might have clashed when it came to a *'who is in charge'* kind of moment.

But as she took one last look back again, she noticed something in the far distance. It looked like a figure, a human-like figure, turned about with its back facing her. She stopped for a moment, telling Dillion to do the same and pointed to it.

"Look, over there!" She beamed. "Is that... is that him?"

"Allen!" Dillion grinned, as he now observed him as well.

The figure look like it was turning slightly, as if it wasn't sure where to look. Katelan seemed puzzled by his reaction.

"What the hell? Why doesn't he turn to see us?"

"Maybe his communicator isn't working?" Dillion shrugged.

Katelan wasted no time and started to briskly walk over to the man. Dillion tried to keep up, but Katelan's stride was too great. The closer she got, the more she could make out the shape of the man; the outline of his environment suit and oxygen back pack was becoming defined and the shimmer of the metal on his helmet was giving her confidence that this was indeed Allen. But as she finally came to the point of where he stood, her smile slowly diminished, and gawked in utter amazement.

"What the hell?" She exhaled out.

This wasn't Allen. In fact, it was nothing more than a plant. She moved about to study the oddity; it was a grouping of plants, each leaf had a color that blended together to form an image that looked exactly like a person standing there. Not only that, but from certain angles, one could almost mistake it for an environment suit, as the mimicry was spot on. Dillion slowly approached as he also saw the reality of what it was.

"Holy shit..." He uttered in surprise. "What... uh... what the fuck is this, Katey?"

She went on to look at it, encircling the free-standing tangled plant-form with utter amazement. A slight wind caused the plants to move, giving the illusion of the figure moving as well. She let out a sigh of disappointment and came to a halt.

"I don't believe it." She stated, while lowering her gaze. "I was sure it was Allen, I mean... it looks so..."

"This is creepy, man." Dillion gawked at it. "Why would a plant... a fucking plant, create an illusion like this? It's shaped like a person... like Allen, right? I mean, I'm not seeing things, this really looks like him."

"I know," She acknowledged while stroking the leaves that resembled an arm. "Plants tend to mimic their environment, not people. I mean, sure, I've seen some instants of them looking like some type of predator, usually as a lure or a defense against one, but... not a... a..."

"Human?" Dillion finished for her, gesturing at it. "This is a goddamn human figure, Katey. And, I'm not sure if you've noticed or not, but's even got his name on the arm... shoulder... thingy..."

Katelan studied the part he pointed at. It wasn't really spelled out or defined like a name, but it clearly mimicked the words, if slightly muted. This made her eyes grow wide. It was mind-blowing stuff. The plants were adapting to them, looking like them, even creating the color scheme of their suits. Thinking back, she'd remembered about that moment of seeing something in the jungle before; the humanoid figure in the shadows, moving, and making her do a double take.

"Was that like this?" She wondered. "Are we going to encounter more mimic-style plants as we go?"

Dillion slowly backed away from it. He looked frightened and gestured with his thumb.

"I'm... uh... going to head back to the ship. I don't want to be out here anymore, okay?"

"Dill..." Katelan rolled her eyes at him. "It's not going to do anything, it's only a plant."

"I dunno, man..." He said, looking worried. "If these things are starting to look like us... what else can they..."

"Jesus, Dill..." She bemoaned, "Get a grip, will ya? Help me grab a sample to take back. I need to see what's causing this. It could be some sort of..."

"No... no way, man!"

Before she could even finish, he took off in the other direction. He was so frightened by it he left her there. Katelan shouted at him to come back, but by the time she said it again, he'd vanished into the thick brush. She was so mad at him. She screamed in frustration and kicked a few of the smaller weeds sticking out of the ground about her.

"You fucking coward! Dill! Dill, you pussy! Don't you dare leave me here!"

Dillion's voice repeated over her communicator. "I can't be here... I can't be here... I can't be here..."

Katelan screamed for him to get back, but all she heard was his non-stop heavy panting as he went on to run. She tried again, but it was ultimately futile; Dillion was mind-locked in fear, and too busy staying focused on sprinting back to the ship. Once he was out of range, his communicator cut out, and then, she heard nothing but silence.

"Come back..." She stated passively, believing he could still hear her voice. "Dill? Dill? Please... come back."

Katelan stepped out where the trees, vines and other vegetation wasn't overshadowing her, and could make out the sky above. The murky atmosphere, full of pollen and spores, nearly blotted out the thick white-grey clouds as it masked the tint of the stratosphere's light blue hue. The deafening quiet caused the woman to shiver slightly. The only thing she could hear was the sound of the pumping action of her suit's filters; it wheezed in and out as it pulsed the air, her breath echoing in the confined helmet.

She stood there, stranded, alone in the jungle, with no one to guide her back. And all she could do now was wonder in that moment, "what the hell had happened to Deacon and Allen before we came back?"

Chapter 13

Deacon And Allen

Hours earlier...

"**Y**ou son of a bitch! I could have had a heart attack!"

Allen gripped his chest in hand and rested on the edge of the engineering computer console. Deacon's sudden appearance, and that of his hand placed on Allen's shoulder, had given him a fright beyond belief. Deacon couldn't help but laugh at his reaction, and shrugged unapologetically.

"That's what you get for not helping me out."

"Bastard..." Allen cursed at him.

"Bah, walk it off son." Deacon dismissed as his laughter subsided. He sat on the opposite console and folded his arms with a bitter glare. "Look, I really needed your help in here. Some of that plant-shit came in here and sprouted on the deck. I had a bitch of a time scrubbing it out." He quickly switched topics in that moment. "Hey, uh... is the group back yet?"

"No," Allen grumbled as he acknowledged his question.

"They're still lost out there, ugh..." He massaged his chest slightly again. "I guess we'd better go looking for them. Just give me a second to see if my heart is back to full rhythm."

"I'll do that and you can continue scrubbing down the filters, O2 tank number five is still filling."

"Uh, Earth to Deac," Allen glared at him. "I'm the one in charge here, not you. I'll be heading out to look for them and you'll be the one continuing to do the job."

"What?" Deacon shot back. "The hell you say! I've been doing it non-stop, without a proper break! Meanwhile, everyone else has been on a hike and having a camping trip!"

The two stood staring at one another for a minute. Both were stubborn as hell, and neither would relent to the other. It was a rather peculiar situation they were in. If this had been a military operation, Deacon (and possibly Allen) would have been spaced long ago for such a lack of authority. It was a comment thought that both had shared once, openly and privately to themselves. Knowing what each other was like, they let out a sigh of frustration and let the matter drop.

"Something sprouted on the deck, you say?" Allen stated, changing the topic (again).

"Yeah, come see..." Deacon motioned with his hand. "I don't know what to make of it."

He walked to the next room and proceeded to mockingly signal Allen to follow. Reluctantly, the bemused man strolled behind giving a slight roll of his eyes.

* * *

Allen, upon entering the next section of the ship, instantly gawked at the sight that Deacon showed him. Plant growth was an understatement. Allen cocked his head in every direction as the vines, leaves, and pulsating roots covered the entire room. Deacon also looked about in confusion, as this was something he hadn't expected.

"Woah..." Allen uttered. "How... how long has it been like this?"

"This wasn't like this a few minutes ago..." Deacon stated, still looking around the room himself. "It was only on the ground... over there, by the floor grating. A big ol' flower-like thing sitting in the middle of the room. But this, naw... this isn't what I saw earlier."

Allen tried not to inhale the floating pollen hanging in the air. He quickly covered his nose and mouth with his hands. Deacon, still stunned by the new development, continued to walk about bewildered.

"What-in-the-hell..." He said, spacing out the words.

"If this was only a few minutes," Allen wondered aloud. "What will it be like in an hour?"

"We'd better start cleaning it." Deacon said, grabbing his scrubber nearby. "Give me a hand, okay?"

"Wait, Deac..."

"No, come on, Allen!" The man grumbled while peering back at him. "To hell with your laziness, this is a mess, I need for you to..."

Suddenly, something distracted his gaze as he stood slack-jawed in horror. Allen turned around to see and reacted in terrified surprise. A large plant-looking humanoid was standing in the doorway. It was if someone placed a shrub there and shaped it into a humanoid form. The vines and leaves bonded together tightly to give the illusion of a solid state. It bore a head, hands and even feet. At first, they weren't sure if it was just a trick of the mind, perhaps the pollen affecting them with some sort of hallucinant. But, as they dared to step closer to inspect it, the two men realized that it was real.

"Holy shit! Where did that come from?" Allen said, stating the obvious question.

"Is it... uh... alive?" Deacon gulped in fear.

The two men waited to see if it moved. It did not. Allen was too scared to go any further to it and recoiled back. Deacon, feeling a bit more ambitious, slowly walked up to the mysterious plant-figure and gawked in wonder.

"Damned if I know..." He shrugged after a brief pause in thought. "This wasn't here two seconds ago... really strange, ain't it?"

"Well," Allen tried to grab his arm. "Don't get too close to it, ya stupid shit! It might, ya know, kill you or something..."

"I wonder if it's a life-form of this planet..."

"Deac! I'm tellin' ya, man... step back, right now..."

Deacon snickered at his comment. He turned to say something back to the frightened man, and then, one of the vines shot out of the figure and took a strangle hold around Deacon's throat. Deacon instantly panicked and started choking. The vine tightened with each breath he took and slowly pulled him in towards it. Allen quickly looked about and found a shovel laying on the far wall. He scooped it up immediately and swung it down to strike the vine. Before it could make contact, another thick vine shot out from the plant-figure and blocked his motion.

Deacon continued to struggle, reaching out to Allen for help, but before his friend could recover from the creature's block, Deacon was subdued by more vines ensnaring him and was engulfed into the green humanoid form. Allen dove at it again, violently swinging the shovel as if to use it like an ax, but the creature moved with unbelievable agility and avoided his deadly swings with precision. Allen shouted Deacon's name, shedding tears and sounding crazed as he continued to slash at the intruder. But for all his actions, nothing was making contact, nor was he able to get close to this bizarre lifeform.

With one last desperate thrust, he fell and collapsed to the floor. As he quickly recovered, trying to stand up, he noticed the figure wasn't there anymore. It amazed him. It was only a second of looking away, and now, the being and his friend were gone. He threw down the shovel and started chasing after the being. He assumed it had fled back out of the ship and raced outside without having his helmet on.

"I'm coming for ya, Deac! Hang on, buddy!"

He slapped the button to the outer hatch, over-riding the safety mechanism, and was undeterred when the wind of the planetary environment came rushing in like a gusting storm. He clambered to the ramp and dropped to his knees as tripped on his own feet. Once he was exposed to the intense atmosphere, he convulsed and clutched his throat. He couldn't breathe. The air intensity was beyond his lungs' capacity and he quickly withdrew back inside Skyward Seven.

He immediately launched himself to the airlock door and slapped the button for it to shut. Once the hydraulics finished closing it, the air pressure activated and brought the oxygen to a normal level. Allen choked and coughed as his lungs tried to adjust; the pollen and spore lined his airways with a thick sludge, and he soon vomited it out onto the floor. It was a horrendous feeling, like being smothered to death with a pillow and then having a bowl of snot ejecting out of you soon afterwards. Allen cursed and writhed in anguish. His friend was taken, abducted by some plant-creature, and he had no way of getting to him.

"The-the-Bushcat..." Allen sputtered out in realization.

He'd almost forgotten about it, knowing full well that would have been the smarter thing to use to follow them. He tried to recuperate, gasping for a normal breath, and spat out more of the alien planet's polluted air sludge from his mouth. With as much strength he could muster, the man sluggishly headed to the back of the ship. The emergency lights were flashing everywhere, shimmering their red and yellow strobes, while the whine of its alert filled every corridor and room. The sudden closure of the door had triggered the ship and was now evacuating the extra air that had seeped inside.

"I'm coming..." Allen said while grasping the walls as he staggered on. "I'm coming buddy... hang on... hang on..."

Once he was in the room where the *Bushcat* resided, Allen took out the remote control from his pocket and activated the machine to unfold from its spot. The machine stood proudly once it was fully assembled and Allen dashed inside the diver's seat and closed the door to seal him in. Like a man possessed, his fingers flew about to every switch and tapped every button needed to make the large robotic-looking ride come alive.

"System is online..." A drone male-like voice announced. "Power is at one hundred percent, filters are at one hundred percent efficiency, oxygen levels are normal. Please begin the safety check protocols for activation of this unit."

"No..." Allen responded to it. "Open the lower cargo hatch and detach the safety line from the *Bushcat*."

"Authorization for bypassing safety protocols is needed."

"Damn, fucking bureaucracy..." Allen grumbled.

"That is not a valid code." It stated back.

"Yeah, okay, fine," Allen responded back, rolling his eyes. "Allen five-five-two beta six nine epsilon alpha, override safety and initiate."

"Safety protocols deactivated. Activation of this unit is granted. Have a nice day."

"Suck my dick..."

* * *

The Skyward Seven opened up its lower section, and the Bushcat dropped underneath and scooted out. Once it was clear of the vessel, the heavily armoured explorer rose to full height, giving its legs and arms a chance to fully extend. Allen was satisfied with the final form, he quickly worked the controls and maneuvered the bipedal robot-vehicle out into the jungle. The pace was slow at first, building up momentum, but then soon gained speed as he increased the power. Activating the protruding right arm laser, Allen sliced his way ahead, giving the machine enough clearance to make it through the thick brush.

"I'm coming buddy..." He frantically spoke. "I'm coming... hang on, Deac, hang on..."

Using the internal scanners, with various holographic screens appearing around his head, the panic stricken man tried to locate Deac's body heat signature or even the beacon that all their environment suits had installed in them. He controlled the computer with his voice and eyes, giving commands to the various screens. They scrolled about and zeroed in on anything he thought might be Deac. His breathing was laboured from the panic and stress. The sound of it echoed in the cramped driver cabin only increased his maelstrom of anxiety ten fold.

"Where are you?" He lowly grumbled. "Come on, where are you?"

As he trounced through the thick foliage and slapped the heavy robotic feet on the mushy surface, the robotic explorer was quickly becoming covered in greenish-slime from the constant residue of the destroyed jungle plants; The vines snapped and hung over the structure like loose threads, the pulping effect from the robot's feet on the vegetive floor splattered the windows, puddles of green juice squirted upward and covered the machine like paint. Allen couldn't care less about the damage he was doing right now, he was too preoccupied with finding his friend.

He had snapped the floodlights on earlier, and took brief stops while searching the area. He waited for anything to suddenly pop up or move, but there was nothing but jungle before him. None of it moved or rustled, causing him to scream as he shone the lights wherever he could.

"Deac!" He called out over and over, using the outer speakers to project his voice. "Deac, man, where are you?"

Just as he slumped back in his seat, looking defeated from the attempt, something suddenly caught his eye. He wasn't sure if he actually saw it and did a double take. Then, when it moved again, he spun the robot around to flood the area with his lights. He was about to say the man's name again, but quickly lost his voice mid-way. His beaming smile of relief suddenly dropped to that of sheer horror. The shadow of, whatever he found, seemed to dwarf the tall robotic suit he was in, and blotted out the light reflecting in. Allen was agape in awe and seemed paralyzed to react. As the shadow continued to cast down over him, the man finally uttered a slow, drawn out statement.

"Oh, my sweetest Jesus in hell..."

Chapter 14

They Live

For several minutes Katelan trounced a few steps in the direction Dill was going, but she was still fuming about his behaviour. The man up and left her in the middle of nowhere. Something she just couldn't let go about. Sure, it was scary, and hey, she would have liked to cut and run as well, but they're supposed to be professionals. Leaving a fellow crew member behind (abandoning one at that), was just about the most cowardly act one person could do.

How far he was now? She couldn't exactly know, the jungle was too busy regenerating to show any signs of his footsteps. She quickly regretted not bringing any flares along, or some type of marker to follow back.

"Shame on me once," She frustratedly murmured. "But, twice? God, I'm so utterly stupid. Too much in a hurry to grab something to help me back... smart, Katey, real smart of you... ugh."

Just for a second, she thought she heard rustling from behind. At first, she wondered if it might be Dillion, skulking his way back to apologize for his sudden departure. Katelan was ready to give him an earful. Turning to look, she suddenly jolted back in surprise. What she saw was the mimic-plant, the one that looked like Allen, only this time, it was facing her way, and poised as if was in a mid-walking motion.

"What the fuck?" She said, glaring with disbelief. "That's impossible... I left you back there... didn't I? How in the hell did you..."

Katelan remained to stare at it with a shocked expression. She couldn't believe how much it really did look like an environment suit; similar in color scheme with a chromed helmet, and a face staring from behind the glass shield, or the look of one, anyway. She could almost make out the human facial characteristics, as if there was a real person within it. A shiver of fear crept down her spine in that moment. It had features of that of the one she saw only minutes earlier, but now, as it was facing her... right at her, she could see it had greater detail than before.

"Allen..." She gasped. It really did look like his eyes and face. Katelan gawked at it with horror. "Oh my god, what is this? This isn't right, no plant can do this, can it?" She stepped back slightly and gulped. "Maybe Dill was right... I should... I should... yeah..."

She quickly turned about and started walking. The rustle of the leaves began again, she could hear it clearly this time. Her fear was now of that of sheer panic. Picking up the pace, she increased her steps to more of a light jog. The sound of the leaves behind her was getting louder—she quickly stopped in her tracks, and spun around to confront it. It was to her surprise that the humanoid-looking plant was only a few feet behind with its limbs posed as if were in a running motion with an out stretched hand. She screamed from the sight of it and tumbled backwards.

"What is this?" She shrieked. "What are you?"

The Allen-looking planet remained motionless. She could almost feel it looking straight at her, perhaps even through her very soul. She was terrified and wanted to run, but felt that if she did, this thing would instantly subdue her. Slowly, with careful movements, she rose back onto her feet and kept her gaze at the alien-plant. She dared not look away. If she did, it would no doubt move again. Perhaps it needed to be close, like a Venus flytrap, luring her closer before it could ensnare her. Yes, that seemed to make sense to her, this was very much a predatory plant sort of action.

As she continued to carefully step back, keeping her eyes focused on it, another sound of rustling leaves came from behind. She stopped dead in her tracks and became paralyzed in fear. Was this another one? Was she surrounded? She trembled with fright as it got closer.

"Get down!" A male voice shouted.

She looked back and saw Allen holding a weapon in hand. Without a thought, she did as told, and covered her head. Allen fired his weapon and a bright beam of blue energy shot out at the plant-creature. Within seconds, the humanoid-looking shrubbery was disintegrated; Nothing was left of it other than some burning ash and smouldering stumps of where the legs had been. Once it was over, Katelan rose to her feet and sprang over to hug Allen.

"Thank god-thank god! Oh, Allen! Where have you been?"

She pulled away from him so he could speak.

"You wouldn't believe me if I told you." He grinned, giving the woman a pat on the helmet.

It was in that moment that she realized that Allen wasn't in an environment suit. He had nothing on to protect himself from the strong oxygen environment and instantly became worried about it.

"What are you doing? You need to get a suit on, right away! You must be struggling to breathe right now..."

"Actually, no," He said, blocking her hands from reaching him. "I'm fine, crazy as it sounds."

"I don't understand," She said, trying to touch him again. "You can't be. Let me unhook my air so you can breathe..."

"I can breathe fine." Allen stated. He stepped back slightly and raised his hand out at her.

She gawked at him with disbelief. This wasn't at all possible. Humans can't take this much oxygen, it would cause their lungs to compress and suffocate from the rich atmosphere. Allen turned off his weapon and placed it by his side. He couldn't stop smirking from her expression, he instantly knew all the questions that were about to come, and decided to just tell her outright.

"I had an encounter, it... uh... changed me, in a way, I guess. It gave me the capacity to breathe normally. I ran into it while I was looking for Deac, actually."

"Whoa-whoa, wait a second, Deacon?" Katelan gave a perplexed squint. "I thought he was with everyone back at the ship?"

"No, he's not. Just let me explain, okay?"

Katelan nodded, looking confused and trying her best to follow along with his story.

"We had a problem on the ship while you guys were gone. Long story short—he got taken by one of those things there when it came on board. I chased after him, for a long while, and... well, before I knew it, something jumped me and when I woke up... Voila! I could breathe this air."

Katelan continued to gawk at him with a bewildered, yet, inquisitive eyes. She was utterly perplexed by his statement. The most she could say back with was, "What?"

Allen laughed at her response, he had expected that reaction, and shrugged unapologetically. "Yeah, look, we could get into the nitty gritty of it right now, but... I think we need to get back to the ship and get the hell out of here."

"So Deac isn't the Deac we saw on the ship?"

"Wait, you guys talked to him? He came back?"

"I guess?" She shrugged. "Or maybe it's something else..."

"Okay, well, that's major," Allen groaned in frustration. "We really need to get back there and warn the others."

"Dill..." She suddenly recalled. "Dill ran off into the jungle. We need to find him now and..."

"It's okay, I found him too."

"You did?"

"Yes, that's how I managed to find you. I ran into him while he was fleeing like a crazed maniac."

Katelan gave a relieved sigh. At least Dillion was found. No need to continue searching through this weird jungle any longer. Allen motioned with his thumb for her to follow him. She nodded, but still seemed cautious, she was unsure about Allen and his sudden *miracle* of being able to inhale in this densely oxygenated environment.

"I still don't understand everything," She said. "You ran into something, or jumped you, like you said... and gave you the ability to adjust to the oxygen levels?"

As they continued to walk on into the thick, lush forest, Allen looked like he had trouble remembering the incident. Struggling to think, he answered her with what little he had.

"It was a large... uh... I don't know, plant-like thing... uh... it just jumped out and sprayed me with this thick crud..." He paused in thought and gritted his teeth, still fighting with the memory as he went on. "I had to get out of the *Bushcat* to... uh... get it off... and... uh..."

Katelan could see he was having a hard time giving a description, obviously traumatized by the event, and gestured for him to stop talking about it further.

"It's fine Allen, we'll talk more about it when we get back. I'm just glad that you're okay. We'll have to scan you to see what it's done."

"I told you already..." He glanced at her. "It made me better. I can breathe."

"Right, I know." She nodded. "But, who knows what it's still doing to you now. This world is unlike any we've seen, it's obvious the plants are aggressive and adaptable." She motioned her thumb behind. "Judging from that thing back there, I'd say it's trying to copy our form and maybe even our behaviour. This could be a type of sentience, or instinct based predatory reaction... who knows?"

Allen said nothing back. He continued on without speaking. Katelan could see he was still struggling about something; his skin was rather pale and squinted his eyes while they passed through the varied beams of light that was passing through the dense foliage. He wasn't sweating, not even on his brow as they carried on briskly, that seemed odd to her. Was it because of this bizarre transformation of his? The hot and humid weather would be unbearable outside of the environment suits, not to mention the constant bombardment of the gunk floating about would be coating his skin with a slimy film.

Yes, something about this didn't feel right to her. His

story was too fantastical; the fact he was breathing in high amounts of O_2 (which no human could tolerate), and the lack of perspiration on his body meant that there was something else going on. Of what? She didn't know. Perhaps once they got back to the ship, she could use the lab to figure it out.

* * *

Back on Skyward Seven, Janice paced back and forth as Captain Dan examined the decomposing body of Deacon, or what they thought was him. The plant-doppelgänger definitely had some traits of their friend, facial features being the main ones, but as Dan studied the holographic medical scan, he could see there was more. He tapped on an image as it hovered over the body, causing it to augment the specific section, and then read the scrolling text as it showed the detailed image beside it.

"Well?" Janice asked, still in mid-pace.

"Huh..." Dan simply uttered.

"Huh, what?" She glared while nervously chewing on her nails. "What does 'huh' mean?"

"It means, I'm not a scientist... or a doctor, for that matter." He paused to look at her as she stopped pacing. "I can only tell you what it's telling me. The computer seems just as baffled as we are."

"Great..." Janice motioned in defeat with her hands raised. "So much for the wonders of technology... just tell me as best as you can, alright?"

"Okay..." Dan passively shrugged. "Well, it seems that this isn't Deac, and yet, it is." Janice scowled at that answer. Dan sighed and tried to elaborate for her. "This thing looks like him, has some similar DNA properties, but... it's just a plant. It has a mixture of his cells and its own cells intertwined."

"Oh, come on," She huffed. "Are you telling me this thing absorbed Deac? To do what, exactly?"

Dan swiped down on the holo-projection, causing the image to disappear. He folded his arms in frustration and sighed again.

"I don't know. And before you even ask me, I'm not sure how it managed to absorb him. I really wish Katey was here right now. She'd be better and giving us some answers."

"Or maybe even Allen..." Janice replied. "He did do a minor in biology when he was in the academy."

"Yeah? I didn't know that about him." Dan unfolded his arms and looked at the corpse laying on the med-bed. "Still, I think he would give it to Katey to solve. He's still only an engineer, and definitely one to pass off things beyond his pay grade."

"That's true." She nodded. "So what now? What do we do with this—this, ya know... thing."

Dan mulled it over in his thoughts before responding her. Tapping a button on the side of the med-bed, it enclosed the body with a type of milky-wrap, which preserved the body, and then folded back into the wall and shut down the med-bay area. Dan turned to Janice and seemed distant in thought.

"We'll keep it in storage for now. I think we should definitely contact AirSurge and get some type of instruction from them about it."

"The collector ship is en route," She mentioned to him. "They might intercept it before headquarters does."

"Yeah, probably will."

"They'll be pissed we're not done yet, the air tanks

aren't fully prepped for their arrival. If we let them know about this... they could abandon us, hell, they might even nuke us from orbit just like that incident on Bio-moon five."

"That was a different corporation, and a different government regime, for that time. They're not going to be like that, Jan."

"Yeah, right," She snickered. "All it takes is one little fuck up, and everyone gets trigger happy. I'm telling you... they might leave us here to die. We've been compromised."

Dan didn't know how to respond. She had a point. AirSurge was very anal about their protocols, there was no telling what they would do or how they'd react to something as major as this. As Janice left the room, without so much as turning to look at him, Dan glared at her with concern and cursed under his breath.

"God, I hate this job some days."

Janice entered the cockpit of the ship, slumped down into the main command chair, and placed her feet up onto the front console. She was utterly disheartened about the loss of her friend and crewmate, if that was him, under all that plant-creature. She wept—not so much for the death of him, but of her own fear of what they discovered, and the fact that the corporation might revoke their contract. AirSurge had done so before, not to their crew, but to another that contaminated their precious oxygen cargo.

"All it takes is one fuck up..." She repeated in thought. "And then... bang! Thanks for nothing."

She took a long look out the window. The jungle was crowding the view as vegetation had regrown over the vessel. They would need to clean it all off before they could prepare to leave the surface. That meant a crap-load of time for it, something she didn't care for. She hated being here, she hated Katelan for making them venture off in this god-forsaken greenery nightmare.

"Scientists..." She mocked in thought. "Always the ones getting everyone else into trouble. Typical..."

She was just about to give a final stretch of her legs, when suddenly, she noticed something looking at her through the window. Janice rubbed her eyes to make sure she wasn't seeing things. She took another hard glare and immediately recognized the person looking on.

"Dillion?" She gawked in disbelief. "Dill? Is that you?"

It was Dillion, barely visible through the cluttered vines and plant-life covering the panoramic-type cockpit window. He mouthed to her, "Open the damn door" and walked away. Janice leapt to her feet and scurried out the control room and down the corridor. As she passed by Dan (looking confused as she rushed on), she tried to explain why in a babbling rant that didn't quite make much sense to him. He followed behind and asked her to repeat, slower this time.

"Dill's out there!" She said, as they approached the airlock leading out to the ramp. "He wants in!"

"Wait a minute, Jan!" Dan gripped her arm. "How do you know that's him?"

"What do you mean? It's Dill. I know that smug son-o-bitch anywhere."

Frantically, she started putting on the rest of her suit. She'd taken off the helmet and gloves after they sealed up the ship again, but they were still covered in the planetary slime. She cursed herself for dropping the slippery items while trying to put them on, agitated and exhilarated, she continuously repeated the process until they managed to stay on. Dan again stressed his concern.

"Wait, we can't be sure that's him out there. Remember? That creature we've got in the med-bay looked a lot like Deac too. His suit was masking his face."

"I saw Dill's face." She said, ignoring his warnings. "He didn't have his helmet on..."

Dan nodded for a second, but then did a swift double take. "Wait—what? He's got no suit helmet on?"

Janice quickly finished putting her helmet on, slapped the locks in place, and activated the airlock mechanism. Dan grabbed her hand before she pressed the exit button and glared at her. She looked surprised by his sudden action and gawked at him.

"What are you doing? Let go of me, I've got to get to Dill before he suffocates..."

"What do you mean he had no helmet on?"

"Exactly what I meant," She said, pulling her hand away. "I've got to get out there and bring him in. He's going to die, Dan!"

Dan took a moment to process. Dillion was out there with no helmet on. But, if they did that, they'd be dead in minutes. So, how could he possibly be out there in that environment. Again, he grabbed her hand before she touched the button.

"It's not him."

"Yes, it is." She said, trying to release herself from him.

"No, Jan..." He stressed, tightening his grip. "It's not him. I'm telling you, Dill couldn't survive without a helmet on out there."

"I know!" She stressed back to him. "That's why I have to save him!"

"Jan!"

"Dan!"

She pushed him away, freeing her hand once more, and

slapped the exit button. The door alarms blared, and the sealed exit opened for her. Just as she stepped out of the frame, Dill suddenly appeared in front of her and smiled.

"Hey, Janice... you and Dan want to see something cool?"

Chapter 15

Nothing Is What It Seems

The journey back to the ship was taking too long, Katelan felt. Allen repeatedly seemed to look confused for a minute and then switched directions in which they were going. This wilderness looked all the same, not only to him, but to herself as well. But even with that thought in mind, she still found his behaviour rather odd. What was going on? What exactly did he encounter in this jungle? What changed him so drastically that he no longer needed a proper suit to breathe? It confounded her.

"Nearly there..." Allen said to Katelan.

He glanced back at her and noticed the woman staring at him with deep concern. She seemed overly apprehensive, only giving him a slight nod in response.

"Hey, don't worry, I know what I'm doing, okay?"

Again, she remained silent in response. Allen stopped in his tracks and faced her.

"I know what you're thinking."

"Do you?" She stated, finally acknowledging him in

response. "Must be quite the trick, is that your keen *Jedi-mind* sense? Or is that something new this jungle gave you?"

"What's that supposed to mean?"

"I think you know what I'm implying here, Allen." She pointed at him. "You've been altered by something, and now you're running through an alien jungle world with no suit, breathing an overly oxygenated atmosphere that would kill any biological Earth-born species, and act like it's no big deal." He stared at her for a moment, taking in her words, but said nothing back while she lingered on. "I don't believe it, any of it, I don't think you're even... human..."

Allen's eyes flared for a second. His intense gaze was that of surprise, perhaps even shocked that she even suggested it. Allen bursted out laughing, smacking his hand to his chest and mockingly threw up his arms.

"That's right, I'm not human anymore! Oh, Katey, whatever you're smoking, you'd better give me some of that too. Man, that's a good one. Got to love that scientist humour, right? God! It must be so hard being you all the time, huh? Nobody gets your stupid jokes..."

"It's not a joke, Allen." She glared at him. "You've been running through this overly warm forest for a long time, and you're not even breaking a sweat."

"Maybe I'm just in good shape?"

"Yeah, right!" She mocked. "You use to break a sweat opening a beer bottle. You've never been in the best of shape, certainly not enough to hike through such a place as this."

Allen's smile slowly diminished as he thought about it. Wiping his brow and examining the lack of perspiration, he quickly realized she was correct in the theory. He sauntered about the area with a confused gaze, his mind wheeling about the possibility that something had drastically changed about him. He cried, only to discover, he had no tears to shed.

"Oh god..." He whimpered lowly. "What am I?"

Katelan took out the small hand-held scanner device from her pocket and focused it on him. As she concentrated it on his hand, she gave him a pat and tried to console the beleaguered man.

"Shhh... let me look. Maybe it's the pollen-spores affecting your skin, or a toxin that got injected into your...."

As the scanner displayed the image on a small holographic that hovered over the device, Katelan's eyes grew wide as it showed her the result. The image was a close up of his skin, or (much to her amazement) to something that wasn't skin at all. There were folded micro-leaves, one on top of each other, moving about slowly, keeping the form of solid matter, and keeping up the deceptive appearance of human skin.

Even as she slowly moved the device away from his hand, she could see the leafy-like material with her naked eye. She could make out the intricate patterns as she stayed focused on it; the edges of the plant leaves were so compact they were barely visible, overlapping so tightly and so defined, that it was easy to mistake it for the real thing. She gulped, fearing for her safety, and backed away from him. The look of terror caused Allen to gawk at her with confusion.

"What? What did you see? What's on me, Katey?"

"You..." She staggered back n fright. "You're not Allen..."

"What?" He glared again, watching her cautiously step away. "What are you talking about? I am so Allen. Jesus...

stop being so fucking paranoid, just tell me what you saw, alright? What's on me? What's changing me?"

"Nothing... nothing is on you, it's what you are." Her voice trembled. She looked at him with disgust and proclaimed, "You are not Allen!" She pointed at him in terror and screamed. "You look like Allen, you talk like Allen... but you... you're not Allen, I don't know what you are!"

Katelan's mind broke from the oddity standing before her. This man, no, not a man, something other... a plant-being, that has the form, the shape, even the personality of her co-worker—but this is not him. She couldn't fathom what kind of botanical hell produced this unholy facsimile of her friend.

As she continued to back away further, Allen began to plead and beg to her he was the genuine article. His frustration grew as Katelan's unacceptance made his pleads turn to that of anger.

"I am Allen!" He screamed. "Don't you dare try to turn this against me! You bitch! So fucking smart, Katey, so fucking stupid, more like!" She tried to keep him at bay by holding out a hand to him. Allen smacked it aside as he ran up close. "You fucking bitch! You scientist know-it-all! I'll show you how real I am! I'll show you!"

Katelan forgot that he had the big laser cutter in hand. He'd been carrying it along throughout their journey back to the ship. He quickly brought it up, first pointing it at her, causing her to gasp in horror, and then... with reluctance, turned it onto himself—and pulled the trigger.

The beam sliced through him. Like a match to dry kindling, Allen's body suddenly became engulfed in flame. His deathly scream echoed across the area, as Katelan drew back in sheer terror from the sight of it. The man, or whatever he was, collapsed to the ground in a heap of ash and smoke. Nothing was left of him. Nothing but the smouldering debris that cooled on the dampish-type jungle floor. Katelan couldn't stop shouting Allen's name. The confusion and sudden death made her go mad with grief.

Katelan sprawled along the ground on her back, she tried to stand up, but found it hard to manage as she was overcome with emotion. She couldn't cope with what she just saw. Her tears and moans of loss were overpowering her sense of judgement. If this wasn't Allen, then—what was he? Katelan had to let go of the fear. She quickly spun around to her knees and raised herself up.

"Why?" She blubbered on and on. "Why? Oh, oh god... why is this happening?"

The minute Katelan stood erect, she darted off into the jungle and ran as fast as she could. She had no idea of where she was going, or in what direction the ship was in. All she wanted to do in that moment was to get away as fast as possible. But without a machete, or some type of laser cutter, she found getting past the layers upon layers of vegetation a feat onto itself. She was stumbling, tripping, and getting smacked all over by the hard leaf foliage. They varied in size and shape, and most had razor-sharp edges that nearly tore into her suit. One of those large imposing leaves came back in her face, causing her to fling back suddenly, nearly fracturing her helmet as the woman dropped to the ground in defeat.

Once again, she was alone in this bizarre jungle, not knowing who to trust anymore. She curled up into a fetal position and rocked herself in comfort.

"Nothing is what it seems..." She wept. "Oh, my god... we are so fucking stupid. I should have realize... I should have realized... oh, please... Allen, where are you? Where's the real you?"

* * *

Katelan's ordeal left her tired and burnt out. She didn't have a clue how long she'd been laying there, crying herself to sleep, but when she did rouse, the woman shot up in fright. She was struggling to breathe. Her side vents were thoroughly clogged, and causing her O_2 levels to drop considerably. She tried desperately to scrub them off in a frantic state, hoping that it would be enough so that the air-regulator filter would work, and keep her from asphyxiating.

Once they were clear enough, she managed to draw in a few steady breaths and her panic subsided. Oddly enough, she did feel refreshed from that nap. But despite that, Katelan was still very much fearful of the state in which she and the rest of the crew were now all in.

"I've got to get back to the ship, to warn the rest, and start the lab..." She rambled to herself. "I need to know what that thing was, what this world is doing to us."

She finally looked about her surroundings. Things looked different to her. She wasn't in the jungle-forest, where she had collapsed, but a dark mossy-type cavern hole. She saw the sunlight fading as she looked up, the canopy shading the hole she was in and blocking the view of the sky above. In her mind, she tried to retrace her steps; Allen (or whatever he was) had led her astray in the jungle, so, was this pit near there? As she continued to survey the area, Katelan wondered if she had wandered down here, maybe even falling into this pit, of such.

She noticed that her legs were entangled in some vines. They wouldn't budge when she pulled on them. And when she attempted to stand up, the vines quickly tightened. Its grip was fierce and painful to her—especially every time she moved a muscle. Gritting her teeth from the action, she managed to pull her legs out and snapped the vines as they tried to pin her down. Katelan shot up to her feet and stomped on the vegetation snaking over to her.

"This place," She thought. "Its nothing but a giant pitcher plant. Maybe... maybe that's what happened to Allen... or... something like it."

She turned on her helmet flood lights, and panned the darkened pit-like cavern. She gazed at the detail in awe. Calling it a "cavern" or "pit" seemed incorrect. This was the basin of the larger plants that had very thick trunks. They encased the surrounding like a wall. The dangling vines, large leaves and stems were wide and thick like columns as it lined the entire circumference. Katelan continued to pan the area with her lights. She stopped suddenly and noticed a familiar object. It was hard to make out at first, it had a throng of vines and a moss-like substance covering over it. It was Skyward Seven's *Bush-cat*.

Katelan headed over to examine it. She could see that the mounted laser gun was missing. That accounted for Allen's doppelgänger having it, but was it removed by the real Allen earlier? Or maybe the creature yanked it off after finding this machine. Either way, Allen definitely had been in contact with the creature at some point.

Katelan, watching her footing, and trying not to get snared by the vines again, carefully walked towards the vehicle. As she reached the pilot cabin, she flashed her light into its window. Plants were jutting out of the cracks and shattered areas of the glass, the cockpit was dark, the plants smothered the interior and made it impossible to see inside. As she aimed the lights to the driver's seat and peered inside as best she could. It revealed a horror she was not prepared for.

"Allen!" She shrieked loudly. "Fuck-fuck-fuck... Allen! No! Allen, no!

His corpse sat in the chair, blood stained, decaying, and covered in vines. His eyes were no longer there, instead, there was two blooming flowers sticking out of where they once were. His suit was tattered, torn, and had other plants jutting out of where various wounds had occurred. He was dead. For how long? She didn't know, and at this very moment, she didn't want to stick around to find out. She quickly removed herself from the scene and tried to climb out of the pit. Frantic and terrified, she scrambled to reach one of the loose vines dangling down like a rope.

The more she struggled to pull on them, the more she slipped on them. They were slime-ridden things. It was tough to get a solid grip. Three times she fell off, but instantly tried again and again to climb for her life. More vines reached for her; from the floor below, the walls on the side, even ones that came out of the *Bush-cat* wreck.

"No-no-no! I won't die like this!" She asserted in panic. "I'm not going to be your next meal you son of a bitch!"

With determination (and pure adrenaline), she managed to get out of the maw of this jungle death trap. She scampered out of the hole and started running away from it as fast as she could. Her leg throbbed in pain from where the vines had strangled her, and limped slightly as she carried on. The only thing in her mind now was to get back to the ship. She had to warn the others, if it wasn't too late already.

"Janice! Dan!" She called out through the suits communicator. She repeated it several times, hoping someone would answer back, but only got static in return. "Where are you guys? Please! Dan! Janice! Do you read me, over?"

The jungle was thick and lush, and yet, totally devoid of sound. All she could hear was that of her own breath and of her own feet along the ground. She sobbed uncontrollably. This was a nightmare. Allen was dead. Perhaps Deacon was too. She only hoped the others weren't as well.

Chapter 16

Life Can Exist Anywhere

"Katey? You okay? I've got you, don't worry."

As she aimlessly wandered about the jungle on Dreganon V, struggling to find the Skyward Seven's landing site, her mind suddenly had a flashback of a time when she was with her former professor, Doctor Lim. She'd been attending interstellar online lectures of his, and enrolled in several courses he taught. She'd been a devout student for years; handing in term papers before the due date, sending questions and theories of her own to him, and even helping in some research assignments—all while off-world. But not too long after, an opportunity came up.

The AirSurge vessel she was aboard came back to the SOL system for repairs. It would take a few months and just happened to co-inside with some much needed leave-time owed to her. When Lim heard she was available, he gladly invited her to join his other students as they studied a few rare jungles left on Earth. It thrilled her to meet him in person, and got the rare chance to see Earth's jungles up-close.

The specific memory she reflected on the most, during that rare occasion, was during the last week of her leave. She'd fallen out of a tree while scouting the outskirts of the *Valdivian temperate rain forest*. Professor Lim (or Doctor Lim—as he preferred...) immediately rushed over to rescue her. Luckily, she had dropped right into a thick pool of muck, as the fresh rains had softened the ground, making it feel more like quicksand—sticky and wet. Doctor Lim and the other students used their ropes and gear to lift her out of it and tended to her wounds.

"That will teach you for climbing up so high." He grinned at her. "What have I always said? Treat the jungle with respect... yes?"

"I'm sorry, Doctor Lim," Katelan grumbled in pain. "I just wanted a better view of where we were going."

The surrounding students began treating her wounds; they cleaned the cuts, bandaged her leg, and created a walking stick for her to use. Professor Lim helped her up and patted her on the shoulder.

"Where we're going isn't as important as where we've been." He stated.

"Very insightful, you make that up yourself?" She snickered.

"I can't take credit for it," He smirked back. "I'm just trying to remind you that you can't just simply look for the way out, it can be deceiving, especially in places like this." He motioned his hand about. "The way always looks closer when observed from above. But, when you're on the ground, in the very heart of the forest, you can easily get lost because you perceive the way is closer based on that view from above."

"Okay..." She blankly stared.

Lim grinned at her response and tried to further elaborate again.

"Using our minds, proper magnetic compasses, and getting a general feel of nature, we can direct ourselves where we need to go. As humans, we can use instinct to our advantage. Does it always work? No... but that's only because we forget to respect the world for which we're in. We need to look, listen and let the surroundings tell us which way to go."

"M'kay, sure..." Katelan sarcastically exhaled. "So, what does Mother Nature say about us getting out of here then, huh?"

Lim closed his eyes. He took out a rock from his vest pouch, held it out and whispered something she couldn't quite hear. The man slowly moved his hand with the rock, as if it was guiding him, and then stopped immediately.

"That way..." He pointed to the far left to her. "That's our destination..."

"Really?" Katelan mocked. "A rock told you that?"

"This is no rock." He said, opening his eyes while turning to face her. "This is a magnetic stone. I picked it up during my trip to the Amazon. The stone is a natural magnet, part of the Earth, it gives off a vibration when pointed to the north or south."

"What about east or west?"

"Yes, that too," He nodded. "North is stronger, south is weaker, east and west are low vibrations, and they can be a bit confusing... but it is enough to get you in the direction."

"You're weird." Katelan said as she stood up and supported her weight on the walking stick. "Just use the GPS or call the Artificial Intelligent Locator Drone to guide you back."

"Ah, yes," he passively snickered, and stood up to meet her gaze. "Technology is good, for some things, but when there's no tech to be found?" He held up the rook and showed it to her. "This is the next best thing. Biology is more than just about science, it deals more with how things work; Organisms, botany, genetics, evolution... things that still baffle us to this day. There are tribes of people that still use nature to heal, both medical and spiritual. If we dismiss them, we dismiss ourselves and that of the world we come from."

"I forgot how much of a witch doctor you are," Katelan said, taking a few steps with the wooden support. "All those lectures on linking homeopathy with astrophysics. Planets that can self heal or are bio-compatible with humans so they can merge with our genetics to do the same."

"Glad to see you weren't one of those sleeping through those lectures of mine." Lim playfully smirked. "Seems many of you, including yourself, tended to disagree with my theories and... as you said, witch doctor-ing practices."

Lim and the rest of the students followed behind Katelan as she limped along. She grew frustrated at her own impediment and comically shrugged as she gave her reply.

"Yeah, well... I believe in what I can see. Not in theories that can't be proven or don't show up on an electron-microscope."

The students giggled at her glib remark and nodded in agreement. Doctor Lim seemed surprised by their reaction and tried to reinforce his belief.

"We need to remember that life can exist anywhere, not just this world, but others throughout the cosmos. Heck, even space is not immune to the possibilities that it could contain some sort of unknown interstellar organism. Perhaps particles drifting about that were the building blocks and seeding those worlds. The point being that astrobiology is not just the study for life among the stars, or searching viable planets with ecosystems in the universe. It's about learning about the very fabric of the cosmos; what's in it, around it, and possibilities beyond our sight. So few tend to respect the world we inhabit. That includes you and I, right now, here in this jungle. We must be humble in its majesty, or else we will all perish by our own ignorance of it."

Katelan stopped in her tracks, gave a deep sigh, and turned about. She could see the seriousness on his face, he was a man of deep belief in his own teachings. He sounded less like a scientist and more like a preacher or an over-zealot philosopher. She decided not to carry on this debate, seeing how she was getting tired, and tapped on his hand with the magnetic stone.

"Well, If this majesty can guide me to my hotel, a hot bath and a fantastic restaurant... I'll believe in whatever you say."

Katelan knew he was fond of her, often remarking on her being one of his most 'profound' learners amongst all others. But sometimes she would end up disappointing him, being close-minded to some of the wisdom he imparted on her. She could see he was very unsatisfied with the statement she gave, closing his fist with the rock and looking back to the others as they looked on in awkward silence.

"Well," He uttered after placing it back in his pocket. "Guess it's time to cut this outing short. Come on, everyone, let's go home and try again in the morning."

Katelan seemed surprised by him giving her the cold shoulder, passing by without so much as a glance at her, or a smile, in fact. It was like she had called him the worst name imaginable, and he was utterly heartbroken. She didn't think her responses to him with were that bad, but then again, she often mistook her own sarcasms for something everyone would get. Lim didn't seem to be the sensitive type. What she didn't see, at first, was that the professor had removed the rock from his pocket (again) and tossed it to the ground. Upon noticing it laying in the muddy ground, she glanced up at him and then back at the rock.

It was if he was now ashamed for ever showing it to her, abandoning it there as if it meant nothing to him anymore, which made her feel like she had betrayed his feelings. She reached down, picked it up, and was about to call out to him... but then hesitated once she saw that the group was nearly out of sight. There was no point in embarrassing him any further. Limping behind, trying to catch up, Katelan wondered to herself if this was just a typical characteristic trait she tended to have, refusing to accept different opinions, or, that she was just one of those that like to 'see to believe' rather than 'believe what you can't see'

* * *

Once they were back at their hotel, with full bellies, clean clothes and a long bath to get all that jungle off; Katelan headed over to Lim's room and prepared herself to apologize to the man who had been like a mentor and surrogate father-figure. Before she could even get close enough to his door, three classmates blocked her path and stopped her from going any further. One was a fit blonde girl, the other two, both well-trimmed South American-type guys, dressed in casual clothing and open-toed sandals.

"What?" Katelan glared at them with a simple shrug.

"You've been given the heave-ho." The blonde said. "Doctor Lim asked us to give you the news. He's too tired to debate with you anymore."

"Uh, excuse me? Debate? We've done this kind of thing before, not that it's any of your business, and I highly doubt he said any—"

"He left this for you." The sandaled boy on the left said, handing her a small data pad.

"You're not to read it until you're off world." The other guy quipped. "Prof's orders..."

Once they handed it to her, the trio left. They headed back they way they came and gave stern glances back at her. Katelan stood gobsmacked about that whole confrontation. She couldn't believe it. But, rather than do as *commanded*, she ignored the warning, briskly marched over to Lim's door and pounded on it.

"Doctor Lim? I need to talk to you..." When he failed to respond, she tried again, thumping on it louder. "Please! Doctor Lim... I need to explain. It's not that I don't agree with you, or feel that I'm above you... if that's what you think I'm doing. I'm just not... I mean... I have my own theories..."

She paused for a moment, anticipating he'd respond or open the door, but he failed to do either. There was only silence. That felt like a knife to her gut like no other. She was devastated that he cut her out. It was unbelievable. He just abandoned herm much like that stupid rock. Even now, she rubbed it in her pocket, hoping she'd get the chance to give it back. But no, now she was pissed. She took it out and chucked it down the narrow hallway.

"Fuck you, then!" She screamed. "Fuck you, and this stupid-shit class! I'll finish it abroad, and then you'll see, you'll see that I'm better and finding the answers than you could ever do!"

She stormed away, tears in her eyes and fists balled up

tight. Suddenly, the professor's door opened up, and he stepped out.

"Katey?"

She quickly spun around to see him standing there, keeping a distance and looking concerned. She wiped the tears away and glared at him.

"You couldn't face me in person for something like this?" She said waving the tablet about. "You're going to flunk me or something? Just because I don't believe in your... your... voodoo astrobiology nonsense!"

"Katey," he stressed calmly, holding out a hand to quell her anger. "Look, I apologize... It's not about that at all. I assure you. I'm upset because... well, AirSurge Incorporated contacted me. It seems they want you back immediately. They've suspended your leave, much to my protest, and asked that I finish out the course with you a head of schedule."

"What?" She glared.

"You've been approved to join with a team for a deep space assignment."

"Wait a minute... they suspended my leave?" She said, folding her arms in disbelief. "They can't do that..."

"Oh, yes, they most certainly can. The contract you signed with them clearly states it." Lim gestured at her tablet. "It's all there. I left a message about how sorry I was that you won't be completing this course here... with me. I was so upset by it. I guess I failed to convey that to the students giving you that."

"I'm... I'm... going into deep space?"

"Seems so..." He nodded.

She laughed for a second. It was a reaction Lim was not expecting. She quickly stopped and took note of his perplexed expression. There was an awkward silence between them for a moment, but then, she broke it by asking him a question.

"That incident in the jungle, the one we had... I... I just need to know. Did I hurt you? I'm sorry if I did."

"No, Katey, no..." He said, shaking his head with a smirk. "In fact, I'm very proud of you. I hope you do well out there, proving me... and others in the field wrong. You're getting the chance many won't, to see new life, wherever it may be." He took a few steps towards her and stopped. "I will miss you, Katelan. You've been a great student, the best I've taught in a long time. I'm not good with goodbyes, as you well know..."

She nodded in understanding. "Yeah, I get it... I'll just, you know..." She turned around and held the pad to her chest. Tears started welling up again. "Thanks for everything, Doctor Lim."

"Don't forget, Katey..." He said to her as she walked away. "Life can exist anywhere... even in the coldness of space."

With those last words of wisdom, she walked away; A slow somber shuffle at first, but then, she lifted her head in pride and picked up the pace with confidence.

Chapter 17

Rescue

As she continued to sprint through the endless jungle environment of Dreganon V, Katelan discovered that she'd been crying the entire time. The memory of that moment, between her and Lim, had evoked a strong well of emotions from within. It fuelled her need to get back to the ship as soon as possible, hoping that the crew, along with Dan, were still alive. She huffed and gasped as the air in her suit thinned, the filters struggled and wheezed loudly, trying to pump in the foul-smelling air of the planet. She repeatedly attempted to scrape off the sticky residue covering over it. The marching rhythm of the beleaguered pumps coincided with her hard breathing, and the combined noise inside her helmet was overwhelming her ears.

But that was a minor irritation for her now, nothing, absolutely nothing, was going to stop her from finding out if the others were okay. The more she thought of it, the more she increased her frantic speed. It was time to get off this god-forsaken world. Science or no science, as far as she was concerned, AirSurge could stick it up their ass! She had the sample vile with her, and the ship had at least two full tanks of pure o2 (she guessed), more than enough to satisfy that greedy corporation's needs.

Katelan assumed she had to be in-range by now, she tapped on the suit's communication button on her arm, and called out to each crew member hoping any (or all) would respond. Nothing, nothing at all came back, this made her worry more, and caused her to push her body limit to the max. Somber wails of anguish kicked in. The images of Allen, lying dead in the ruins of the Bush-cat, and then that of his doppelgänger firing the weapon onto itself—overwhelmed her mind to no end. She'd almost given up any hope of finding the ship, when—through the last sprint through the thick brush—she saw the vessel before her. It was like finding a lost ruin on Earth. The ship was covered in vines, sprouting flowers and looked like a hybrid of technology and plant-decor.

Katelan laughed hysterically, running up to it and groping the leg, like a lost child finding her mother. She passively patted it with tender-loving care, and then proceeded to the main airlock side. The ramp was still down, but the doorway was covered in greenery. Using a tool from her left leg pocket, she held the small laser cutter and methodically trimmed the area to free the door.

"Dan?" She said into her suit's microphone. "Dan? Can you hear me? Janice? Deac? Anyone?"

The doorway took shape as she continued to remove the overgrowth, and once it was finished, she approached the side control panel and punched in the sequence. The LED screen fizzled to life; the keypad flashed sporadically, struggling with power as it acknowledged her code. The doors slowly opened up, as the hydraulics whined and whirled, trying to retract. Katelan stepped in the minute it opened enough for her to go through, and quickly headed for the second access door. To her surprise, it was clean. The vegetation wasn't anywhere around this access point. She tapped her code onto the flat LED panel. It was working fine, and not at all struggling like the outer version.

The doors slid away with ease, the sound of air rushing in, and practically pulling her right into the ship. Once she was clear, the door shut tight and the air pressure returned to normal. Upon viewing the inside, she saw that it was in pristine condition. Nothing had gotten in to this area. She was about to pull off her helmet when suddenly, she saw someone standing off to the side.

"I wouldn't do that just yet..."

Katelan recognized the voice and glanced up. It was Captain Dan. He stood in the ship's archway corridor, leaning against the wall with arms folded. He bore a smile at the sight of her and motioned his head at her.

"You should leave that on for the time being, just to be certain..."

"Dan!" She gasped in awe, and beamed at his presence. "I'm so glad you're okay. Why didn't you answer me? Where's the rest of the group? Do you know about Allen?"

"Hang on a sec..." He said, stepping away from the wall and guiding her to a chair to sit down on. "Take a load off for a minute. There's a lot to go into."

"What the hell is going on here?" She glared impatiently. "We've got to get off this planet! Send out the rescue call..."

"Whoa-whoa-whoa!" He motioned at her. "Let's just take a moment, please, huh? For me?"

"Why won't you let me take this suit off?"

"It's just a precaution." He stated back.

"For who?" She retorted, raising a brow. "For you or for me?"

Dan grimaced at her for a second. He rubbed his face in frustration and quickly sat next beside her.

"Look, the truth is, I don't know if you are... you know... you. First, are you really Katelan? Or are you a plant-clone-thingy like the others?"

"Dan..." She glared at him with a scowl. "I'm Katelan, I'm not one of those beings that... wait a second—" she paused in thought. "How do I know that you aren't one as well? Why should I trust you? What in the hell is happening here?"

Dan gave a long sigh and allowed her to remove the suit. She gave a relieved look and asked him to help remove her helmet. After it came off, Katelan crinkled her nose in disgust. The changing odour, from suit to ship, caught her by surprise.

"What the fuck is that awful smell?"

"That's the solvent I used to kill the surrounding plants in this ship." He placed her helmet down on the table they were near and elaborated further. "Our vessel was exposed and overrun with that spore-pollen shit. Once I had the chance, I found a chemical that could kill it on contact and spread as much around as possible. It's sulphur based, I think, hence the awful smell."

"So, this stuff was inside?" Katelan glanced about.

"Yeah," Dan nodded. "Inside and spreading like wild-fire. I tried to save Janice from her exposure... but..."

"What happened?" She said, looking at him directly. "Where is she?"

"She's... uh... she's dead."

Katelan recoiled in horror. Another crew member gone, just like that. She shook her head remorsefully.

"Who else? Is Deacon dead too? Dill?"

"Yep..." He dryly stated. "All of them are dead. Those plant-things copied Deac and Dill. I managed to kill Deac, or his weird alien version of him, and then I had to kill Dill as he grabbed Janice coming out of the airlock."

"Janice..." She sombrely spoke.

"She died instantly," Dan said, looking ashamed. "The thing ripped her helmet off and exposed her to the atmosphere. I grabbed a small container nearby and launched it at his head, that's what that chemical was... that sulphur based stuff, instantly melted him and the plants around the door. I kicked him out with my foot, Janice's body tumbled out with him, and... well... the jungle took her and him. Those fucking vines dragged their corpses into the thick of it."

Katelan couldn't believe it. This planet had no other life than plants. And yet, here was an aggressive species of life, killing her team. She wasn't sure of anything anymore.

"We're all alone here." She uttered sotto voce.

Dan gently held on to her shoulder. His face showed compassion and even seemed to reflect her sorrow. There wasn't anything they could do, no way to bring them back, it was a tragic loss that washed over them both. Katelan stood up, pushing his hand away, and glared at her surroundings.

"We can't stay here. This place is going to swallow us up and... and..."

"I send out a rescue beacon." Dan said, leaning back in his seat. "I managed to get the AASSD to carry the signal and relay it back to AirSurge. With any luck, the Purification Cargo Cruiser will pick it up and try to increase their speed to get to us."

"They're how far along are they?" Katelan asked without to face him.

"A month... maybe two..." Dan shrugged. "But, if they get our signal, within a day or two, then, they could increase the timeline and be here within a few weeks... three at max. That's only if they use full throttle, mind you. Somehow, I think they might just stay at the same speed and send a signal back to us to 'keep calm and wait'... worst-case scenario, of course."

Katelan started removing the rest of her suit. She was careful not to touch any of the green sludge covering the outer casing, and then placed it to the ground as if it were mere trash.

"I was so worried about you..." She sniffed. "I was afraid that you... you... had..."

"Katey..." He said to her, looking on with concern.

"I love you, Dan... I didn't want anything... to... I... just love you..."

"It's okay, hey... I feel the same way, I love you as well, you know that, right?"

"Yeah," She sniffled again. Still not turning around to face him. "I know you do. I was just afraid to give into it... to... aw, shit Dan... everyone is dead!"

Dan stood up, walked over to her, and placed his hands on her shoulders again. She didn't shy away from it. Instead, she spun around and cried into his arms. He hugged her tightly and kissed her head lovingly. The emotion flowed out between the two of them; they were full of tears, sorrowful moans, and embraced one another in comfort. Trembling lips of woe turned into passionate kisses of two lovers. Time was fleeting and death was all around them. But for this moment, in this very moment, they decided to succumb to their long lost desire. Passion turned into heated ecstasy. Together they headed for the pod-beds and lay down in one as they continued their unstoppable sexual desire.

They professed their love to each other, over and over. Katelan quivered to his touch, the feel of his warm body next to hers, she wanted nothing but him in this moment, just as he wanted nothing but her. The emotion of fear and loss had turned into that of unbridled passion. And for now, that was more acceptable to either of them, and the only way to deal with it as best they could.

Chapter 18

A Closer Look

Katelan wasn't sure how long she slept. The vigorous exercise Dan and her had shared wiped them out for a good duration of time. She was still naked in the pod, covered with just the thin white sheet that outlined her form. While it might have been slightly uncomfortable making love in a cramped pod-bed like this, she didn't seem overly concerned that her muscle ached from holding on throughout the ordeal. Better to stay stable than fall out and break a limb, or something. She let out a soft sigh, refreshed and recharged, and sat up as best she could in the pod. Her legs draped over the side and her feet firmly planted on the freezing cold floor.

"Good morning..." She stated to Dan.

Dan was dressed and sitting at the table with his back turned. He was working on her suit; using the chemical to wash off the green gunk, and seemed nearly complete in his task. He turned to look at her with a smile.

"Good morning yourself... although, I think good evening might be more appropriate, if we're going by the measure of time on this planet."

She concurred with that, stood up (letting the sheet fall away), and walked over to her clothes laying on the ground nearby. She quickly got her underwear and bra on, and looked at the rest of her garments with concern.

"Maybe I should put on some fresh clothes. This is sweaty and gross."

Dan nodded, but then tapped his upper lip in thought.

"Uh, not sure if I cleaned off those things in there, our lockers, I mean... could be covered in that crap as well."

"Right..." she stated. "Well, I'll let you know."

She walked over to the lockers, found hers, and opened it up. She let out a sigh of relief. Nothing was covered in the spore-like goop. As she picked out an outfit, she talked to Dan, hoping her voice wasn't blocked by the metal lockers between them.

"We should think about blasting off this planet." She said with a grunt, while pulling on her pale-blue overalls. "We can stay in orbit while waiting for the rescue."

Dan finished cleaning her suit and brought it over to her. He leaned against the lockers and watched her finish dressing. She eyed him carefully and noticed his growing smile.

"You are... so beautiful, you know that?"

"Dan, I think one time is enough for now." She snickered.

"One time? I think we had several..."

"That counts as one..." She grinned while shutting her locker door. "One with multiple positions."

"Amen to that," He winked playfully. "As to us blasting off this giant garden, I've had time to check out the status of the engines and so on."

"And?"

"And," He said, folding his arms. "The plants got into

the main manifolds, they've choked off the supply to the fuel."

"What? Shit!" She uttered. "I thought Allen secured that so it wouldn't?"

Dan shrugged. "Maybe he took them off while we were out. It is his job to inspect it regularly."

"Son of a bitch..." Katelan murmured.

"Gets better..." Dan motioned with his finger, requesting her to follow him. "Let me tell you about what I discovered out the window this morning... night... whatever it is..."

Katelan zipped up her overall jumper and quickly followed behind.

* * *

What they both saw out the cockpit window was the lush jungle forest and a small clearing in front of the ship. Standing there like scarecrows in a cornfield, was four figures in environment suits; Deacon, Allen, Janice and Dillion. Katelan was horrified by the sight and noticed their lifelike detail instantly.

"My god..." She uttered. "Did they prop the corpses up or something? Is this a warning to us?"

"I don't think those are them..." Dan scrutinized. "Their plant-equivalents, maybe? But, here, use this to get a better look..."

Dan handed her a pair of high resolution-binoculars, and pointed at the one that looked like Janice. Katelan zoomed in on her face, past the plexiglass-type helmet covering it, and noticed the lifeless gaze of the cloned woman. It sent a chill down her spine.

"She's almost an exact copy... my god, so real... are you sure that's not..."

"Katey..." Dan sternly said, lowering his eyes. "Her head exploded from the pressure... yes, I'm sure that's not her."

"Fuck..." Katelan uttered in disbelief. Taking another view, switching from Janice, to Deacon, and then to Dill, Katelan glared at them with confusion. "So, why aren't they doing anything? Why haven't they tried to board the ship again? What is their motive?"

"Do they really have one?" Dan shrugged.

Katelan thought for a moment and lowered the binoculars. "Instinct..." She simply stated. "It must be more based on instinct. Like any predatory plant... or animal of low intelligence, it must be purely instinctive to seek a host or source of food."

"So, there's no intelligence?"

"I don't know... I'd need a specimen to find out."

Dan snapped his fingers in realization.

"I just happen to have one for ya." Dan motioned his thumb. "In the back, we've got the Deac... er... whatever that thing was, that I killed. It's still in the med-bay."

"Shit, why didn't you tell me that in the first place, ya dummy!" Katelan proclaimed. She handed him the binoculars and darted out of the cockpit.

"Well, uh... I didn't...."

Before he could say anything more, Katelan was well on her way with him in hot pursuit behind.

* * *

The body of plant-Deac was still well preserved by the time Katelan got to it. She transferred the body over to her lab, where she and Dan set up the whole thing and got it fully working. The lab was impressive, if not tightly spaced, but Katelan was finally in her element. Using the beakers and various liquid compounds to break down the tissue samples, it was like watching a mad scientist at work. The equipment at her disposal was of the latest kind; quantum spectra-scopes, DNA sequencing AI computers, Micro-genetic sequencers, and the list went on and on. Katelan analyzed and studied every particle she could get her hands on. She even uploaded the scanned images from her hand-held microscope.

Dan let her work for hours on the specimens, taking a nap while she worked diligently, and with her getting little rest in-between. When she was finished, she called him back and presented her findings. Dan, trying his best to stay focused on all that techno-babble of hers, listened intently while she spelled it all out for him in a nut shell.

"Oh, my god... Dan!" She started with an enthused expression. "This is fucking amazing! This plant... is exactly what I thought it is. I mean, sure, Earth has a great variety of vegetation, animal, insectivore... and they all have some sort of common link in the genome, right?" Dan's eyes failed to budge. She continued on. "But this, this thing? This is all one giant plant itself. None of these things are remotely individual in genetics, biochemistry, even in their osmosis... if you can even believe that."

Dan still seemed un-phased in his reaction, expecting the point (at some moment) would rear its ugly head. Kate-lan's huge grin seemed to show this was a big deal, so he nodded slightly, as if understanding it. She nodded back and returned to her presentation.

"Okay, let me simplify it even more for you. This world... isn't a world. Ya got me? This entire planet, isn't even a planet... it's a fucking plant! One big, colossal sized, mother fucking-huge vegetation!"

Dan's eyebrows raised slightly. "Pardon?"

Katelan rolled her eyes at his bemused response, even letting out a disgruntled sigh. She tried again.

"Everything on this world, which isn't a world, is one plant; All the vegetation, all the seemingly diverse varieties, and even the slimy goo pond we took a sample from... it all comes from one source—and we're sitting on it." Katelan turned on the holo-projectors and showed the information she gathered. "See here? This is the cell of a sample I took from this plant just outside the ship a few days ago... now, this one," She flipped the image to another. "That's from the body of Not-Deacon, he's composed of the same cells... if you can believe it. Every thing on this planet, that's not a planet, is intertwined and created from the same source. It makes its own air, it produces its own moisture to feed on, it literally is a self-sustaining organism that's been around for millions of years."

There was dead silence between them for a few seconds. Dan eyed the holo-images and then her, then back at the images, then her again. He then raised a hand, almost mockingly.

"Question..." He flatly stated. "If this thing is one massive plant, as you suggest... why is it trying to kill us? Hm? If this thing is self-sustaining, why does it need to feed on us?"

"Okay, yeah... right..." Katelan nodded, giving an awkward finger point. "You raise a good and very valid point about that." Dan raised his brows again, waiting for the answer. Katelan glared at the information and then back to him. "Well, I do have a theory..."

"Oh, god..." Dan exhaled. "A theory, great..."

"No, no... hear me out on this." She sat next to him and patted his leg. "I think us being here was a disruption in the harmonious balance of this world. Our presence and actions caused it to react. It saw us as a threat and tried to eliminate the virus..."

"Virus?"

"Yeah," She nodded. "Like our bodies when a foreign virus invades us. The antibodies seek to destroy it and get rid of the infection. Well, this is like that... of a sort. You see, we're the virus... but it also incorporated our nutrients into its cells. Our genetic make up was absorbed into it and hyper-accelerated its development. This living plant has to adapt constantly, and I mean fast, so quickly that it mimics to better understand complexity and enhance the progression. There are so many blooming flowers out there, I bet each one is unique and a variant of the other. It has a means of experimentation, giving rise to intelligence and intricate patterns of creative design."

"You're really enjoying this aren't you?" Dan glared at her.

"Damn right I am!" She grinned enthusiastically. "This world is adapting, mutating, changing at a speed few other organisms could even hope to accomplish. It's copying us, because it learned from us, it's trying to become something more, evolve and adapt... my god, man, this thing is going to surpass us at this rate. Imagine it..." She held out her hand to the ceiling and gazed up in awe. "We could be responsible for a new breed of intelligence, just out of pure chance."

Dan looked at her with concern, stood up, walked over to the terminal, and switched off the holo-images. With a deep inhale, he tried his best not to seem too annoyed with her.

"Katey..." He said. "People have died because of this thing, our crew mates, our friends... AirSurge isn't going to give a god-damn crap about a new form of intelligence we may—or may not—have inadvertently created. What they want, scratch that, what they demand... is only this world's abundant source of oxygen, plain and simple."

Katelan stood up and looked deep into his eyes.

"I don't fucking care what they want. All I know is that this is everything I want in a profound discovery. This is my moment, the major find that will make me a legend in the astrobiologist community. The fuck with AirSurge, don't you see? I'm going to be famous... we're going to be goddamn famous. They can't stop any of it. You and I, we'll be the most talked about couple in the entire galaxy!"

"You've lost it." Dan glared at her with concern. "Listen to yourself... just listen to it... sweet merciful crap, Katey."

He pulled away from her and laughed. Only this laugh wasn't like one she'd ever heard him make before, this was borderline on hysterical. This was unlike him. Never had he ever lost his cool to the point of crazed maniac before. She waited for him to finish, keeping some distance away, and saw him turn about with equally crazed eyes.

"You... have got... to be... fucking kidding me!"

"W-w-what?" She sputtered.

"I defended you!" He screamed at her. "I said, 'no, of course she knows what she's doing. She's a brilliant girl, that one'. But the truth is, they were right... everyone was right—Deac, Janice, Dill, hell... even Allen. They all said you were a hypocrite, a fraud, a small minded-scientist that thinks they're better than everyone else."

"They said that?" Katelan glared in bewilderment. "They thought I was a... a... fraud? And now you think that of me?"

"What can I say, Katey? This is made up bullshit!"

"Dan!" She asserted. "Please, I'm telling you the facts, this is all the truth. Everything in the data confirms it. You of all people should know that I'm absolutely..."

"Bonkers?" He cut in. "Off their flippin' rocks? Jesus, woman! You're nothing but an egotistical nightmare full of delusions of grandeur. Why did I ever trust you? Why did I ever believe in you? Now we'll have no money, no crew, and no life whatsoever!"

Dan picked up an object from a nearby table and held it in his grip. The anger swelling in him as he held it out to her and pointed it with malice.

"We may have fucked and had a good thing going, but I'll be damned if I'm going to lose my money, AirSurge will make sure of that if you tell them that crackpot story."

"What... what are you..." She cowered back in fear, as he grabbed the shovel he used before on the plant-deacon. "Dan... Dan... put that down..."

"I've lost it all, because of you." He growled. "I didn't want you at all... I wanted the money! To stop living this awful life in space! I can't stand it! You hear me, bitch? I can't stand it... but most of all, I can't stand you!"

Just before he was about to launch the shovel on her in full fury, a bright blast came through his head, leaving a gaping hole and singed flesh. The man dropped to the ground instantly, with Katelan screaming in panic from the sight. Her scream came after looking upon his face, his eyes turned up and the smouldering hole still sizzling from the cauterization of the laser beam.

"Fuck you, alien bastard!"

Janice stood there at the doorway, still holding the weapon in hand. Her suit was dirty, slime ridden, and had tears up along her right arm. The suit was barely keeping her alive, sputtering and wheezing with her every breath as she came closer to inspect the corpse that lay before her.

"Janice?" Katelan asked in surprise. "I thought you were... ya know..."

"I'm not dead. I almost was!" She said, kicking the man's body. "But, I managed to get out before that Dillion-look-a-like nearly tore my arm off."

"Wait, you called him an alien..." Katelan said, pointing at Dan.

"Uh-huh..." The woman nodded in response. "Dan's the one that died, sweetie. This son of a bitch took his place. I watched in horror as it grew out of his body."

"I don't understand..."

"Well then," she said, propping her foot onto a chair and leaning onto her leg. "let me fill you in on what happened, lil' miss smarty-pants..."

Chapter 19

The Spawning

Hours earlier...

"Hey, Janice... you and Dan want to see something cool?"

Dillion blocked Janice's way before she could step out. She glared up in surprise as he stood in Skyward Seven's archway's outer airlock. His sudden reappearance caught the woman off guard (momentarily). She stumbled back, catching a breath, and held onto her chest in fright. Dan was equally unprepared for Dillion's quick entrance, and shouted a mild curse in reaction.

"You fucking Dick!" They both screamed in unison.

"Holy shit!" Janice went on. "God... asshole! Where the fuck have you been?"

"With Katey, of course..." Dill grinned.

"Oh, man!" She panted, still clutching her chest as the fright subsided. "I nearly dropped a load, god!"

Dillion snickered as he repositioned himself to stand in-between them. "Come on, I want to show you something, both of you."

"Wait a minute," Janice slapped his hand away, just as he tried to reach for hers. "Where the hell did you and Katelan go? What took you two so long? We need her here to examine Deac's body."

"Deac's body?" He frowned. "He's dead?"

"Duh!" She rolled her eyes at him. "I just told you we've got to look at his body. He's dead and something else replaced him..."

"Uh, okay..." Dillion said, looking over at Dan. Dan shook his head to confirm what she was saying. Dillion restated the fact as if to clarify it further. "Huh... dead you say."

"Yes, Dill, he's dead, for the love of..." Janice grew frustrated at his reaction. "Stop being a fudge-head and get Katey on the horn... geez, what's with you?"

"So crabby, as always..." He smirked back. "Katey is busy."

"Busy?" Dan shrugged. "Doing what, exactly?"

"I dunno..." He shrugged back at him. "Science stuff, you know her. Anyway, what does it matter? Come on, what I got to show you is really cool..."

"Dill," Dan said, joining them at the door. "We're not going anywhere until you explain what you two were doing, exactly."

Dillion looked frustrated as he glared at them both. But that soon subsided, as he gave a simple shrug and motioned about with his hands.

"Well, Katelan wanted to explore, and I agreed to tag along. But, you know how she gets, so deep into the work, but then, she started acting stupid..."

"Oh?" Dan cocked a brow. "How so?"

Dill came closer to Janice. She glared at him with questioning eyes. His movements were slow, even as he tilted his head, scanning the both of them as they stood there. He gave a slight click of his tongue, and shrugged while he leaned against the door frame.

"She thought she saw Allen standing in the jungle." Dillion snickered. "It was absurd. I mean, it was a plant... just a plant, doing what plants do... mimicking what they see to adapt to the environment. Or in this case, to something they like or want to emulate."

"Emulate?" Janice snorted. "What the fuck does that mean? Emulate what?"

"Us, of course." Dill winked, as he went on giggling.

Dan seemed perturbed by Dill's incessant and bizarre giggling, even as he lovingly stroked Janice's arm, strangely. He wasn't sure, but, something wasn't quite right with the man. He acted, well, very un-Dillion-like. He was eyeing Janice, as one might a meal they've never really tried before. That alone made him very paranoid and quickly grabbed onto Janice's other arm.

"Hey, uh... let's go inside here and we can talk about it more. Right, Janice? Oh, uh... you too Dill, buddy."

"But I need to show you something..." Dill stated.

"Ah, right, yeah," Dan nodded. "I know, but... let's come in for a bit. Man, you must be tired after walking all that way. Come on, Dill... Janice..."

Janice conceded and turned to head back inside. Dill held on tighter to Janice's arm, clutching it hard with a scowl on his face. The quick glimpse she gave back him, one of suspicion and concern, caused Dill to shake his head, giving a disappointed few clicks of his tongue in response. Dan sensed the danger again, and continued to pull the woman his way again. Janice felt the pain as the men were grasping tightly on either side. She uttered "oof!" as they proceeded to pull back and forth.

"Hey, I'm not a piñata, dimwits!" She scowled at them. "I like the attention, but, come on boys... I might have to file for abuse in the workplace!"

The two continued to pull—neither one letting go or showing Janice any sympathy for her cries of pain. Dan could not set her free. Dillion, on the other hand, managed to pry her away from Dan's grip in one swift tug. Surprised by his strength, Dan fell to the floor and watched helplessly as Dillion lifted her up over his head. Even as his hand still embraced her and snaked about unnaturally. Dan could see that Dillion's arm had now coiled around hers; it had multiple thorns stuck out of it, like those from a rose bush, and started piercing her suit.

Dillion (insanely giggling) dangled Janice close to the ceiling of the outer hatchway. Her look of surprise, combined with that of sheer pain, grew as she hung overhead. From the swift force of his deadly grip, she let out a cry of unbridled agony. Dan snapped out of his shock and tried to free her from the twisted alien arm. It was a futile effort. Dillion smacked the man away with his free hand and then followed it with a powerful kick to his upper body. Dan fell to the floor. It stunned the man, and he struggled to keep conscious. Janice screamed again in agony as the being continued to tighten his tentacle-like arm to hers. He walked out off the ship with her in tow.

"Dan! Dan! Help me!" Janice shrieked.

Dan found the strength and recouped from his injury. Her beckoning plea fuelled his adrenaline, making his rage skyrocket into a tyrannical roar of revenge. He bounded on to the Dillion doppelgänger, climbed up to Janice hovering above, and mustered enough force to pry a few coils away to get her free. Janice wasted no time and launched her self to the ground below. With her free, Dan could now turn his attack back onto Dillion... or... whatever this thing was. Dill was quick to react as his arm now tried to snatch Dan. The captain repeatedly used his foot to contact Dill's head, causing the Dillion-creature to fall back and drop to the ground. Dan was airborne for a second, but recovered quickly as he landed safely to his feet. He wobbling slightly after touching down and shouted at Janice as she watched in disbelief.

"Go Janice! Go find Katey! Get out of here!"

"Dan!" She screamed back. "I'm not going to leave you..."

"Get out, I say!" He scowled at her. "I'm your Captain, Goddamnit! Do what I say, understand!"

Just as he turned his attention back to the creature, Dan was impaled by a thorny tentacle. The forceful thrust sliced right through his chest and out of his back. Janice screamed in horror from the sight. Dan's blood splattered across the green floor canopy, with chunks of flesh and bits of his enviro-suit smacking against the side of the ship.

"Dill..." Dan uttered in shock. He gazed upon the blood splattered face of the creature that mimicked his crewman. Eventhough it wasn't really him, Dan felt the need to say something as if it were. "I'm sorry... buddy... I'm so sorry for bringing you here."

The Dillion-plant create said nothing back. There wasn't even a smile on his face as he stared at the dying man before him. The illusion of what he was, as Dillion, slowly disassembled as the creature unfurled from its human form. It grew into its true shape. Janice remained stunned as she gawked at this being revealing itself. Dan was equally wide-eyed, even as he could feel the blood draining from his body. The alien continued to keep him in position and unfurled more of itself. A massive jumble of thorn-like tentacles, broad leaves, and a central blossoming flower head, completed its final form. Never have either of them seen anything like this in their lives. An organic being purely composed of plant-life.

"Jesus..." Janice uttered in horror.

Dan, feeling the life drain out of him, went limp. His skin turned pale. His last breath was that of his final thought.

"I... love you... Katey."

Janice shed a tear as she witnessed him die. It was horrible to know that Katelan would hear his final words, a confession of love, just for her. The plant-creature brought him closer to its blooming head, it shot out a spore all over his body and continued to do so until he was covered in it. Janice wasted no time, there was nothing more to do for Dan, now that he was dead. She bravely sprinted into the ship and tried to search for a weapon. Overcome with the grief and pain, she rambled on to herself while running about.

"Got to find a gun... a cutter... a... a... tool... Jesus! Some-thing! I got to have something here to kill that mother fucking..."

Stepping onto the bridge of the ship, she gazed out the side window to where the plant and Dan were. In that moment she glanced over, the spores covering his cadaver expanded like mini-balloons, then popped over his dead flesh. It was a gruesome spectacle to behold. It almost caused Janice to wretch on the spot. The spores contained millions of tiny seeds. All of which drilled into Dan's body, peppering him with holes that caused more blood to ooze out from their impact. His body twitched, wriggled, and writhed, as it split apart like a ripe banana. A bloody mass of discarded organs and bones plopped onto the ground. This time, Janice did hurl into her helmet, several times over. She then bolted out of the bridge and fumbled about in a daze.

As she managed to reach the next section of the ship, she collapsed and sprawled out on the floor. She wailed uncontrollably, with quick gasps of air in-between, and realized that she was practically swimming in her own puke. It was all too much for her to deal with. Despite all that was going on, including the overpowering stench of her own vomit, she noted a panel on the nearby wall that read:

Emergency Contingent - For Ship's Captain Use Only.

Janice thought back for a moment. There was a time when Dan had mentioned, very briefly to her, that the corporation installed certain items for their captains to use on long missions. He would never exactly state what it was, only that it was meant as a "necessary deterrent for problematic crew". The fact that she'd never seen it before, in all the time she'd been aboard, confounded her in that instant. Well, for one, the writing was rather small in print, of course, now that's she's seeing it, but... to never have notice it?

She snickered lightly, "Fuck me, you slippery shit, Dan. I thought he was just kidding about that."

She had more questions of the why and how, but, those concerns would have to wait for another time. She quickly smacked the panel with her fist, causing it to pop open, reached in, and pulled out a hand-held, standard-issue military grade energy pulse gun. This was no mere deterrent. This was a weapon that could clearly take out anyone and possibly every thing, if it came to that. Even as the fumes of her own stomach acid burned into her nostrils, the look of surprise upon discovering this weapon gave her a momentary pause.

"You sons of bitches..." She stood up, causing the slurry of vomit to drain from her helmet and down the inside of her suit. "Never trusted us, did you? Well, I'm going to put this to better use, right now."

She boldly ran out of the vessel and aimed the weapon, she was about to press the trigger and the huge alien plant-creature, when she noticed someone standing just below it.

"Janice? What are you doing?"

It was Dan. He was alive, fully suited (except the helmet), and looked at her while giving a shrug.

"Dan?" She said, a look of confusion.

"Yeah, it's me, stupid." He snickered while stretching out his arms to her. "What the heck do you think you're doing? Put that down, will ya? And how did you know where that was, anyway?"

"No..." She blinked, looking terrified. "You're not Dan... he died, this is his blood everywhere. You're a... a..."

"Janice..." He scowled mockingly. "Seriously? This was all a hallucination. We inhaled some of the spore and..."

"No!" She shrieked, pointing the gun directly at him. "Don't you give me that shit you-you-you fucking plant-thing! I'm on to you... you adapt, you learn from us, maybe absorb who we are... yeah... yeah, that's it. Katey's not the only one who can figure things out..."

"Where is Katey, Janice?" Dan glared at her. "Why not call her?" He took a few slow steps towards her. "Have her join us..."

Janice flinched from his sudden movement, causing her to pull the trigger, and took out his right shoulder. The beam of energy disintegrated it instantly. A loud chattering came from the giant plant-being; Janice forgetting that it was standing there behind Dan, patiently. A tentacle shot out from it and grabbed her arm holding the gun. Once again, the thorns dug into her, causing her to wince from the pain of their needle-sharp points.

"That was uncalled for Janice..." Dan uttered as he looked at his non-existent shoulder. "That weapon is for emergencies only, I'll have to report you to the company, you could lose your job over this..."

"Bite me, Dan-or whatever the fuck you are!"

The tentacle tightened again on her. Dan gave a disappointed glance at her and proceeded to grow his shoulder back. The vegetation knitted together at a rapid pace and solidified his flesh once more. The mimicked skin tone returned, and even his suit patched itself up to complete the overall look of the man. Dan grinned at her shocked reaction, seeing his transformation was utterly horrifying to her.

"Make no mistake, Janice," He stated, still grinning at her. "I am Dan Sebastian Fruger, captain of the Skyward Seven Explorer vessel. And..."

Janice quickly kicked a tentacle off of herself, repositioned the gun (still in her grip), and fired it—the beam sliced through Dan's morphed arm holding on to her. He let out a high pitched shrill as it dropped away. Janice, now free, used all of her might to runaway and untangle herself. Dan was too busy tending to his wound to charge after her, giving the woman the opportunity to flee into the dense jungle and hide. The struggling air ventilator on her suit caused her to gasp repeatedly. The pollen had thickened over the small ports, restricting her air flow, and was now causing her to asphyxiate.

She considered taking off the helmet, even going so far as fiddling with the latches on the side of it. But, when she realized the problem with doing that, with the ultra-rich oxygen smothering her to death, she quickly stopped herself and tried clearing the vents instead. They were slimy and goopy to the touch. Her gloved hands weren't able to clear away a good portion of it.

"It will do..." She thought, reaching to swipe them, trying to free up an air valve. "Got to find help... got to find Katey... or anyone still alive!"

Chapter 20

Planning Ahead

Katelan finished listening to Janice's explanation of what happened to her and Dan. She was perplexed by the oddity that occurred. The horrific end to her lover and captain, Dan, was a tough pill to swallow. She didn't know what to do first; cry for his loss, get mad for not being there for them all, or scold Janice for not securing the ship first. Katelan pondered endlessly about what could have been, or what they should have done instead.

But even as she sat there, saying nothing to her surviving crew mate, she had to take command of the situation and hold all those emotions for later. They were the only two left to deal with this problem. Both she and Janice would have to think of a solution to get themselves off this world.

"What's the state of the vessel?" Katey stated to her.

"It's fucked..."

"That's not the answer I'm looking for, Janice."

"Okay..." Janice nodded. "The ship is really, really fucked. That any better for ya?"

"Jesus, Janice..." Katelan stated, giving a disapproving facepalm. "Can you please, for once, in your life, just act like a professional? Huh? Did you inspect the ship before that whole incident?"

"Oh, hell yeah," Janice snickered. "Uh, right after I tried not to get killed... what kind of stupid question is that? Look at me! I'm a mess! You really think Dan and I had any moment to..."

Janice quickly stopped for a second and looked away from Katelan. There was a spark of thought occurring and pointed to the other section of the ship.

"Wait a minute..." She said. "We took a scan of Dillion... or, whatever he was."

"Yeah, I know..." Katelan nodded. "I managed to take a closer look at that. My theory is that he and the rest of these plant-beings are actually the same. This entire planet is one big singular life. What kind of life? Sentient or non-sentient? I'm not sure."

"Well, they must be pretty fuckin' smart if they're talking like us and acting like us." Janice paced about with her hands waving in the air. "One minute I'm talking to Dill and Deac as if they're them, then, the next minute, they're all acting weird and trying to kill me! I'd say that's a good case for intelligence..."

Katelan stood up and stopped Janice from pacing about. She looked at her until the woman met her gaze. Janice was ashamed of herself. Her eyes gave it away as she started to tear up. Katelan gave her a comforting hug and patted her head gently. Janice sobbed.

"I tried Katey..." She blubbered on. "I tried so hard... so hard to..."

"Shhh... I know, Jan, I know..." She reached to pat her head. "I feel the same way. But, we've got to get it together.

We've got to come up with a plan to stop them and get off this world. It's up to us now, you understand me? It's up to us now."

Janice pulled herself away and wiped her face. She felt slightly embarrassed for crying. The woman re-composed herself and let out a breath to ease her emotions. Once she took another deep inhale, she glanced over at Katelan and apologized. Katelan said nothing, merely held up a hand as if to say, "Forget about it".

"So..." Janice shrugged. "What is our plan, anyhow?"

Katelan folded her arms and started thinking. The analytical mind was at work. She tried to think of how they could distract the plant creatures, prep the ship for take off, and contact AirSurge for an ETA for a pickup point. She motioned to Janice to follow her as they headed to the medical bay section. Once there, Katelan activated the computer and used the holographic projectors to show her results of the autopsy.

"There's a sort of symbiosis with the separate plant-forms, the ones looking like us, and the planet itself. It's evolved so rapidly, that I think there's connection... pheromone or psychic, I'm not sure which. Maybe both... perhaps..."

"So it is intelligent." Janice glared at it.

"In a way, yes..." Katelan flipped the image to another. "Here's a spectrogram of the osmotic, there's a kind of chemical irregularity, one I wasn't sure of what to make of, until I finally understood..."

"Understood, what?"

"That's us..." She pointed at it. "We were adding our own biogenetic to its evolutionary process. Giving it a new code to rework itself. A foreign body introduced into a constantly changing environment. Now it wants to keep evolving with our unique pattern and bio-diversity."

"Uh-huh, truly fascinating..." Janice rolled her eyes. "I'm sure this is really blowing your little scientific mind and all, but, how is this helping our escape plan here, Katey? What's your point here?"

Katelan seemed annoyed by her lack of understanding. Everyone, even Dan, constantly belittled her observations. It was frustrating dealing with them. She felt like they were punishing her for being so brainy. Maybe she did come off as a tad too smart for her own good, sometimes, she could admit that, sure. But when giving explanations or detailed information that is just plain fact? Man, dealing with these knuckle heads was just hard to cope with sometimes. It made her question why she stayed with them at all.

"The point I'm getting at is..." Katelan rolled her eyes slightly. "That we need to use a chemical or signal that can counter act with the communication process."

"A gun works just as well..." Janice said, presenting the weapon to her. "Fry the fuckers... that will cut them off."

"That's just a temporary measure..." Katelan said, pushing her hand down. "These things can manifest them-selves rather quickly. That link remember? It's like muscle memory or instinct, it just forms a new version to compen-sate. I had to kill a version of Allen twice now... each time he improves, evolves into a new form with greater detail."

"Then, I say we take off, and nuke the place from orbit..." Janice stated with a firm glare. "Only way to be sure..."

Katelan groaned at the apparent movie quote being referenced. Janice and Dill had been big fans of that classic old film, and now, this was her attempt at being funny in the moment... or was it?

"Ugh, please... you're not some fictional character with nukes conveniently at her disposal. Besides, we don't have anything like that on board."

"Well—we should." Janice stated back. "It would help us a lot, especially now."

"Fuck, Janice..."

"Fuck yourself!" She harped back. "We're the only ones left. We need to get out of here—now! Let's just go into orbit and wait for the Purification Cargo Cruiser to show up."

"Wait? For how long?"

"I dunno..." Janice shrugged. "All I know is that we'd be a lot better off in orbit of it than surviving on the surface of it. Especially since this thing is trying to kill us for our genetic material."

Katelan was about to argue the point, but held back as she mulled the situation in her mind. She was right (albeit, in a frantic sort of way). They needed to be off this world. She gave a defeated sigh and passively gestured at the woman.

"Fine, you're right. We need to go. This place is too dangerous to stick around any longer."

"Damn right I'm right!" Janice stated, slapping her hands forcefully. "What's it going to take to freak you out? As if killing multiple Allens and sleeping with plant-life beings isn't enough?"

"I said, okay!" Katelan stressed back, giving a glare.

"Great, get your stuff on and let's get this mother fuckin' ship ready to go."

Katelan stood up, grabbed her environment suit and started putting it on. The filters were still working (within reason, anyway), but the smell inside of the helmet, after she clasped it on, well—it was foul. She winced from the odour and gagged from inhaling.

"Yeah, I know..." Janice nodded in agreement. "Trust me, you don't want to be in mine right now."

"Sorry, Janice, I forgot you've got some stuff sloshing around in there as well." Katelan glanced at her. "But, I thought mine would be aired out enough after taking it off."

"We've been in these things for a long time." Janice passively gestured. "Usually, we clean these suckers before heading out again, but... with all that's happening..."

"I get it."

"Are you sure?" Janice inquisitively glared back. "If you'd rather we do a quick wash out of them... we could just..."

"I'm fine." Katelan scowled, slapping on the power button to start the filters. "Let's get this over with already. We need to check out the ship and get it ready to take off, like you said."

* * *

The two women cautiously stepped out of the vessel, glancing everywhere and anywhere for any sort of surprise. They couldn't trust anything in this nightmare of a world. Janice couldn't help but feel she was being watched; she turned sporadically, jumping in fear as if something caught her eye, but there was nothing there. Katelan did her best to remain calm. She preferred to keep eyes fixated on the engines as they both toured about and inspected them. When Katelan saw the state they were in, she let out a mild curse.

There was a thick green mossy-like substance that filled the entire lining. Reaching in with her hand, and giving it a thorough feel all around, she could tell that all the major components were clogged. She tore a few chunks off, giving a feel to the consistency, and wondered if it would ignite if she tried to start up the ship's power. It was really damp and sticky, it would take a lot to burn this out.

"Fuck, I thought you said you covered up the engines, Allen..." She muttered to herself in mid-thought. "What in the hell possessed you to remove them? Unless... you were thinking the same thing..."

She tried to get Janice's input on the matter, but the frightened woman wasn't really paying attention to her. Janice was too freaked out and in no condition to offer assistance. Ultimately, it was her own decision on how to proceed, knowing full well this substance might not come off entirely, or enough to give them the full thrust needed. If that doesn't work, well, they're pretty much out of options. That worried her greatly.

Janice was growing even more erratic as she turned about wildly. Her eyes were wide with fear, and kept the weapon out-stretched in hand as she was ready to fire on anything that so much moved or even twitched.

"Come on Katey..." She said with uneasiness. "Let's make this quick, girl..."

Katelan pitched the clump in her hand and turned to face the nervous woman.

"It's not going to work." She stated.

"The fuck you mean?" Janice turned with a crazed glare.

"This moss... it's all inside here. It's too moist and thick. We'll have to fire the engines for a good while before we can get enough off. Then, and only then, we'll get enough momentum to rocket away."

"Shit..." Janice lowly cursed.

"The cutting lasers underneath the ship could be removed, and we could use them to cut the growth, but..." Katelan said, folding her arms in frustration. "They're hooked in to the ship's main power. We'd need to rig them to a portable power pack, one with just as much juice to be of any significant use."

"So I take it that's out of the question, then?" Janice huffed as she darted her gaze about.

"Yeah, I'm afraid so." Katelan grumbled. "Which sucks, because it's the back engines here we need for additional thrust. The boosters underneath can only get us so far. We need the main drive ones to get us into orbit."

Janice tried to think. Her mind was too engulfed in fear, and couldn't give any critical input. All she could respond with was with a quick simple nod and continued to keep her gun focused on the jungle layout. Katelan took a few glances back at the main engines again and threw up her hands in defeat. What more could they do? It was just the two of them, and neither one was well versed as an engineer. Allen was the only one who knew how to figure this stuff out (except for Dan and Deacon). He'd more than likely have some sort of brilliant inspiration on how to handle all that veg blocking the engine's thruster vents.

"Well, let's get back inside..." Katelan shrugged. "Maybe we can come up with a better plan in there, or—at the very least, have some sort of safety."

"No argument from me..." Janice quipped back.

As the two made their way back to the ramp and headed for the outer airlock, a large vine sprung out of the ground and wrapped itself around Janice. The woman panicked and started firing her weapon, she was aiming for the source of the lively veg, but before she could shred it with her laser fire, another and another came up and pinned her to the ramp. Katelan screamed at the sight, and refocused her efforts on freeing her friend from the attacking vines.

"Katey! Take it!" Janice screamed as she flung the weapon to her. Katelan caught it instantly. "Shoot them! Hurry!"

Katelan wildly shot at the continuous vines popping up all around her. Each blast removed one, but then two more would appear and snaked around Janice. The woman struggled as best she could, but the vines grew tighter and tighter.

"Get... to... safety..." Janice struggled to say to Katelan. "Go!"

The vines tightened more, the suit was starting to rip, and her helmet was cracking from the sheer pressure from the plant's strength. Katelan kept firing at the alien plant-life, but found that her efforts were futile. Janice continued pleading for to her to leave, and as they locked eyes, Katelan mouthed, 'I'm sorry', to her. Janice couldn't respond back, the pain was too much for her. All Janice could do was give a sharp nod in acknowledgement. Katelan quickly turned about and bolted into the heart of the jungle. The pain intensified as Janice was still being slowly crushed. The creature turned her around, brought her upright and pulled her in close to it. The figure began morphing, taking a human form, as a face started to appear.

"Hey there, Janice..." It said, in a jovial manner. The face was detailed, and she could see that it was Dan, or a facsimile of him. "You ladies are so hard to get a hold of... well, in a manner of speaking," He snickered.

The creature's face and body morphed into greater detail (with skin colour, hair and sprouting clothes around his naked form). Dan brought his face up to hers and grinned. She shook in terror as she looked upon this being of pure evil.

"We've got time, though." He continued on. "We can be patient... but for right now, I think you'll do."

"Eat my shit, asshole!" She spat at him.

"Alright," He chuckled while absorbing her spit. "I forgot you're not one for small talk, are you? Fine, let's try this then, how about—I see what *you're* made of!"

Janice felt the vines squeezing her like a powerful closing fist, and screamed in pain as it pulverized her instantly.

Chapter 21

Escape

Katelan ran through the jungle as fast as she could. The echoing scream of Janice's demise caused her to cry uncontrollably. The poor woman didn't deserve such a horrid death. This jungle was ruthless in obtaining its victims. But even as she sobbed for her friend, whose howl of agony sharply ended, she had to remember that this giant living plant-world was only using them all for its own need to survive. Evolution was the main goal for this bizarre life-form, they were just a bonus to its advancement. Still, she was terrified nonetheless, and running for her very life in this endless vegetation. She was all alone now. No one was left but her. This increased her panic ten fold and made her collapse in sheer dismay.

"No-no-no... please!" She nervously spoke to herself. "This can't be how I die... oh, god! I've got to get out. There's got to be a way off of here..."

She curled up into a ball, rocking back and forth with the weapon in hand, and tried to self-soothe, while listening for anything approaching her immediate location. The jungle was quiet as ever. Nothing by the sound of a gentle wind rustling the of oversized leaves of the thick-stemmed growth. Katelan could only think of poor Janice in this moment, undoubtedly being absorbed like the others now. A template for the plant-being to copy and take her form. If only they hadn't set down on this ill-gotten planet, none of them would have perished, and they'd be onto a less horrific world with lots of oxygen to harvest.

"Wait..." She suddenly thought. "Oxygen..."

Her intellect kicked in to the forefront and started spinning those wheels in her head.

"Pure, concentrated and compressed O_2. We've got lots of it. I could use it like a booster rocket, enough to propel the ship off the surface and bring it into orbit. But, how much would I need specifically to achieve such a thing? That's the question..."

The more she pondered on that theory, the more her analytical brain began calculating the actual numbers needed to make it happen. She put the gun into her open right side-leg pocket, and started scribbling in the air with her fingers. It was like she could see it—visually, moving the numbers and calculations in frantic motions. A slow growing grin came upon her face, she could see the idea would work and continued to shuffle the non-existent permutations around until it finally make sense. Once it did, Katelan pumped her fist with a pleased motion and nodded with a smile.

"As long as there's enough in three or four of the tanks... yeah, it could work." She recalculated the math in her head. "Uh-huh, that's just enough to lift that sucker right off the surface."

The pressurized O_2 in the tanks were designed for maximum storage. That would be like launching a billion balloons at once or hundreds of compressed air tanks strapped to a car, causing it to launch down the road at unfathomable speeds. But, the main problem, which even Katelan had to acknowledge, had to do with this type of planet's air; it was far more dense, and extremely flammable if ignited. She'd have to take care in that regard. One small error, in take off or the mixture, and tanks could very well blowup instantly, and that would end her escape rather abruptly.

Using the pressurized air, as extremely compressed as that, would certainly give her the accession necessary, but once the ship got to the stratosphere, well, things get far more tricky. The friction would increase dramatically, for one, she'd have to control the rate somehow so that it eases her into space with no hiccups. She let out a breath of frustration on that thought. It was doable, dangerous, and rather labour intensive, but, it had to be if she wanted to leave this place.

The tears remained on her cheeks, and she tried to remove them, Katelan forgot that she was sill in her environment suit.

"How soon we forget about those natural motions of the hand." She quipped to herself. "Just instinct... stupid, foolish human instinct."

The astrobiologist stood on her feet and kept hidden behind a tall stump that she scooted over to nearby. She quickly glanced around for a second, and looked for any sign of the creatures, or movement of any kind. She even listened to hear for any snapping or rustling of branches. Once she was sure the way was clear, she took careful steps and slowly headed back to the vessel. She hoped that the beings were not still there, that they were out searching for her instead. Maybe she could get inside and quickly close the door before any of them could get back in.

"I still can't believe I fucked a plant..." She self mocked. "Talk about loving your work too much," she tilted her head in thought. "I should have known it wasn't him... cause he was never really that good, not like that." She glanced up at the sky and winced. "Sorry Dan..."

The jungle continued the eerie silence, even as she tried to be just as deafeningly mute as it. An impossible task, even as she chose her footing carefully. With no one else there to help guide her, she was on her own... alone—on this alien world. That sudden reminder of being the sole survivor struck a nerve. She was totally and terrifyingly all on her own. That caused a panic to set in quickly. A wave of uncontrollable sobbing hit her immediately; it was the grief, fear, anger, and shame all rolled into one pinnacle emotion.

"No-no-no..." She said, trying to subdue the passing thought. "Don't you dare do this now, Katey! You've got to be strong. Survive... yes... survive for them. Get to the ship and get the fuck out of here."

Desperately, Katelan tried her best to muffle the sound of her faint sobs, clasping a hand to her mouth–"Damnit, the suit..." She grumbled, realizing her mistake. "God, I've got to get control..."

With a few deep deep inhales, as the suit still struggled to process the ultra-condensed air, Katelan calmed her mind and tried to focus on what to do next. The creature must still be lurking about near the ship. But how long could it wait there? Was is patient? It must understand that she needs it to fly out of here. She squatted down low and scanned the jungle with her widened eyes. Much like Janice was earlier, now she was experiencing the height-ened sense of alertness.

"I wonder if it can sense me." She thought. "If the jungle is part of its whole being... perhaps it can... feel me, maybe?" Katelan balked at her own theory. "No, I doubt it has that kind of tactile nature with so much of itself. Even when we were vaporizing the mutated form, it didn't continue to attack. It could've just sporadically come at us from any angle."

Skulking along the ground, continuing to keep low, she moved to another thick, oversized stem and listened. Katelan felt it was useless to even do this action. The plants were quiet, always. She realized it was only they, the crew, or now, her, making all the ruckus on this world—just a bunch of noisy humans stomping around the living planet.

"Hmm..." She said, reflecting on that internal thought. "It couldn't hear us, feel us, or move on us until it was formed. That means, it had to generate and rebuild its conscious mind to that host. Transferable brain patterns? That would be a first, in any species of plant. It must be trying to continually adapt and improve on itself. Weird..."

She noted the darkness beginning to set in as she looked up at the sky. The long hours was still hard to adjust too, but once the light was gone, it would be next to impossible to move through the jungle without seeing what's in front of her. The helmet lamp was small and not very powerful. Enough to see a few feet, sure, but not so much to see much in the way of detail. This concerned her greatly. As Katelan moved again, she tried to lessen her steps and take them cautiously. She had to get onboard the vessel, and get off this world, before the darkness consumed everything around her. Would that plant-creature be waiting for her? Could she sneak past without it jumping out and taking her?

With those questions in mind, she gave a determined

sigh. "Okay... okay, then... it's now or never Katey, you can do this—keep it together girl, you can... no, you will do this."

She slowly kept a steady march through the greenery, taking careful, firm steps with each foot, and made her way back towards the ship——and to the danger that surely awaited for her. The light seemed too dim with each stride she made, the jungle was turning darker and darker as she went along. There was no turning back. If this was to be her fate, then, what better way to go than making one last attempt.

"Here I come, ya dumb weed..." She snickered. "One last stupid human, doing one last stupid human thing, how's that for irony for ya?"

Running away from the ship doesn't give one time to note one's surroundings. Nor does it help to know just how far you might actually be from the spot you came from. Based on this, Katelan was sure that it had been a full half hour before she saw even close to something she recognized. But, once she was in the familiar, and saw the ship coming into view, a wave of relief came over the woman. The darkness was now total. The ship, having an automated light system, gave the area enough illumination that she could see the surrounding. Taking a few last careful steps, just at the edge of where the light's reach stopped. Katelan inspected the way and peered with apprehension.

There wasn't anyone about. The ship ramp was still down, the door open, and there was no sign of the creature lurking about. Of course, that was to be expected. She knew it was curious, it seemed to like mimicking the individuals and their personalities.

"So," she thought, "if it was trying to be Dan-like, then it was busy scoping out the ship, right? And quite possibly... maybe... doing a pre-flight... check?" Katelan balked at the very idea, giving a slight snicker of the absurdity of it. "Yeah, okay, sure... and he's sitting down having a coffee while writing a report for AirSurge too."

She did another scan of the area, stepping gingerly into the lighted area. She continued to ponder on the matter as she slowly approached the ship.

"Hmm, well, maybe he is? If it was (or is) copying him in every way, then... yay, it probably is doing what any captain of a space vessel would do. This life form, or entity, of sorts, enjoys taking on the role of the human it absorbed." She paused for a second, scrunching her nose with a curious eye. "Wait, is absorbed the right term for this? Maybe cloning, or downloading memories and brain patters is more accurate." She shook her head. "Damnit, stop being a scientist right now. Focus, girl, focus..."

The closer she got to the ship, the more her heart pounded. Somewhere, out in this dark lush jungle canopy, was the creature. Probably eyeing her as she continued on with her odd, slow-paced steps towards the ramp leading to the open hatch. Her luck was running very thin. Even though nothing jumped out at her, trying to hinder her escape, she still felt there was too much danger at the moment. Yes, she's on the ship and she survived that ordeal outside... but now, what was there to discover inside the vessel? Reaching to her right side leg pocket, she quickly discovered the weapon was gone.

"Shit!" She cursed. "It must have fallen out... no-no-no-no... goddamit!"

Her mind raced to think of another alternative to combat this alien plant-life. There were a pair of oxygen canisters off to the side of the inner hatch, strapped in their cradles, but, that wouldn't do much. Blasting it with compressed air wasn't going to do anything, seeing how it loves concentrated o2 in abundance. Katelan needed to get to the mini-lab and look for other chemicals that might do some damage.

"If only I had a big honkin' jug of weed "killer... yeah... acidic phosphates! I've got a few compounds like that. If I mix it with a few other types, it could be strong enough to burn through organic matter..."

With that in mind, she opened the next hatch into the inner vessel. The doors slid open, and she stepped in with a confidant stride. Why she wasn't afraid of what might be beyond the door, or if something was waiting there? That didn't seem to phase her in the least. Her mind was too busy thinking of the right mixture needed to create her plant-killer acid she wanted to make. But before she could get to the next section, she instantly noticed a monumental change of the interior.

"What the..." She glared wildly, "It's clean. It's all clean in here."

Not a speck of mossy-laden green adorned the walls. No vines were tangled about, or plant-life of any kind sprouting out like it was before. The ship appeared immaculate, as if it had been stripped and washed of every spore and microbe that dared to adhere to the white plating. She touched it with her hand in amazement. Katelan was stunned by it. She couldn't understand how it could have been cleaned off so quickly... unless...

"Hey, Katey..."

Dan's voice caused her to halt in fear. She didn't know

what to do in that moment. He was standing behind her, perhaps a few feet away, but, did she dare turn to look and see?

"Dan?" She said, quivering in fright.

"Yeah, it's me... welcome back, Katey... welcome back."

Chapter 22

Blast Off

"I can't believe you came back, Katey..." Dan said, as he approached her cautiously.

His movements were slow, his hands outstretched, and kept his eyes lined with hers as she finally turned about. The terror stricken woman was fumbling about as she backed away. How she wished that gun was still with her in this moment.

"D-d-don't... stay there..." She responded, lips quivering and her hand out defensively. "Just leave me alone!"

"Shhh..." He responded. "It's okay, don't be afraid. I'm Dan, you know me, right? I'd never harm you. Oh, Katey... we share a bond, something far deeper and more intimate than any of those others did."

"Don't you dare..." She glared at him. "You don't get to say things like that to me! I know what you are, you're not Dan, that's for damn sure. Dan would have killed himself before harming any of his crew."

"Oh, yes... very true." The Dan-plant creature nodded. "But, how else could I have gathered enough information to become... well... what I am now?"

"What about something less destructive?"

"I think you gave the right solution..." He smirked.

"I fucked a plant!" She hysterically proclaimed. "That's what I did. I gave you DNA the old-fashioned human way... now you want to take more? By killing me? That's perverse! Do you have any concept of these things? Is this just part of your instinct? A survival mechanism?"

"I didn't say anything about killing you." He frowned. "Why would I kill the woman I love?"

"Love?"

"Yes," He grinned. "You and I are the perfect mates."

"What?" She paused in her steps. "Mates? Love? Oh, my god..."

She was getting closer to the next section of the ship. A quick glance behind showed that she wasn't far from the storage tank control centre, she could shut the doors on either side and remain contained inside the room. Allen always referred to that as *The Hub*, she never understood why, until that moment. *The Hub* could do everything (if need be), they could control the tanks, but also navigate the ship as a backup system, should the bridge ever be compromised. AirSurge tried to have contingencies and fail-safe systems in the event of mutiny, asteroid damage or hull ruptures.

It could also contain the high levels of oxygen, should the tanks suddenly crack or leak. Making it a perfect self-contained unit for any situation; well, for right now, it was the only solution Katelan had available to her. She tried to stall the *Dan-creature* by asking more irrelevant questions.

"I don't understand... please, please tell me, why? Why are you doing all this? What more do you want?"

Dan stopped moving towards her and placed his hands

down. "I want... what all of you have ever wanted: To explore, to continue, to become better and grow."

"Grow?" She mocked. "You're a fucking plant, of course you're going to grow."

"You know what I mean." He stated, his face giving no signs of emotion behind the words.

"Okay... yeah... right." She nodded. Her eyes glanced backward and saw that she was getting closer to the threshold. "So... so you want to travel beyond this planet... er... yourself... I mean. You know that will never work."

"Of course it will." Another voice projected from behind him. "I am capable of so much more now."

Janice suddenly walked up and joined Dan. She was soon followed by others—Deacon, Allen and Dillion. The crew stood side by side and glared at her. There was nothing in their faces, no emotion, no sign of their personalities shining through, just empty eyes with expressionless faces.

"I can now be all things, and all beings." Deacon stated.

"My mind is limitless thanks to you and the others." Dillion motioned to them all.

"Evolution and thought has taken me to a new level." Allen spoke. "Where else is there to go but out there," he poised a hand up, "and to every new world in the infinite cosmos."

They said it all without missing a beat. From one person to the next, as if they were of one mind. And they were, of course, of one singular mind. Katelan was horrified by their unified thought and made her final steps into the O2 room. She found the emergency switch on the side of the archway, slammed it with her palm and let the partition wall come sliding down to seal off both sides of the room. Twisting the large round locking mechanisms on the doors, she assured her own protection and denied the alien plants from getting in.

With only a small rectangular window to see them from; a thick, shatterproof glass, she gave them the finger and laughed. She finally got the upper hand. They simply stood with blank expressions. Dan walked up the sealed door and peered at her through the window. There wasn't a sign of frustration on his face, just a look of mild concern as he tapped on the door.

"You're only hurting yourself, Katey." He said. "The ship is magnificent. Such complexities, and strange new materials to bond too. But, I've learned all I need to fly this thing. And before you try to open the oxygen valves and thrust us into the atmosphere, I should tell you that your plan simply won't work."

"Try me fucker!" She bitterly snarled.

Katelan marched over to the controls, punched in her access code, and started the process to release the oxygen out of the tanks. But to her surprise, nothing happened. She blankly looked at the screens and re-punched the sequence again... but, nothing happened. Stepping back in shock. She heard him tap at the door again, with his forehead pressed to the pane of glass.

"Told you..." He grinned, stretching out the words like a melody. "I have all the crew's access codes. It took awhile to understand, such interesting and alien thought patterns, I really had to re-spawn over and over to get the thinking right." He looked at her again, giving a slight sigh. "Perhaps you noticed. I really believed I was your friend Allen, for a time."

"Transference," She glared at him. "You absorbed his mind? How? That's impossible..."

"Mmm—not really," Dan shrugged. "For me, it was

fairly easy. Understand Katey, I've been at this... uh... what did you call it, evolution? That's it... I've been in evolution for a very long time."

"Survival instinct..." Katelan said, giving a nod of understanding.

Dan smiled at her. Who else would understand but someone like her—an astrobiologist. She knew of the complexities any biological life needed to change and adapt to its surrounding environment. This world was nothing but one giant plant. Millions of years of rapid growth, creating its own breathable air, feeding on its own moisture and cannibalizing on itself was the only way to ensure survival when no other option was available. Yes, she understood completely. Dan stepped back from the door and motioned his hand for the other selves (Allen, Janice, Deacon, and Dillion) to leave.

Without so much as an acknowledgement, the group headed for the bridge. This time, Katelan came to the window and looked out at him. She could see the others leave and him standing there with pride. This was a nightmare. What could she do to stop this? Nothing it seemed, nothing at all.

"So what now?" She sheepishly shrugged. "You want to keep me as a mate? A fuck buddy for all your DNA needs? Think again, ya sicko plant!"

"Humans..." Dan smirked. "Always thinking with your biological needs." He tapped on his crotch area and snickered. "Oh, but then... so does all life, right? You call us plants... an odd name, but, we're an organic life much like you."

"We're not the same..." Katelan grumbled.

"You would know, I suppose." He shrugged. "Ever the scientist, eh?"

"I'm not going to be some shitty-ass love slave to you. Get that out of your chlorophyl-filled brain right now. And I won't help you spread to other worlds to start some sort of seeding or pollination invasion."

"Find a chair, Katey, and strap in." He winked at her. "Time for us to go."

Before he turned to leave, Katelan pounded on the door and caught his attention.

"You have no way to lift off! The engines are saturated in wet moss and pollen. You're not going to get any thrust."

Dan folded his arms and shook his head at her. "Aw, sweetie, I know that. You made it abundantly clear to Janice. But, you see, thanks to you and your plan—which we're going to go with, of course—those tanks of air..." He glared at her with contempt. "And that is my air you're stealing, by the way—I'm going to lift off the surface using it. Just like you had originally planned."

"But you need the proper calculations," She said in a stumbling frantic behaviour. "You don't know the variables, the-the-the angle of departure... pressure limits, and... uh... oh... the rate of speed needed to..."

"Calm yourself..." He sharply stated. "I understand it all, perfectly. Dan was a skilled pilot, his knowledge of such things is everything I now possess."

Katelan was taken aback by that fact, but realized that it must be true. Even though this wasn't Dan, yet looked like him, the creature had mimicked everything about him. Through trial and error, the plant-being had perfectly absorbed and cloned human engrams, memories, and even personality traits. The speed in which this jungle planet processed the biological data was leaps and bounds ahead of any created artificial intelligence. She didn't bother to question it anymore, the fact was that this facsimile, this version of Dan, was in fact a pilot as he claimed. Katelan couldn't help but be slightly fascinated by this sort of rapid transformation; a plant that could duplicate and possess the complicated functions of a human brain.

The Skyward Seven suddenly came to life. The sound of electronics powering up, circuit breakers flipping on and the air tanks depressurizing, caused the woman to stir. She glanced at him with a dumbfounded expression, as Dan, beyond the small door window, waved casually in a goodbye to her. Angered by that gesture, Katelan ran up to the door again and pounded on it in hysterical rage.

"You can't do this! Let me out of here! You haven't got the experience of how to fly a ship! Let me out of here you fucking plant-asshole! You're going to get us all killed!"

No matter how much she punched, shoulder checked, or kicked on the sealed door with her environment suit boots, there was no way it would ever come loose. This was a hermetically sealed room now. Frantically, she looked for any override button, a kill switch, something to provide her with the means of stopping them from leaving the surface. But, as much as she wanted to rework the controls from where she was, the fact was that those creatures on the bridge had full access, and nothing she had in that room was available to her now.

"You'd better strap yourself in, Katey." Janice said over the ship's intercom. "Cause we're about to get a very large jolt."

Katelan broke out of her crazed mental state. The feeling of movement and the air tanks rush of release, caused her to launch over to a nearby chair, slap on the harness belt, and lock her self down as the ship rocked about. With one last tank opening up, the ship suddenly catapulted upward like that of an uncontrolled elevator, heading straight up to the top floor. The G-force from the blast was making it hard for her to move. Her body felt incredibly heavy. Her arms felt like they wanted to merge with the floor beneath her, and her head pressed into the back of the suit's helmet uncomfortably.

Dealing with extreme forces was all part of the training when signing on for space missions. AirSurge trained all crews and staff on the rigours of spaceflight and the dangers that came with it. Katelan had only been in a simulator once when they switched off the gravity plating, and spun out of control and pinned to the interior of the artificial ship wall. It made her nauseous, of course, but she knew enough that it wasn't real and managed to ride it out flawlessly. But in this instant, where the crushing gravity is causing her to lose consciousness, was nothing like that simulation at all.

On the monitor to her right, she could see the surface of Dreganon V zooming out as they entered the stratosphere at a record pace. The tanks that contained the pure oxygen had performed just as she predicted. They were like booster rockets, with enough parts per million to send them into a high orbit within minutes. The hiss from each tank, slowly quieted down, and the feeling of weightlessness kicked in. Looking at the monitor again, she could see the curvature of the planet. They'd successfully made it into space and propelled Skyward Seven into orbit. But it wouldn't last long, Katelan knew that if they didn't restart the engines and move further away from the world, the ship's orbit would decay and they'd fall back onto the surface.

She released the belt and hovered over her chair. Being weightless was always an incredible feeling, but if one didn't know how to navigate themselves properly, they'd felt helpless and drift about in a panic. Being experienced (and well trained), she managed to head for the controls and checked the computer for the status of their engines. Tapping on the monitor, she was surprised by what it stated on the screen:

Fuel Status: None
Reserve Fuel: None

"What?" She breathlessly choked, eyes flared wide. "That can't be right! We had lots of fuel... we never touched the reserves."

Katelan maneuvered herself to the other controls around the air tanks, and checked all the gauges. The air tanks were all bottomed out, just like she had figured, but she still hoped there might be something left (even if it was only a few micro-bursts) to get the ship out of this doomed parking spot.

"Stupid fuckers don't know about the gravity plating, I guess." She snickered while trying to stay stable over the console.

She hadn't heard a peep from them since they got here, making her wonder if something happened.

"Did the G-forces crush their plant-bodies? Maybe they didn't survive?" She shook that notion off. "No, they live on a world with concentrated air pressure. I'm sure they've adapted easily." She then glared over to the door of the room. "But if that's the case, where are they?"

She floated over to the door and glanced out the small, retangular window. There was no one there. No one had come to check on her. Not that they would or even cared about her enough to do it, nonetheless, there wasn't anyone. She was trapped. With no access to the ship whatsoever. It was time to get creative again, and figure out a way to get out of this room and off this ship.

Chapter 23

Survival Mode

Skyward Seven hung in orbit of Dreganon V as it stayed in the planet's rotation. The singular light source from a distant star faded as the ship crossed into the terminator of night. It would be several hours before Skyward Seven would be visible again. As the time continued to pass, Katelan steadily worked on trying to find a way out of her predicament. The attempt to use her access code on the computer failed, though she couldn't understand why. It was constantly rejecting it and returning to the main menu. She then tried to yank out the wires from underneath the control terminals (hoping to ignite a reboot), but again, there was no progress in that attempt.

Everything she was doing had little to no impact. It confounded her. There was power, that much is for sure, but for some reason, she couldn't get anything to work like it should.

"What am I doing wrong here?" She stated out loud. "Why can't I get anything to work?"

She took a minute to calm down, tapped on her helmet for luck, and started the process all over again.

"I'm not going to be the bride of a plant!" She stated, gazing up at the small camera fixed in the corner of room. She knew they were watching her, and raised a middle finger up at it. "I'm going to stop you, fucker! Bet on that."

* * *

On the bridge of the ship, Dan and the rest of the Skyward Seven cloned-plant crew (Deacon, Janice, Allen and Dillion), familiarized themselves with the controls and chuckled at Katelan's ongoing battle in the hub by herself. Dan shook his head as he watched the monitor, he brushed his finger on the image of her, and smiled.

"Such persistence," He snickered. "That's why I chose you, my sweet Katey..."

He looked up to the surrounding crew and returned to smirk. There was no individuality in them, they were all interconnected with Dan, and the planet below. If it wanted to channel their personalities, it would speak through each individual one. But there was no need to do so. If they came into contact with another vessel or wanted to pretend for Katelan's benefit, then they would act like their former selves. As a collective mind, the jungle of Dreganon V, this outwardly dramatic display was unnecessary.

"I can feel them all." Dan said, gazing out to the planet visible from the bridge's main window. "Such differences, so many thoughts, it's hard to believe they could ever truly get along at all."

Suddenly, Deacon, who was seated opposite to him, shot up out of his chair, and began writhing uncontrollably. Dan felt the shot of pain and winced from it. Deacon glanced over to Dan with a look of terror, and then collapsed to the floor. His body colour changed to a brown tinge and fell apart into a plant-like bio-matter. It was a puzzling scene for the *Dan-creature* to witness, he was still feeling the effects and headed over to examine the body. Then it happened again, this time Janice and the others did the same odd behaviour. They rose out of their pilot's seat, and suddenly burst like balloons full of green goo. It splattered across the consoles and main window as the droplets hung in the air from the weightless environment.

Dan, feeling all of it, writhed in pain and quickly tried to back out of the room. He started wriggling like the others had. His eyes grew wide from the intensity of pain and bolted from the bridge as fast as he could. He instantly sealed the door, collapsing on the other side of it and began flopping about as his skin deteriorated.

Since reaching the planet's orbit, Katelan found it odd that none of the plant-creatures had come to check on her. Dan, or whatever plant-being had taken his form, had already been and said his peace, of course. And yes, they had the camera, so there was no need to physically come down to check. But, it would have been nice if one of them (any of the his plant-clone colleagues), came to keep her company. If they truly did possess the personalities and mental traits of her crew, then surely, just one of them would have been so inclined to come and see. It was like they didn't care at all. Emotionless plants with human forms.

She tried calling them over the intercom, but even that, as much as she couldn't believe, wasn't working right, either. Something was wrong. Where the hell were they? Why isn't anything working? She couldn't put her finger on it, but, something just didn't seem right. Despite this feeling, she managed to locate some minor tools to work with. She continued to pull off paneling, floor plates, and even tampered with the pipes leading into the air pumps. The more she disassembled the more she became distraught. Nothing was working, nothing would function like it should. She couldn't figure out why.

Exhausted and frustrated from her actions, she maneuvered to the wall and slumped down against it; her arms and legs freely drifted up and down as she relaxed them. Katelan was sweating profusely, as the beads drifted about in the weightlessness. She occasionally batted an eye, or moved her head slightly to avoid the floating bits of perspiration. Katelan's depression finally set in. She chucked the small tool in her hand to the far side in defeat. The need to survive was starting to dim for her.

Even though AirSurge's Purification Cargo Cruiser was on its way, it still wouldn't be in range of the system for a few weeks, maybe even months... she wasn't sure; only Dan or Allen knew the schedule with greater accuracy. And even if, by some miracle, it did show up early, the cruiser would need to link up with Skyward Seven's beacon before entering the planetary region. The two ship computers would have to sync and log through endless data streams, and once that was done, they would issue a standard *grace time protocol*. That was to give the harvesting crew time to prep the tanks, recheck the levels they've siphoned, and readied the load to be picked up. Then they'd have to mull through tons of documents, sign each one, and then... only then, they could dock with the cruiser.

"Jesus..." Katelan thought.

She absolutely hated the bureaucracy of it all. It's no wonder it takes so long for any crew of mining (oxygen or asteroid) to get paid and given the next assignment. But, that's what it's like working for a corporation like AirSurge or any other mining operation for that matter. They're all about time, product purity, and letting harvesting explore teams do all the hard work. She sat in her spot, staring off into nothing, wondering if she made the right choices in life, especially joining this team, whom now are all dead— except her. She focused her attention to the wall across the room, where exposed pipes and wires stuck out from her fruitless efforts of pulling them apart.

As she focused her gaze, concentrating on the wall itself, she noticed something. Katelan didn't know what it was, not at first, but there seemed to be a brown spot flaking away. She floated over to examine it closer and pondered at it. It looked like a flake of rust. Yet, it wasn't quite metallic as it flopped in the air. Katelan brought herself in closer, as close as she could (to get a good look), and touched it with her finger. It wasn't metal. It was... a leaf. Her eyes widened upon the discovery. She plucked it off and studied it with intensity.

The leaf was part dead and part... metallic? That didn't make any sense to her. She glanced over to the wall from which it came and felt it with her hand. Some of it was smooth, but as she continued to brush along, more of it flaked off.

"What the–?" She stated, floating close to the wall again. "What is this?"

Upon examination, she slowly noticed the fine detail in the metal. It looked familiar to her, as if she'd seen the patterning from some place before—or rather—a certain someone.

"Oh, my god..." She uttered in realization. "No, it can't be... that's not possible."

The more she looked at the wall, and the other parts of

the interior, the more she discovered the tightly woven pattern embedded in the structure. They were tiny leaves, almost microscopic to the naked eye, but the same ones she'd seen on the plant-imposter of Allen and Dan's skin. Skyward Seven, in every mechanical detail, was that of the plant life of Dreganon V. The more she rubbed on the surface, the more it peeled away and flake off. Her mind raced from the sheer impracticality of having an entire ship (a non-biological object) copied right down to the very electrical components and computer programs used to run this vessel.

Wildly she gazed about the room, the ceiling, the chairs, the window pane on the door—everywhere she looked, the pattern suddenly became visible to her eyes. The ship, Skyward Seven, was a facsimile, a plant-like chameleon, just like the crew had become—and it was now in space, of all places. Was this even the real ship? Did they modify it somehow? Is that even possible? Could it have adapted to such a vacuous environment in mere minutes or hours?

"No... that's not possible," Katelan thought. So many questions were burning in her brain right now. She had to explain it to herself to make sense. "Organic vegetation simply cannot survive in the vacuum of space, it's a fact of nature. You can't change that fact. Right, of course. But plants need several things to continue to thrive; Sunlight, moisture, and... oh..." she paused in realization, "Wait-wait-wait a second... oh, god! No, oh no!"

She quickly shot herself over to the door and frantically pounded upon it. The window was tinted with frost. Katelan noted the glass and quickly felt at the air vents on her suit's helmet. She raised up her gloved hand, curiously eyeing it, and saw ice crystallization. It was from the carbon monoxide vapour expelling out, as the suit continued to regulate her air, and froze instantly. It was a sign that the ship's interior temperature was starting to grow colder, so much so that it was now at a freezing point. Her eyes flashed. There was only one reason for such a drop. Again, she wildly pounded on the door.

"Dan! Dan! Or... whatever you are! You can't survive out here!" She called out to the top of her lungs. "You've got to bring the ship down! You can't live in this type of environment! You've got nothing to keep you from..."

Before she could finish her words, the plant-imposter of Dan appeared. He was walking irregularly, as if drunk or badly wounded. His feet were dragging as he clumsily made his way over to the door she was staring out of. She watched him with amazement. He wasn't floating about and weightless like she was, his feet were on the floor and looked oddly sticky underneath. A layer of thick mucus remained attached between, looking overly gooey as it followed his steps.

"So, that's why there was no need for gravity plating for them." She thought. "Sticky sap feet... amazing."

Dan pulled himself up to the window and pressed his head against it with a crooked smile.

"You... you knew this would happen..." He slurred at her. "You... scientist, you..."

"What are you talking about?" She glared back. She could see his plant-like appearance taking shape again. The structure of leaves and tightly wound vines loosening and falling off of his skin.

"The minute we came into orbit... we... I... felt something burn, my spawn dying instantly..."

"Radiation..." She stated. "There's tons of it out here."

"You failed to tell us... in your minds..."

"Duh!" She mocked. "It's called space for a reason... I

thought you would have figured that out. I mean, you've managed to grasp just about everything else. Taking all that knowledge out of my friends..." She paused momentarily, remembering them, and how they died. She shook off the thought and continued on. "Such an evolved mental capacity you have, huh? Didn't you understand the concept of what space was? You mimicked our minds and personalities... but couldn't understand the complex science behind it?"

"Not as smart... then... instinct to survive... took millions of turns of world to adapt, change... become..."

"Evolution, you kept evolving over and over."

"Long time..." He smirked.

"So now, we gave you more thought, greater speed to understand... you absorbed my crew to speed up the process."

He nodded, concurring with her, and tried to speak again. It took him a few tries, taking deep inhales of the diminishing air, and then pressed his face on the window again. The browning tint of his skin colour gave her a moment of pause. She knew what this was. Plants quickly decompose when deprived of natural resources; be it water, light, nutrients and, the most important, air. Without such things in abundance, organic life (plants especially) will wither and die. The stupid plant-being launched itself into space and didn't have enough intelligence to know there was nothing to protect it from the lack of those resources. But most of all, no protection from the bombardment of cosmic rays.

Pity would have crossed her mind, seeing it suffer the way it was, but since it did not respect the lives of her crew, Katelan felt a sense of justice coming back to bite it in the ass. The lights flickered throughout the ship as Dan's painful rasping gasps for oxygen synchronized. The symbiosis with the vessel waned with each inhale. She crossed her arms in delight and shrugged at his misfortune.

"Well, isn't karma a bitch, huh, asshole..." She mockingly stated with a smug attitude. "You took the lives of my crew, and now, you get to experience what that's like."

"You... have to... have to help... me." He struggled to speak. "I need... I need... to return. You have to do it for me, come back with me..."

"Not a chance," She snorted. "I'd rather die out here than let something like you live."

"You need me... just as I need you..."

"Doubtful..." She smirked. "But, hey, why not just do it yourself? You're a pilot, right? You can aim the ship yourself."

"Not... able... to... think..." He choked again, struggling to speak. "Need to re-spawn to... a better form..."

"Ahhh..." She responded, nodding slightly to him. It was becoming very apparent to her now. She glanced away for a second, processing the thought, and turned back to face him. "So, you transferred the main part of your consciousness to these forms... to this ship as well?"

"I attached, studied form, what you call pollen or spore..."

"Right, cause that's all of you. Everything is you. Which means the entire world is like a big brain, the more you absorb, adapt and evolve, the smarter you become; So, let me guess, you want to go down there, reboot the form, and maybe strengthen your structure to survive the conditions? And then what? Spread to other systems, seeding other worlds and continue your existence?" Dan said nothing to her. He didn't have to, she understood perfectly. "I see, wow, brilliant," She winked at him. "A survival mode, if you will. Like any struggling organic life form, you wanted to grow and expand, to become more than what you are."

Katelan stopped grinning for a minute. The description sounded oddly familiar to her. She glanced at her own reflection in the frosted window—an epiphany suddenly arose.

"Thats... kind of like, us... humanity, I mean. We're spreading across the galaxy, making new homes on other worlds, consuming the resources, expanding our knowledge... trying to..."

"Survive..." He said, finishing her thought. "See how humans are such hypocrites. You came to me, taking my air, all that I needed to survive. You are just as monstrous..."

That caught her off guard and glanced up with surprise. This creature was intelligent, more so than she had initially realized. That feeling of satisfied revenge was dwindling, and pity finally took its place. How utterly foolish she felt in that moment, an astrobiologist's dream was to make this kind of discovery, and here she was savouring its demise.

"You have the only air supply left..." He said, taking long gasps, struggling to inhale. "Sealed in that room... but not for long. The form is... dying... soon..."

Looking at her surroundings, she noticed more of the interior breaking down. Like falling leaves from a tree, the skin of the walls and ceiling peeled away and floated about with her. The colour was browning and becoming frozen with ice. There wasn't much time indeed. She flipped up her right arm suit control and started tapping on the buttons. Two flaps on her back opened up like large vents and started sucking in the cold, icy-like air. She had to quickly fill as much as she could to survive. Then, once the meter registered full, she deactivated the pump and closed the vents.

The suit automatically converted when she doubled tapped on the flashing red button on the arm display. This closed the protruding vents on her helmet and turned it into a temporary spacesuit. The air swirling about was frigid and causing her to shiver. It felt like pins and needles in her lungs, but she would have to endure it in order to survive. Looking up at Dan, she could see him breaking apart.

"I'm sorry, Katey..." He said. "I'm sorry for leaving you like this."

Katelan said nothing back and just looked at him. She almost believed that was Dan, speaking through that doppelgänger, as if he was still somewhere deep inside that thing's brain. She wanted to say something back to him, but, she couldn't find the right words of comfort. As if on cue, the ship split apart. The *Dan-creature* launched out of the open section and was hurled away. Then the rest of the ship imploded, it sucked Katelan inward with the rest, but then thrusted her out as the entire vessel disintegrated into its organic components. The crystallized debris of the massive dead vegetation shot about in a wide plume.

The *Dan-plant creature* was shot back into the planet's atmosphere, sending him into a fiery re-entry. He burned into oblivion as did many other pieces of debris from the wreckage as it fell back onto the surface below. Katelan was more fortunate. The force of impact had knocked her unconscious, and jettisoned her away in the opposite direction. She narrowly missed several large jagged chunks of the former vessel, as her body floated away from the planet. Katelan was in an uncontrolled spin and headed out into deep space.

Chapter 24

The Void Of Space

Katelan's unconscious mind began focusing on memories as she drifted out into the black. They fluctuated from past to present; from her childhood, with family, friends and relatives, to her adult years; Studying with Doctor Lim, walking through various jungle environments, and then her experiences on Skyward Seven. Those were the moments she seemed to remember most. Flashes of the crew laughing together, telling stories, playing cards, and enjoying the work as a team. Allen and Dillion would always be playing practical jokes on her or Janice, especially when they were working, eating, or trying to get some sleep in their own bunks.

The crew were like an extended family, full of good times and bad, especially when it came to working in such confined spaces. But, they always managed to solve their problems and continue their jobs like professionals. And then, there were the thoughts of her and Dan; she remembered the time they met, after signing on with AirSurge, Dan volunteered to take her under his wing and show her the *ins* and *outs* of the job. She wasn't too fond of him at first.

He tended to be slightly chauvinistic and rude, but slowly, over time and missions, she discovered there was another side to him. He could be sweet, caring, and a romantic at heart. The more they spent time together, the more they bonded and understood one another. Dan wasn't like the rest of the crew. He was never condescending about her title, not like Janice was, and seemed rather impressed with her curious mind. He always made her feel like she was part of the team and never an outsider.

She remembered when they shared their first kiss and intimate embrace. They were on a space station overlooking the newly colonized world of Epsilon Minor, nestled in an obscure solar system just beyond the Tau Ceti sector. It was a gorgeous planet that had a brilliant hue of blue and green, like an angelic halo surrounding the world. Their luxurious room had a magnificent panoramic windowed view of it, making it the most romantic spot both had ever witnessed.

The beauty and awe of such a scene sparked a sexual moment, whether it was from the effect of the planet's aura, or just the relationship taking another bold step, neither one was absolutely certain. But it didn't matter. She and Dan were right for each other, physically and mentally. It would have happened eventually, in that room on the station or on the ship in mid-journey. Katelan took the chance and threw caution to the wind.

Recollection of that lustful night played over and over. His passionate play fuelled hers and the two intertwined like wild beasts. And as the lingering moment continued to play on, Dan's tenderness suddenly stopped. He forcefully placed himself over her and grabbed her arms roughly. She laughed at his aggressiveness, but when gazing up at him, she noticed his face had changed. Instead of a handsome smiling face, there was a tangled weave of leaves and vines that contorted about. It appeared to be Dan's face, but resembled more of the alien creature from that dreaded jungle planet.

"Don't struggle, Katey!" It said, wheezing out the words to her. "You will be with me... forever!"

"No!" She screamed. "No-no-no! Let go!"

The memory had turned into a full on nightmare. Out of his mouth came a tendril vine, sliding into her mouth and nose, with more coiling around her body and into her exposed areas. She tried to break free of this vile act, and found that her struggle was only causing more to happen. Dan's body engulfed hers and the two merged into one. All that was visible to her were vines and foliage as it moved about. Suddenly, Katelan found herself in a swirling vortex of it, holding her over the spinning apex. She could feel herself dropping inside of it, taking her back to the planet as it appeared out of the bottom and sucked her into its domain.

The vines continued to hold on to her, pinning her in place, and sliding downwards into the thick dense forest of the surface. It was just like the dream she had experienced on Dreganon V before, being rushed towards an open chasm that seemed deeply black and as void as space itself. Drum beats echoed about. The more she focused on the sound, the more it thumped away like a beating heart. Was it hers or others collectively beating as one? The crew perhaps? Or maybe it was the jungle, reminding her it too was alive and forcing her to listen to it.

It continued on, louder, faster, as the vines pushed her forward; rushing her along the never-ending canopy floor of the lush vegetation. The jungle was swallowing her in.

There was no escape from the vine's stranglehold all over her, nothing to grab on to as she sped past, its leafy-tendrils shoved her into an awaiting pit-like maw of Dreganon's jungle domain.

As she fell into the darkened pit, she could hear the distant voices of her former crew; snippets of haunted conversational moments she'd had with each of them. An echo of the friends she'd lost along the way:

"When have I ever listened to instruction properly? Or you, for that matter?" Said Allen.

"Well, they must be pretty fuckin' smart if they're talking like us and acting like us." Said Janice.

"What a place," Dillion exhaled, "I don't think it's worth the effort to get all that oxygen from here, to be honest."

"Look at it, floating in the air all around us." Deacon stated. "It's so light and minuscule, I bet the breeze brings in a continual cycle of this stuff."

The final voice was that of Dan, it seemed closer to her than the others did. As if he was whispering it into her ear.

"Don't let them get to you. I love you... I love you Katey... I love you."

There were quick memory flashes of him smiling at her, kissing her, walking beside her in the jungle in their suits, and even moments on the bridge of Skyward Seven of where both had shared an embrace. Dan was the only one that understood her the most, and now, he's dead. The crew perished because of her curiosity. If they had just collected the air and left, like all of them wanted, perhaps they would have survived. It was only because of her, AirSurge's overly curious astrobiologist, that needed to take samples and record data for that greedy company.

No, the company wasn't really to blame, it was all her. It

was her suggestion to take samples, to bring back the data, to extend their time on that planet. Unknown to Dan and the rest of the crew, prior to their assignment, Katelan had taken a meeting with the CEO of AirSurge. Based on her findings on what the probe picked up on its initial fly by of Dreganon V, they agreed more study needed to be done on the ecosystem and felt the crew didn't need to know the added details. Katelan kept the secret from all of them, even Dan. The company would only inform him of what needed to be done upon arrival, but not of the true intent behind it.

They could have just easily taken the air and moved on, but no, Katelan wanted to be famous. She wanted to have a legacy. She wanted to be recognized as a true scientist in her field.

"All for nothing..." Her mind echoed. "All for nothing..."

Katelan slowly dipped into the darkness feet first, as it enveloped her slowly, rising and over her legs and torso. The thumping heartbeat sound that echoed over and over slowed, the rhythm paced out and faded as the shroud of dark crawled up over her face. Her right hand was poised over her head, reaching for someone to save her from this pitch black abyss. But there was no one, nobody at all, just her and the unquenchable void that consumed her into its depths.

* * *

In that utter darkness, where nothing could be seen, a faint beeping sound pulsed on and on; a muffled voice accompanied it, repeating in tone and length. As it continued, it started to becoming more audible, it was a woman's voice, it grew stronger and more discernible. Katelan's face returned from the pitch black, as if rising out of an ocean of ink. She strained to hear the words as they continued to repeat louder and louder.

"Skyward Seven, this is The Scallion, do you copy? Over? Do you copy, over? I say again, this is AirSurge's Purification Cargo Cruiser, The Scallion-IPS 44, do you copy?"

Slowly, Katelan's eyes fluttered open. The voice seemed to force her to regain clarity of thought. But was it real? It can't be. She felt it was just part of her imagination, now that her dream-like state was ending. When her eyes fully opened, Katelan could see the reflection of her own face staring back at her. No longer was she in the utter darkness of her mind, but facing the ghostly mirrored image of herself inside the spacesuit's helmet, with the pitch black of deep space behind it.

The memories and nightmares faded out, and reality of her predicament soon became apparent once more. She could feel the pain again, at the base of her skull where she'd been struck, but strangely, it wasn't as sore as before. Her breathing returned to a steady pace and could hear it from the enclosed helmet she bore. The remaining collected chilled air in the suit was thin and very hard to breathe.

She wondered how long she'd been out of it. Her body felt strange, she hadn't the strength to move a muscle. Perhaps she'd been floating for hours or days? She couldn't tell. The fog of being in that state of unconsciousness confused her senses. All she could make out was the faint stars in the distance, they were blurry and streaked about as she spun. Dreganon V, though much further away, was a mere greenish dot that scrolled over and over with the rest of the stars as her uncontrolled spinning continued.

"I'm going to die out here." She whimpered, her voice

was dry and raspy. "I deserve it... for what I did..."

She could feel the ice build up on her tear ducts, the frozen air had chilled her considerably. Her skin was pale and frost laden. The suit heater wasn't working anymore. She figured the suit shutdown all internal systems with only the air pump working to keep her alive. This wouldn't last too long. Eventually, the suit would turn off completely, spending its remaining back-up systems, and then—she was done.

Katelan made peace with her death. Feeling it to be a sense of justice for the harm she'd caused that world and her crew. She closed her eyes, hard as it was with the ice covering them, and uttered, "Goodbye..."

In that moment, she heard that repeated unknown female voice again.

"Skyward Seven, this is The Scallion, do you copy?"

Katelan's eyes quickly popped open in realization. The voice wasn't part of that bizarre dream she just endured, nor was it from the onset of hypoxia, giving rise to a hallucination or delusion because of it. No, it wasn't a dream or a memory, this was happening right now. Even as the stars swirled, and the distant hue of Dreganon V looped around, there was now a massive metallic wall appearing before her.

She giggled, slowly at first, but then belted out a hysterical mad-like laugh. As she gazed upon the structure (each time she came around) she noted the familiar grey-black patchwork of the hull. The words on the side of it were hard to make out at first, but as the large imposing ship cruised closer to her, she could make out the insignia and massive white letters adorning it:

The Scallion-IPS 44
AirSurge Purification Cargo Class Cruiser

Chapter 25

Recovery

K atelan wasn't able to determine what was happening after the shuttle crew recovered her from space. They brought her back to the massive Purification Cargo Cruiser and things got a bit fuzzy once she was onboard. There were quick flashes of light in her eyes from all directions, and the feeling of being rushed through the large, spacious corridors of the vessel. The frantic medical staff spouted off technical terms and procedures in various raised voices, but it was hard to make out what they were all saying, it sounded muffled to her, as if her ears were doused in water.

Like bees swarming a nest, they scurried around her, hooking up machines to aid in her recovery. Her limbs could barely move. They felt like slabs of granite. And she still felt extremely cold, despite having blankets thrown onto her. From time to time, she could feel things poking her, an air mask being adjusted on her face, and a heat source emanating from something surrounding her body.

As she dove in and out of consciousness, Katelan had fractured visions of the nurses and doctors working on her.

They wore masks that covered the lower half of their faces, and bore long white surgical gowns. The doctors were being handed various med-tools, as the staff catered to their every request. She could make out a few things they were saying as she became conscious for a few seconds.

"Bring up the heart monitor!" A doctor ordered.

"She's thawing out..." A nurse proclaimed.

"Take that suit to the labs and have it checked out..." Someone directed in the distance.

The last thing she remembered before conking out again, was one of the nurses looking down at her with a look of concern. The woman was black, that much she knew, and had extremely beautiful brown eyes. Katelan figured the woman must have been very young and gorgeous underneath all that garb. Probably a woman that got a lot of attention outside of her job. But, that look she gave seemed to bother Katelan, even as she drifted off into slumber.

"Why was she looking at me like that? How bad of a situation am I in? Wait... what did she say? I couldn't quite make out that last bit... what... what did she say?"

Katelan's eyes closed. Sleep was all she was craving now, and as all the voices and visions blurred out, dissipating into nothingness, Katelan managed to utter a last thought.

"I don't want to die..."

* * *

Hours later...

Katelan awoke and lay in a clean-looking, well polished all-white room. She wondered if she had in fact died, and was in the afterlife. Of course, she didn't believe in that sort of thing. Religion and the concept of place people go after death was delusional thinking, as far as she was concerned. But even so, the thought did strike her mind as she roused from her slumber. She quickly noted that her enviro-suit had been removed, and she was now wearing a long white, short sleeved hospital-type gown. The velcro straps on the back kept it secure enough for her not to have her backside visible, she was thankful for that, at least.

The one thing she noticed was that it didn't feel cold anymore. There was warmth on her skin. Even the room was warm and comfortable to be in. The bed she was lying in, looking more like a simple cot, was attached to the wall. She rose from her position and scanned the room. It became apparent that the bed was the only bit of furnishing in this space. Perplexed by her surroundings, with the lack of decor, Katelan got out of her bed and tried to get her bearings. Her limbs, still having some atrophy, caused her to wobble and stumble about, as if she was a newborn baby fawn trying to stand for the first time.

The white room had no windows, none that she could make out, anyway, and the walls were as smooth as glass, yet warm to the touch.

"Heated..." She guessed in her mind. "For my benefit, perhaps?"

The only thing out of place in that room was the upper ventilation. It looked small, slender and deeply honey-combed. She thought about it for a moment, and then concluded that this must be a decontamination chamber; a way to assess if she was carrying any impurities before being reintroduced into the ship.

"This is The Scallion, right?" She wondered aloud. She lifted her head up and hollered it out louder. "I'm aboard

The Scallion, am I not? Can I talk to someone here? Hello? I know you're there, watching me..."

The far right wall produced a door that pushed inward and slid to the side. An enviro-suited individual stepped in and waited for the door to close behind them. Katelan seemed surprised by their sudden appearance, backing away slightly from them and giving a curious glare.

"What's going on?" Katelan said. "Why am I in here?"

"Good morning, I'm glad to see you awake, Miss Driscoll."

Katelan realized that it was a woman talking. The helmet was covered with a reflective face shield. She'd only seen those types of suits when there was the possibility of radiation or biohazardous contamination. Their suit even had its own oxygen supply strapped on the back, keeping that person perfectly self contained with their own air. The rhythmic breathing gave it an ominous sound and made it very imposing to Katelan. The enviro-suited woman gestured to the centre of the room.

"Please, have a seat."

Out of the floor rose a square table and two rounded stools. With yet another gesture of the woman's hand, Katelan reluctantly shuffled over and sat down upon the opposite side. The enviro-suited woman took to the other seat and rested her hands flat on the table. A holographic projection appeared in-between them. It was flat and scrolled multiple images of the crew, Skyward Seven and hi-res planetary scans of Dreganon V.

"To answer your question," The woman finally disclosed. "Yes, you are indeed aboard The Scallion. You were lucky we showed up earlier than expected, otherwise you would have floated out into the deep black and we would have never seen you at all."

The voice sounded familiar to Katelan. She eyed the individual carefully and shrugged in response.

"I didn't have the beacon on me. So how did you?"

"Process of elimination, and like I said, blind luck, really. But, we did use Skyward Seven's outer marker buoy for us to trace back to this area. Your enviro-suit does have an ident-chip installed, and we just pinged it, since there was no response to any of our hails to the Skyward Seven."

"What outer buoy?" Katelan said, giving a double take in confusion. "I don't remember us doing that."

"No, not you," The woman responded. "It was launched by your ship's computer. It's a protocol that all deep space explorer class vessels have. Your captain was probably aware of it, but since it's so common place, it probably wasn't worth mentioning to the rest of you."

"Okay," Katelan blinked, still looking unsure about it all. "So, why am I in here, in this room? Shouldn't I be in medical right now?"

"You were, Miss Driscoll."

"Call me Katelan."

"If you like..." The woman nodded.

Katelan tilted her head at her. "And who are you? What's your name?"

"You can call me, Vivian."

"Nice to meet you, Vivian. So... I'm out of med, and now I'm here." She glared with confusion. "Has something changed? Am I contaminated, or something?"

"It's procedure," the woman said, crossing her legs and folding her hands together as they rested on the tabletop. "But, before we can release you, we'd like for you to answer some questions, if you please."

Katelan looked about at the walls again. The woman stated, 'we'—as if there was more than one person with her.

She wondered if there were others were watching from another room, possibly next to this one. The walls did look glass like in appearance. She clucked her tongue at the thought, glanced back at the suited woman and then gave a sarcastic nod.

"Alrighty then, if you'd like. I suppose it's going to be about what happened to the crew, or if we managed to secure enough pure oxygen, or even if I still have any samples of the plant life in my possession."

"Something like that." Vivian acknowledged. "Can you shed some light on any or all of those points? How about we just start with the crew then... whet happened to them and the ship?"

"That's a loaded explanation to give..." Katelan stated, giving a wry glance.

"What do you mean? Can you elaborate?"

"Look," Katelan glared at her. "Before I start, can I at least get a sense of whom I'm talking to here, on a one-to-one basis? Do you have a title or what, Vivian?"

Vivian nodded agreeably and tapped the side of her helmet. The visor's upper section crystallized clear, showing only her eyes and forehead. The lower half of the visor remained mirrored, probably covering the breathing apparatus and microphone from which the woman was talking with, Katelan assumed. She gave a look of satisfaction. She'd seen those eyes before. It was the nurse, or staff member, that had gazed upon her prior before going unconscious. Those beautiful brown eyes drew Katelan in like a magnet.

"Is this better?"

"Yeah," Katelan nodded. "Thanks for that. So, tell me, are you a nurse?"

"Not as such, no..." Vivian snickered slightly. "I'm The

Scallion's representative of AirSurge Incorporated, specifically in the Bio-science division."

"Oh..." Katelan replied with a cocked brow. "That's uh... that's a quite the position, I guess you know of my credentials then."

"Yes, Katelan, I'm well aware."

"So, let me guess then," She exhaled, folding her arms in frustration at the corporate woman. "I'm in deep shit, and this is an integration. Right? Or do they call it a debriefing? Whatever the term is to see if an employee is at fault."

"I didn't say that you were at fault, Katelan. The company just wants to know what happened, to you, and the crew. And yes, they want to know about the cargo and samples. But, let's put that aside for now," the woman said as she leaned in and relaxed her elbows on the table. "Can you please just give us the details about what transpired on Dreganon V? Just that... for now, and then we'll talk more on the rest of it."

Katelan laughed and shook her head disapprovingly. Yep, she was in deep *doo-doo* with the corporation alright, she figured. They sent a representative in to get all dirt and possibly cover their asses from this incident. She took a moment to gather her wits, eyeing Vivian in the enviro-suit with those pretty eyes looking back, and shrugged at her submissively.

"Okay, sure. Where do I even begin?"

"Well," Vivian leaned back a bit. "How about just after you set down on Dreganon V? Where did you land the ship? What did you do once you set foot on the surface?

Katelan snickered. "Oh Viv, I hope you've got a lot drive space on that holo-recorder of yours, cause... lady, you're going to hear a lot of interesting and really wild shit."

Chapter 26

Decision

Two Hours later...

Standing on The Scallion's observation deck, facing the panoramic window that overlooked the vast, sprawling industrial city-like vessel, was Captain Theodore Hasad Jalal. Jalal (in his standard issue AirSurge grey-beige uniform), was a tall, middle-eastern man who had commanded The Scallion Air Purification Cruiser for many years. And while he's been to many worlds with rich sources of oxygen before, this one was by far has had the purest source he's ever encountered. The vibrantly green planet of Dreganon V was coming into view over the ship's mighty bow. From his vantage point, most of what he could see of it was obscured by the labyrinth before him; nothing but pipes, tall silos, and multi-layered supporting struts as they sandwiched between either side of the vessel's thick wall-like hull.

Holographic projection was playing behind him. It hovered in the air with a video of Katelan and Vivian in the all-white chamber.

"So... Vivian, that's what happened to me..." Katelan's voice stated. "Now that you know all this, I assume I'm free to go? So, when the hell can I get out of here?"

Vivian, having since finished her long interview with Katelan, sat at a long black-glassed table in the centre of the room. She was indeed an exquisitely beautiful ebony woman, with luscious hair pulled back into a ponytail. She switched off the holo-vid recording of that debriefing. The floating holographic over the tabletop disappeared. She then eyed the captain still standing there in deep contemplation. Vivian passively observed the reaction of the other five people sitting at the table with her; two senior crew members and three personnel of the AirSurge company vessel.

"So..." Jalal finally uttered. "Is her story believable?"

"I'm not sure." Vivian responded. "We're still analyzing her uniform, waiting for the lab to send us back the results, and the medical report from Doctor Williams."

"I see..." Jalal exhaled in frustration. "So, we might have come all this way out for nothing."

"Nothing? I think it's more than that, sir." Vivian said. She took a short gaze at the others before adding more. "This could be the discovery of epic proportions. Life on other worlds... of an entire world itself... that's mind bogglingly huge."

"We've found life on other planets before, Vivian." The captain sighed.

"Not like this, sir." She stressed, tapping her finger to the table. "Like I said, this world is one gigantic life form. A living plant world."

"I agree." Dr. Raymond Saimai, sitting across from Vivian, acknowledged with a nod. He was the chief scientist on board, one who was not only established in astrobiology but also an accomplished astrophysicist as well. "I believe the planet has enormous potential. Not only is it abundant in O_2 in its purest form, but Dreganon V is self sustaining and could be used for increased production on other AirSurge acquired worlds."

"Well," Vivian passively gestured to him. "I won't argue that it isn't, but, I think we need to take precautions here. And besides, Katelan Driscoll has a legitimate claim to the find, and the most qualified astrobiologist AirSurge employee to study it further."

"Vivian, please..." Sally Truman, The Scallion's first mate, brushed back her short crop of blonde hair and rolled her eyes. "You can't trust her word, I'll bet the whole thing is a cover up to her murdering the crew."

"That's not proven yet..." Vivian glared.

"The observation drones are nearly done scanning the planet." Saimai openly stated. "They've got the technology to do high resolution scans from orbit, no need to clog their instruments on the surface, so we'll soon find out the truth... eventually."

"Wait, shouldn't we contact AirSurge HQ first?" The young, red-haired second mate, Scott Mezzart, glanced about. "They need to be informed of this."

"They will..." Tai So-Fala quickly stated.

She was a slender bald Indonesian woman with high cheek bones, and sat poised at the opposite end of the table. So-Fala adjusted her thin glasses while glancing over to her corporate cohort seated beside her. He was an elderly Asian gentleman with a pensive stare, and quietly absorbed the conversation taking place. Takara Nautsobishi was the authority of the pair. The administrative arm for AirSurge Incorporated and The Scallion's resident *big-wig* that acted on the corporation's behalf. Both he and So-Fala wore finest business attire, setting themselves apart from the rest in the room.

"We can give them every detail when the information is ready to do so." So-Fala included.

"For all you know she could be lying." Takara stated coldly.

"A possibility, yes..." Vivian conceded. "But, why would she? There're obvious signs of trauma, both physically and psychologically, she's been through quite a lot. But, then again..." She paused for a moment, hesitating to speak.

The captain turned about and faced her. "You found something?"

"I... uh..."

"Don't hold back. Tell us."

Vivian waited until he sat down in his chair. His focus on her was paramount and leaned in closer with anticipation.

"I was there during the medical examination, when she was brought on board." She nervously tapped on the table. "And... well... there was something off about her."

"Off? How do you mean?" Takara glared over to her.

"I think my colleague, Doctor Saimari here," she gestured over to him, "can fill you in on that, right Saimari?"

He quickly glanced up in surprise, not prepared to be put on the spot so soon, and fiddled with his hands for a moment before resting them on the table.

"Thanks for that Vivian..." He said, giving her a frustrated squint. "Uh, yes... so, um, both of us were present at the examination. For all intents and purposes, Miss Driscoll was supposedly well enough..."

"Supposedly?" The captain arched a brow.

"Forgive me," Saimari held out a hand, "poor choice of

words on my part. What I meant to say was—uh... was that... oh, wait a second, here, let me show you instead..."

The holographic projection appeared over the table again, a flat screen that all sitting at the table could see clearly enough. It displayed a detailed visual of Katelan's body as she lay on medical gurney while in the med-bay. The image then zoomed in to her left hand and stopped on the closeup. Saimari pointed to her index finger and the dark spot on it.

"We're not sure what this is. It's not a freckle, it's not cancerous, and from what we know of her medical history... it's not anything she's ever had on her before."

"So..." Jalal shrugged at him. "What is it then? Discolouring? A bruise?"

"To be honest..." Saimari exhaled with frustration, flashing a quick glance over to Vivian. "We're not entirely sure. Furthermore, when we went to look at it again, to examine the blemish, we couldn't find it."

"Can't find it?" The captain squinted with confusion.

"Then it must have been just some particle of debris." So-Fala stated. "That's probably why the scans missed it."

"Yeah, that's what we thought at first. But, that's when Vivian looked down at Katelan after the scan and... well..."

The captain and the others turned their attention on her. Vivian felt all their eyes on her and quickly gave an answer.

"The black dot, or line... whatever it was, suddenly moved up into her eye. I saw it dart up there as if... well... as if it knew we were looking at it and wanted to hide."

"You're joking?" The second mate scoffed. "Tell me you're joking. A dot moved from her finger to her eye... and you witnessed that?"

"Yes," Vivian nodded at him, with a slow blink of reassurance. "I witnessed it myself. In fact, I told the team that just as Katelan's eyes closed. It moved very quickly. That's why we've contained her. Just in case she's brought something on board."

"You mean..." The captain motioned with his hand, trying to understand her explanation. "You believe she's contaminated, infected with something, right?"

"Something... maybe," she nodded.

Everyone glared at her for a moment, saying nothing in response. Takara inched back in his seat and poised his fingers together in thought. It lasted for a minute as he swivelled about, contemplating the matter. The first mate was about to say something to the captain, but Jalal quickly held up a hand to stop her. He knew interrupting Takara in his introspective thought process would be a mistake. People had been fired for less, but some, having done so in the past, were almost ejected into space.

Once the corporate man was finished thinking, he gave a nod to the captain, then one to his colleague, So-Fala, and then stood up from his chair as he walked over to Vivian.

"She's still in the decontamination chamber, yes?" He inquired to her. Vivian nodded in response. Takara pursed his lips as he stood before her and gave a light shrug. "I think I'd like to have a closer look at her myself."

Chapter 27

What Happened On Dreganon V?

In an adjacent room, on the other side of Katelan's decontamination chamber, Takara and the others from the meeting had come to observe her. She sat there on her stool, looking tired, bored, and continued to casually glance about the room she was in. The captain and Takara stood closest to the window. It was wide enough for them to see her and most of the chamber she was in. A view that only they could see on their side, and not on Katelan's. To her, it was just a long white-frosted glass wall, with no translucence whatsoever.

At the back of the darkened observation room, So-Fala and Doctor Saimai conversed lowly to each other about the impact this would have on the company and its other investors. They seemed disinterested with Katelan and chose not to study her like the others did. Sally and Scott leaned on a wall next to the window and kept a watchful eye on Katelan. They weren't convinced of Vivian's interview and medical scan of this woman. They felt that this was all a big waste of time. Passively, both mentioned it to each other and seemed to agree that she was guilty of murdering her entire crew.

The captain ignored their glib comments. He was more interested in what Takara thought.

"Should we tell her about everything?" Jalal lowly said to him.

Looking back at Jalal, Takara shook his head. "No, that wouldn't be a good idea, captain. I think for now, we should just say as little as possible to her. I'll wait for the medical and lab reports before proceeding with anything drastic. Vivian is looking at them now, answers will come soon, we'll just have to be patient."

* * *

Katelan could only see the white glass wall from her side, she didn't and couldn't see or hear anyone at all. It was perfectly smooth and seamless, from the ceiling to the floor. Decontamination rooms like this were standard on many ships. She'd been in several over the course of her career. But this was much more streamlined and well made, easy to clean and keep any pollutants from escaping.

"I only wish I had something like this on our ship to stop contaminations..." She mused. "The Scallion must be the pride of the fleet."

That thought gave her a moment of pause. The Scallion was an impressive vessel, the most advanced she'd ever been on. But, in order to get here weeks in advance, they would have to have launched way before their ship. So, why did Dan think there was going to be a delay? Something wasn't adding up. The more she thought on the matter, the more she realized, they'd been planning to be at this world just as the crew of Skyward Seven would be completed their harvesting.

"Those preliminary scans from the satellite must have made quite the impression." She figured. "They must have been eyeing this place for some time, waiting for my research results and to make a move on it fast."

Looking back at her cot and the small table with the two stools on either side. She wondered what was taking so long to get her out of this place.

"Surely, I've passed all their protocol requirements. Why am I still in here? What's wrong with me? Maybe something was still on the suit or…"

Jalal found it strange to be looking at this woman, knowing that she couldn't see them all staring at her from behind the one way glass. Did she know that they were? He knew Katelan wasn't stupid, she had to know they were. Still, Captain Jalal seemed rather bothered by it, nonetheless. He shook his head slightly as the feeling of reservation set in.

"Did you honestly believe all that? What she was on about, I mean? An intelligent jungle?"

"Yes, it is a rather fascinating tale," Takara mused. "No doubt she believes it firmly, so, until we can prove otherwise, her story is all we have at the moment. But, it does seem like she had quite the adventure, regardless."

"More like a nightmare." Jalal surmised.

The door to the darkened room opened up. Vivian casually walked in and headed to the captain and Takara. She stood before them with her hands clasped behind.

"I've finished reading the reports…" She stated to both of them.

"And..." The captain inquired to her.

"And..." She sarcastically repeated back to him with one eyebrow raised. "That is Katelan Driscoll, Skyward Seven's astrobiologist." The two men gave a barely audible sigh of relief. Until, Vivian quickly went on, "However... uh... the medical scan... um..."

Takara noted Vivian as she hesitated to finish. She looked unsure on how to continue. Takara reassured her with an interested smile and nod. Vivian twisted her lips slightly and finally confessed.

"This isn't really her."

Both men seemed puzzled by that and glanced at each other in confusion. Jalal rubbed his upper temple in frustration.

"You... you just stated that she was."

"I know what I said. Yes, that's her, but, that it's not the actual her. Do you understand what I'm saying?"

Before Jalal could speak again, looking very annoyed, Takara asked her a better question.

"Are you implying that this woman in that chamber there, is not the genuine article?"

"In a manner of speaking," Vivian nodded in agreement. "Yes, absolutely."

"What? You're joking..." Jalal sneered. He pointed at Katelan still gazing about in the other room. "That's her... right there. She had a real suit on... she survived the ordeal."

"The suit was real, yes." Vivian nodded to him. "But, the individual inside of it, no—that's not the real Katelan Driscoll of Skyward Seven."

"How can you be so certain?"

"The medical scans," Takara interjected. "They showed something, didn't they?"

Vivian nodded again. "It was a minor thing, that black

dot I mentioned about before, they saw it and inspected it. It was there. The magnification had to be very strong to have a look at the structure. I must admit, it is very refined, and very impressive."

"Oh, my god..." The captain uttered as he glanced over to Katelan.

Vivian ignored Jalal's reaction and proudly cocked her head up. "This is going to be the most significant biological find humanity has ever come across."

"But, the ship... Skyward Seven..." Jalal looked at her with confusion. "It broke up in orbit, it died from lack of oxygen and all the cosmic radiation. How did she manage to avoid it all?"

"As I mentioned previously, the enviro-suit, that was real." Vivian firmly stated. "Yes, there was some radiation exposure from being bombarded by the deadly cosmic spectrums—but, the suit is shielded enough to protect the wearer for a duration of time. She said that she had refilled the suit's air supply using whatever was left on the ship, before it disintegrated. It would have been very frigid, and somewhat painful to breathe in her lungs. A freezing effect would have begun in the capillaries, decreasing blood flow and slowing her heart rate down. However, by doing that, she managed to preserve her body as it lowered in temperature."

"Like a stasis pod... of sorts." Jalal nodded as he thought about it.

"I see, so, the oxygen," Takara included, "even if it was freezing, was still enough for her to use for sometime, I'm assuming."

"Correct." Vivian smirked. "The slowing of the heart, the shallow breaths of the trapped air, all of which aided in her preservation. Of course, had we not shown up when we did, I believe she... or this... thing... this copy of her, would have died eventually once the air supply depleted."

"No, I don't believe it. This is insane!" The captain balked. "That is a real person. She's flesh and blood. There's no way that thing could survive as her."

"Calm yourself, captain..." Takara motioned to him.

"The scans are wrong." Jalal pointed at him. "There's no way this could happen."

"What about the others?" Takara said to Vivian, ignoring Jalal's emotional outburst. "They had real suits too, didn't they?"

"I've seen the autopsies of them too," Vivian glanced at Takara. "The bodies were located from our orbital satellites. Those scans confirm a lot of what I was saying. But, the ones that are dead on the surface, the crew, are still wearing the actual suits. They all died sleeping in an area not too far away from the vessel."

"Wait, what? It's there? Still on the surface?" Captain Jalal gawked. "That's impossible..."

Vivian handed him a clear tablet from out of her coat pocket, and touched the surface with her thumb. The device expanded out, widening large enough for him to hold it with two hands. Images popped up on the translucent display and showed the surface of Dreganon V. Takara stood beside the captain and eyed them as well.

Vivian aided Jalal as she helped to tap on some images he was focusing on, and zoomed in on the bodies. "As you can see here, it appears their suits were systematically... uh... forced open, as the plant-life penetrated many areas it could enter the body."

"Fuck..." Jalal uttered in horror.

Vivian tapped on the tablet again for them, and showed more of the medical file. The images had text overlapping them, giving more detail about each one, and pointed to all the spots she'd just mentioned. The entire crew were in a state of decomposition and had multiple plant-life sticking out of their cadavers. Where eyes once were, blooming flowers and thick snake-like vines protruded out like a nightmare. The name plates on their suits confirmed each one. Out of the four still propped up against the tree-like vegetation, only one was out of a suit. The image identified the corpse of that of Katelan Driscoll.

Takara stepped away and placed himself in front of the viewing window. Stroking his fingers in thought, he watched Katelan with deep interest. Jalal seemed bewildered by the facts, he was starting to look pale, and left the room immediately. The other Scallion crew members followed him out and tried to catch up. Vivian, placed the tablet on an empty seat, stepped carefully over to the reserved Takara, and clasped her hands behind her back again. She stood beside the man, keeping quiet, and looked out at Katelan as well.

* * *

Katelan placed a hand on the centre of the wall she was facing. The warmth was still there, as the glass seemed to give off a gentle radiance. The reflection of herself became noticeable as she concentrated her gaze upon it. The more she looked, the more detail she could see. But as she stood there, giving in to some mild vanity, she noticed something in the corner of her right eye. There was a blemish, a dark spot, something that the doctors might have missed in their examination of her. She'd have to make it a point to tell them, if they ever came back to let her out, that is.

But as she continued to examine the spot, the brightness of the room helping her, and angling her head with lighting in such a way to do so, it became even more noticeable. She tried to remain focused on the area and kept her stare upon it. Katelan then brought her face in a little closer, adjusting the angle and examining the blemish spot with intensity. It was miniscule. A dot... no, more like a thin line, or something like it. Her other hand came up and widened the eyelid back gently. She finally got a better view of it.

The dot-line suddenly moved. That caused her to flinch slightly, but continued to concentrate on it. She could see a shape within that micro-shadow of it. There was a form, like a crinkled leaf edge, an outline of one, and it caused her to gasp at the sight of it. She stepped back in fright. The denial come swiftly, making her laugh slightly and the oddity of it. But as it finally sunk in, of what she was, Katelan panicked and screamed loudly from the horrific discovery.

"No! That's not possible... that's... that's just not possible!" She glanced about the room hysterically. "No! I'm not a plant! I'm not a plant! I can't be! No-no-no, I'm not! Do you hear me? I'm not!"

* * *

Takara and Vivian continued to look on as Katelan pounded the walls in hysteria. Vivian was saddened to see her upset it and tried to look away, while Takara remained stoic.

"What happened to the other two that weren't with the other crew in that area?" He asked Vivian. "The engineer and the technician, what were their names?"

"Allen and Deacon..." She said, pursing her lips. "They had a similar fate. Deacon was found merged to the jungle's floor, and Allen was found in his *Bush-cat* land walker in a deep trench just a few miles out from where the original Skyward Seven was."

Takara was utterly confounded by it all. He shook his head in disbelief.

"She thought she found her own ship and got on board of it. And it worked, like a regular vessel, no less." He tilted his head back slightly and watched Katelan as she collapsed to the floor in tears. Takara gave a drawn-out sigh and glanced over at Vivian. "How the hell did it manage that?"

"I'm not quite sure." She said. "I've never encountered something like this before. It has an amazing property of adapting to whatever it can consume. It did it all with such incredible speed. That's more than anything any of our technology could ever do. Even our AIs can't adapt as quick as it did."

"You sound like you admire it."

"No, actually, I'm quite terrified by it. Being able to mimic an individual so perfectly? It's no wonder Katelan or the others couldn't tell the difference. Before I saw the med report, I thought for sure I was talking to Katelan Driscoll. This planet did quite the number on all of them... even her."

"It played her." The man snickered. "The damn planet strung her along for all that time. Making her think she was real, that the crew, who probably thought so as well, were all just puppets to its whim."

"No, I don't think that." Vivian passively exhaled. "I think, it was purely instinctive. This world... this giant plant that thinks it's a planet, needed to feast on something other than itself. So, how do you lure in your prey, how do you get them to come willingly so that it can feast? You make it appealing, desirable, something to come an explore—then, when they're in, you consume. Just like any other carnivorous plant would."

"Incredible," Takara stated. "But, was it purely instinctive, or was from a latent intelligence emerging upon their arrival?"

"I don't know." She shrugged. "We probably helped it along in that regard. Maybe that's just part of its evolution, like Katelan said." Vivian snickered at her own words. "Like Katelan said... my god, even I can't stop referring to her as the actual person. I can't believe it did all this just to get her the off planet. It almost seems like, it wanted this scenario for her to believe. Jesus, an astrobiologist that becomes the plant she's studying, shit man... that's just fucking bizarre."

"Yeah," the man smirked at her. "Bizarre—and quite possibly, very, very profitable."

"I beg your Pardon?" She squinted at him.

"Oh, yes,' he grinned. "Self replication, continuous air production, spontaneous and rapid cloning properties... oh, yes, very, very profitable, my dear." Takara walked over to a communication panel on the side of the glass and tapped on it. "You may proceed gentlemen, I want lots of samples."

"What are you doing?" Vivian glared at him.

"Thank you very much, my dear." He grinned at her. "I was hoping for this kind of turn out. I will, of course include you in all the research, as stated in your AirSurge contract. You and I are about to become the most important people in the entire company."

Vivian glanced at him with surprise. His smile sent a chill down her spine. She could see the greed forming in his face, a corporation tyrant planning to prosper on something they had in their possession. Looking back at Katelan in the other room, she saw her stand up and head over to the wall they were facing. They were practically face to face, with only the thick glassed wall separating them. If only she knew she was there, that they were all there, and what they were planning.

* * *

"Let me out of here!" Katelan screamed to the top of her lungs and she pounded on the white glassed wall. "I'm not a fucking plant! I'm not a fucking plant! Let me out! Let me out!"

The seamless door to the room opened up. Katelan turned about quickly as she thought her calls for freedom were granted. She smiled and made a B-Line to the opening. She suddenly halted in her steps as she witnessed two biohazard enviro-suited individuals enter. One aimed a weapon at her, pointing it defensively, while the other individual held two cylindrical silver containers; each container had a biohazard symbol etched in the metal and the red stamp of the AirSurge logo over top of it. Katelan trembled at the sight, stumbling backwards, and backing herself into a corner of the room.

"Stop! No! Please! I'm not that thing! I can't be that thing! I'm Katelan Driscoll! Do you hear me? I'm Katelan Driscoll!"

She glanced about frantically, with tears flowing down her cheeks. There was no where she could go, no escape from the two individuals moving towards her slowly, and she continued to assert who she was, looking catatonic and whispering to herself.

"Katey... I'm... Katey... I'm Katey... I'm Katey..."

What Am I?

***

"If you step into the jungle, showing little respect for it, there's a good chance you won't ever come back."

I wish I had taken that phrase to heart just a bit more than I did. I don't know what I was thinking, believing I could single handedly become the foremost expert on the subject. Now, I've become that subject, the one I so wanted to study and understand. Dreganon V was the chance for me to shine, to get my name up there with others in the field and maybe create a long-lasting legacy among the science community. I don't know why or how this planet managed to get the better of me. I don't even recall how I died. Maybe it wasn't a dream I had, that day we fell asleep in the jungle while trying to get back to our ship. Perhaps that actually did happen, and it wasn't a dream I had, more like the memory of what truly occurred. But to make me think it was a dream? Holy shit, that's just twisted as fuck.

The thing I can't make sense of, what bothers me the most about all this, is how the hell I managed to keep my personality intact and my own mind. I think I am Katelan, I act like Katelan, I'm even as smart as she was... as I was. There's a theory going around, amongst the scientists, and other astrobiologists coming to study me from AirSurge Incorporated; the ones that have been poking, prodding, and slicing chunks off of me. They believe that the planet took longer to figure me out. Am I that complicated? Dan probably thought so. Janice and Deacon might not. But, they're not here anymore to say otherwise.

I still feel sad for them. I miss them a lot. But, am I, as the plant-being, the one feeling sadness, or is it the real me... the downloaded version of me, its brain, the one feeling it? So many questions, so little answers. Why was this planet doing this in the first place? Maybe it was trying to lure us there. Well, I'd say that it did a good job, huh? But to recreate us, make us interact, to give a false sense of being? That's bizarre!

Some of these corporate geniuses said the world was probably duplicating us over days. Just like some of those unfinished ones Allen, Dillion, and I discovered. The group of us that woke up, the ones that got lost and slept in the forest area, were actually clones of us, duplicates, in fact. That's how the planet survived, by duplicating and repli-cating the same form over and over, creating multiple hosts for itself to thrive. The difference was that humans, what I once was, had complexities it had never worked with before. Our cell structure and biological chemistry awoke the planet into a new intelligence. It was only surviving before, but now, now it had the chance to expand, grow and evolve into something new.

But why did it have to be me? Why did it choose to keep me the way I was? To make me... just like it? I'm guessing that was part of the whole evolution process as well. Much like humanity does, it creates off-spring through impregnation, recombining DNA genetics to improve and give variations to the next generation. Great, I'm the mother of a new species. How do you like that? Well, I suppose I am, in a way. Instead of being pregnant, with a protruding belly, I've been popping off pods from my back and getting some weird Franken-babies. It's disgusting. And yet, I still feel sad every time they take them away. I know they're ripping them apart and using them for genetic experiments. It's like I can feel them, somehow, like we're connected. It hurts, I feel their pain, and when they die, it's like part of me did too.

What the hell am I? Who am I? What kind of life is this for me? I beg for them to kill me, to let Katelan Driscoll die and end this torment. But they ignore my wishes. They don't even listen to my observations, having once been an astrobiologist and studying the very jungle planet that I've spawned out of. Why should they listen to me, right? What practical insight would I have? I'm just some weird fucking plant to them. Someone they would have respected and listened to; a colleague, an intelligent and well educated woman that's long gone. I'm only an echo, a copy, something made to look and sound like her in every way. And I guess, this is exactly who I am and what I am. I'm just a plant that thinks it's human.

I get strapped to a table, practically every day, sliced open with no anesthetic, and bleed out for hours before I'm patched up and placed back in my glass room cage. I'm a lab rat to them, but I think they're rats get better treatment than I do. Maybe I should try to escape, and kill a few of these assholes that treat me like shit. I know it would make me feel better. One day, perhaps... when an opportunity comes. I guess for now, I'll play their game. Let them do the science and try to create others. Stupid fucking humans, huh?

And what of Dreganon V? Well, it turns out they're sucking that planet's air supply dry from orbit. They placed a stationary factory over the world, sucking up the O_2 and filtering it from there. The pollen and spores get spaced, die, and fall back onto the surface. Why bother trying to understand or communicate with a planet that's actually a singular form of life? Especially one that can mimic anything that it absorbs.

See what I mean? Humans, total morons of the universe. No respect for anyone or anything. It's a wonder we... or rather, you... are still alive at all. I'm not Katelan, or Katey, I'm not even human anymore. Once I stepped onto that jungle planet, I never returned. Not because I didn't respect it, or that I was a stupid, foolish human that should never have gone there in the first place. No, I didn't come back because I belonged there, I've always belonged there.

I am the jungle, and the jungle will always be me... forever.

Thank You For Reading!

Did you enjoy this book? Was it something you would recommend to friends, family or other readers of the genre? Then why not give it a review and let everyone know you thought of the novel. It's the best way to communicate to the author and show your appreciation for the work.
Go to Goodreads, Bookbub, and/or any other social media review site and help spread the word for this title.

Look For These Other Titles
Coming Soon

Our future soldiers are those who are marked for death. Violent and dangerous criminals who have no choice but to fight a war on Earth's behalf. **Look for this book in 2024 or 2025.**

FROM THE AUTHOR OF *THE LONG LOST WAR* AND *OUTER RED*

SPACE ROCKERS

DANGEROUS PROSPECT

JEFF WALKER

Space mining is a dangerous job, but when the crew of The Calista are assigned to mine a specific asteroid, they'll soon discover that it's more than just your average rock in space. **Look for this book in 2023!**

About the Author

Jeff Walker is the author and self-publisher of such titles as: *The Long Lost War, Outer Red, and The Mysterious World Of Professor Darkk And Miss Shadow.* He has written seven titles, short stories and novellas, most of which are now available as audiobooks. His contribution to many fan fiction titles have spawned his writing career into the direction of creating original characters and shaping new worlds of his own imagination. Living with him is his wife and two children in a small town of the province of Ontario, Canada.

For more information/contact - visit his official website: http://www.jeffwalkerbooks.weebly.com

And please - go to Bookbub.com, Goodreads.com, Facebook Review sites and leave your review about this title or others by this writer. It is the best way to spread the word and tell the author of what you thought of his work.

Also by Jeff Walker